The Heart of Stone Adventures

Fool's Proof

Power's Play

Doom's Daze

Spring's Eternal

Praise for Eva Sandor's books

A perfect escape from the real world—
funny, engaging and brilliantly written.
—Andrew Shanahan, author of Before And After

A breath of fresh air, just waiting for a reader to escape
into a world of magic, miscommunication and magpies.
—Sydney Rappis, Reedsy Discovery

The uncommon words and lyrical dialogue are a joy...
you will not find any of your boring old
cliché-driven fantasy fiction here!
–John Derek, Netgalley

Many surprises to delight literary fantasy readers
looking for far more than an adventure story.
—Diane Donovan, Midwest Book Review

If I were wearing a hat, I'd take it off to Eva.
— Jim Webster, author of the Tallis Steelyard series

SPRING'S ETERNAL

Eva Sandor

ISBN 979-8-9877723-2-4 (Paperback)
979-8-9877723-3-1 (eBook)
Library of Congress Control Number: 2021908578

Cover illustration and book design by Eva Sandor
Printed in the United States of America
First printing 2023
Published by Huszar Books

Visit us at www.huszarbooks.com

to the bestest horse

HERE COMES LIFE,
bringing wonder and terror, horror and splendor.
Let it all in.

— *Reynar Murri Arilka,*
Advice to a Scribe's Apprentice.

CHAPTER 1

THE PLUM BLOSSOM FESTIVAL MARKED the very start of spring, and spring is notoriously unpredictable.

Some years, the Festival sagged under curtains of rain, with cold gusts from the harbor flogging vendors' barrows and sending trinkets flying; in others the sun got the upper hand, making revelers wish they'd chosen lighter robes, breezier pantaloons, hats with shady brims. But sometimes, Ye Gods smiled upon the ancient city of Coastwall with its sandstone twistings and turnings: smiled, and nodded, and got it just exactly right.

This morning was golden, and smelled clean. Birds sang. In a public park— for, like many cities in the Brewel Country, Coastwall had lately been graced with public parks— mothers and daughters went about their broadspear practice in a zestful Plum Blossom spirit, striking at straw targets painted pink and white just like the flowers bursting forth on the branches overhead.

One little girl was particularly aggressive, continuing to thrash a target with the handle of her broadspear long after its wooden practice blade had broken loose, and shouting out a list of typical brats' grievances as she did so.

"*That's* for face washing! *That's* for hair brushing! *That's* for no honey-bons till after dinner!"

"For shame," growled her mother. "Learn to control yourself. Your blade is all the way over there in the yellowleaf hedge. Go get it and let's start again on the basic diagonal strike."

"No-o-o, mama! That's *boring*! I want to slay a monster!"

At an outdoor café bordering the park, a gentleman looked up over the news bulletin he was reading. From behind thick spectacles his eyes met those of the dismayed mother; he was just calling out to her when Coastwall's bell, high in the square tower known as the Lantern, began its great, deep, bronze morning peal.

By the time that had faded to a faint shimmering hum, the family was seated together: or, rather, the gentleman and the mother were seated, while their brat walked in circles around the table, devouring an enormous plum cookie.

"Oh, I wouldn't call it *spoiling* her, my dear," said the gentleman. "Let her have her fun. This whole week *is* a holiday, after all. You relax, too— would you like me to read you this bulletin?"

The brat stopped chewing and threw her mother a glare, because of course reading was for *boys*, and listening to it was nearly as bad; she coughed a few crumbs and smacked the newly-replaced blade of her weapon against a lamp post, picturing it as the neck of some frightful beast.

And so the gentleman read aloud, and the birds sang, and the rest of the women in the park went about their ladylike practice, and all around them Coastwall—from the top of the Lantern to the mouth of the broad brown Denna— began to think of spring.

On the Denna's western bank, opposite the great ivory-tiled palace of the de Brewel family, a small knot of the very men who had created the news bulletin stood fidgeting and muttering, in their own way craving adventure as strongly as the brat had.

They wore jackets covered with pockets for wax tablets and styli, the tools with which they scribbled the words and scrawled the pictures that were to become plaster printing blocks. From these would peel copy after copy, selling till the blocks wore flat— though some stories or images would show such popularity that their blocks would be re-cast, and sold anew labeled *MULTI-EXTRA*. To originate a multi-extra news sheet was the dream. But hunting it was chancy and arduous— as difficult, in its own way, as hunting the firewyrm, the meldragore, the wish-granting nullicorn.

One of the news hounds lowered a pair of twin spyglasses from his eyes. "This could be big. I just saw the Nameless Lady, boarding her personal ferry. She'll be across in a few minutes."

His neighbor was new to the pack and squinted across the estuary of the Denna as though he could identify anyone at such a distance. "Really, the Lady? Hope the Prince is with her... not the baby Prince, I mean... I'm talking about the other one..."

The oldest of the news hounds turned on the new fellow in exasperation. "Hoy, Popper," he snapped. "See any nullicorns around here? No? Then quit makin' wishes."

As the rest of the men laughed, the new fellow hung his head. He'd been a scribe's apprentice till just that week. Contracts and receipts and Harbormaster's paperwork didn't laugh at you—but then again, no scribe ever experienced the thrill of chasing a story. Literally chasing it.

The oldest news hound took pity. "Aw, Popper, I don't mean to bust your beans. But anyone who's seen the Trickster Prince this past month or more has seen the back of the moon. Never you mind— whatever his Lady does, it sells sheets galore. Now get set, fellas! Fling a leg over them hurry-horses."

The horses he referred to were not animals, but crude vehicles consisting of front and rear wheels with seats slung between them, propelled by the rider's feet scrambling at the ground. Hurry-horses were hard to maneuver and often ended up colliding with trees, shop fronts, or other vehicles such as ox carts and sedan chairs, but they let even the clumsiest man move as swiftly as a professional foot messenger— at least on straight stretches, of which Coastwall admittedly had precious few.

So the men straddled their wheels and waited. All were silent except Popper, who continued babbling.

"About the Nameless Lady, though... I've looked into what the Prince calls her and it's entirely fictitious... she hasn't really got a Doktorate in anything at all... yet they say she's a fiend for books... though maybe she only carries them for show... these fashionable types get up to so many fads..."

"Rotsy," groaned the spyglass man to the oldest news hound, "can you tell young Popper to shut it? I'm tryin' to think up some headlines."

"Tell him yourself. You know how it is."

Just then the spyglass man let his lenses drop to the end of their neck loop. He grabbed the handlebars of his hurry-horse, gave the ground beneath him a furious push with both feet and away he rolled. Within seconds the rest were after him, racing for the riverbank— all except the unfortunate Popper, who didn't know that how it is, is this: friendly chat is well enough, but when the chase is on it's every hound for himself.

THE NAMELESS LADY WAS HIDING in plain sight.

Her hair was covered by a scarf, folded diagonally and wrapped around her head. Her eyes lay behind a pair of sun goggles— the modern kind, not mere old-fashioned slits in a whalebone strip but the frames of a scholar's spectacles, fitted with ovals of darkened glass. And her ferry had high, boxy walls which blocked any view of the vehicle she was seated in.

But she was tall; above the boxy walls her torso rose up lean and broad-shouldered, with the breeze ruffling her fine and simple robe. And she was striking: she carried her head with an elegant bearing, as though putting the strong line of her jaw and the proud jut of her nose on display.

A documentary artist skidded to a halt at the ferry landing beside the spyglass man, pulling forth his tablet.

"Damn it deep— be nice if she'd unwind that scarf and pull those lids off her weepers. What rig you think she's drivin'? White ponies, put to a cart? Open top sedan chair?"

The spyglass man didn't have to answer. The ferry touched, its gangplank fell, one wall of the box swung open and out shot the Nameless Lady in a brass-fitted, red-painted blur.

Her vehicle had no team, no bearers. Its four whirling wheels were large, but the wooden body between them, which held only a dashboard and two seats, was tiny. As it sped away, it emitted an intricate ticking sound and left behind a smell of fresh varnish, metal polish, and lubricating oil.

"Aw, blisters!" moaned the artist. "That was too fast! I wasn't ready!"

Off surged the pack. At the rear, Popper paddled his boots wildly against the pavement and suddenly remembered having copied some paperwork earlier in the month— documents that had to do with the import of a new Tekology from the Whellen Country. "I know what that is!" he cried. "It's a power carriage!" And then he clamped his tongue between his rearmost teeth, appalled at himself for nearly giving away his exclusive, his potential multi-extra.

But he wanted an interview, and chasing it took all the energy he possessed. The sluggish, thuggish old heart of Coastwall might have been a dirty nest of alleys, barely wide enough for carts or barrows, but the city had bigger and newer and cleaner streets too, and the Lady was flying up one of them: Coastwall's most fashionable boulevard, a straight broad promenade shaded by plum trees. She twisted the throttle of the power carriage and swung its steering tiller with expert precision, threading through a flow of flashy coaches, gleaming sedan chairs, briskly trotting horses and smoothly ambling mules, crowds of ladies and gentlemen whose social cachet demanded that they ignore everyone and everything around them, only later to learn about it in bulletin sheets.

Higher and higher uphill climbed the boulevard, and Popper's heart felt ready to burst; yet he was young and zealous, and followed bravely, and to his own surprise found himself at the front of the pack, panting and sweating not ten yards behind the Lady, whose way had been cut off by a barrow with plum cookies painted on it.

The wench pushing the barrow was bent down low, putting her back into the job, oblivious. Popper's hurry-horse slipped easily through the crowd. He could almost touch the Lady's power carriage... in a moment she'd be all his to question...

Once, twice, three times, a brassy bray split the air. The Lady was squeezing a rubber bulb attached to a trumpet. Its honking made the barrow wench leap to attention. A gap opened in the traffic and the ticking of the power carriage rose to a whirr, then to a hiss; the Nameless Lady surged away. As she vanished, she turned back to face Popper and one corner of her mouth curved upward into her trademark halfway smile.

Popper was too startled to move. He was sure that smile was meant as a special gift for him alone. While he waited to catch his breath, the rest of the pack overtook him.

"Don't just stand there, fella!" cried the oldest news hound as he rolled past. "Come on up here— she's as good as caught!"

At the top of the hill, the boulevard terminated before a magnificent set of gates, which gazed down upon the city in much the same complacent way that Brewel Hall lorded its presence across the broad brown Denna. Trudging toward them, the exhausted Popper wondered what old Rotsy could possibly have meant. As good as caught? More like good as gone: the gates marked the entry to a Royal District, governed not by the laws of the Brewel Country but by the House of Castramars, and once the Nameless Lady passed through them she would be as inaccessible as though she'd sailed across the Midland Sea.

But now he saw it. In front of the gates sprawled an elaborate snarl in traffic— runaway mule, sedan chair crash, coach with a broken spring— all suspiciously theatrical and completely halting the Lady's flight. The chase was over; the hounds closed in and attacked.

"Tell us about this *thing* you're driving!"

"Zat a book there, on the seat beside you?"

"Read us a storytale from it!"

"That's right— from 'once there was, and now there's not' all the way to 'they lived happily until always'!"

The Lady said nothing. She only smiled— halfway, her special way.

Against the din of questions, the documentary artist crept up close to her. "Hoy, Lady. Take pity on a poor scribbler— strike me a pose. It's this or draw courtroom diagrams."

To his astonishment, the Lady turned to face him. She pulled her sun goggles a fraction of an inch down her nose and sent a glance over the top of them, lifting one eyebrow.

The artist whooped in glee. "Sweet gods a-mighty!" he shouted, as his hand leaped into action and curls of wax rained from his tablet. "What a pic! This'll be a multi-extra for sure!"

"Pocks to dreary diagrams," said the Lady, hooking her elbow over the door of the power carriage and raising her chin into a sleek profile. "Here. Have another." Her sleeve draped in a picturesque arc; a red and yellow enameled ring flashed on her pinky; the artist drew ever more furiously and the rest of the news hounds went wild.

"She's wearing his ring!"

"Nice! But when are we going to see some wedding bracelets?"

"That's right— where *is* the Trickster Prince?"

"You keeping him busy?"

"Keeping him quiet?"

"Will he be joining you at the theater tonight?"

"What's going *on* with you two?"

A squad of hard-faced wenches in red and yellow livery emerged from a guardhouse beside the gates. Their jaws were clenched on quids of maidenroot and their fists gripped broadspears with gleaming steel blades; the drivers of the make-believe traffic jam decided they'd earned their pay and fled. The gates swung open. The news hounds howled their final questions.

"What's back there, Lady?"

"We hear you and the Trickster Prince have a pretty sweet palace."

"That's right— a regular pleasure-dome!"

"Does he give you a private show? You been jingling his bells? No, Lady, wait! It was just a joke! A *joke!* Like the kind His Highness used to tell. Back when he was— aw, boilsores."

THE BOULEVARD HAD BEEN A lovely stretch of road, but what lay behind the gates was immensely more gracious. The trees here were not flowering plums but baslins, blackbuds, and whitewoods— newly planted and yet to leaf out, but already shapely and strong. Yellow hedges glowed and bright red crocuses blanketed slumbering lawns. The paving itself was a work of art: stripes of brick alternating with golden stone, punctuated by lozenges of crystal-white marble.

As she drove past a sculpture of the Castramars magpie, the Lady removed her goggles and stowed them in a compartment. Passing another sculpture— a golden man with his laughing face turned up to the sky— she tugged open the knot of her scarf.

On she rolled, with the sun in her eyes and the wind in her hair, thinking. But eventually, she did have to squeeze the brake: the Lady had reached the end of her driveway.

Two town houses faced one another across an intimate plaza. They were of the most thoroughly comfortable elegance, and neither was taller or grander than the other; neither had better gardens or brighter windows or a more welcoming entry. They were in fact exactly alike, as perfectly matched as reflections in a mirror— except for the words enameled on plain, unpretentious plaques.

HIS, read one. HERS, read the other.

The Lady stepped from her carriage, slammed its door, picked up the book and carried it with her up a neat brick walkway to the plaza.

There she stopped between the houses, took a deep breath, and chose.

CHAPTER 2

LISTEN TO A STORYTALE— ONE that's very true. It begins like this: once there was, and now there's not, war in Midlandis.

That was three generations ago, going on four. Back in those days the countries of the Kingdom were less well united, and through various combinations of greed, vengefulness, and ambition a series of trifling incidents escalated into the bloody spasm that historians refer to as The Grand War.

The Grand War was vast and tragic, but it was the last war the Federated Kingdom of Midlandis has known. After the dust was down and the House of Castramars emerged victorious, the people in the lands around the brandy-black Midland Sea found they had lost their stomach for military conflict. Crossbows came home and were hung over hearths; broadspears were put to use hunting firewyrms; knights hitched their horses to plowshares.

But in some of the world's further places dwell people who have not a distaste for war, but a hunger for it. And one of them— a bleak, distant, secretive country, hidden behind airless mountains and scoured by a ceaseless icy wind— calls itself Abode.

Isolated as it is, scholars still do not know exactly how Abode became aware of Midlandis. But through the backward-facing lens of history, it is now sadly obvious that they had their eyes upon the natural wonder known as the Heart of Stone: a spellbound monolith, the size of a moderate town, that rotates like a vast mill wheel. The Heart of Stone generates limitless motive power and brings the people around it a quiet but impressive prosperity. Abode longed for control of it, and cultivated a plan to conquer the country where it stood— indeed, to conquer the entire Kingdom— by means of their own unique possession: the Weapon.

The Weapon was a perversion of Alkemy, an unimaginable force. The new reality of its existence exploded earlier generations' understanding of war. Whoever commanded it would own the world.

But the storytale of history is filled with unlikely twists. And after a series of them Midlandis— peaceable Midlandis— was left in possession of the very last Weapon.

So. Maybe all was well.

Or maybe it wasn't.

Maybe the Weapon that Midlandis held was not the last one after all. Maybe Abode's capability to build more had not been destroyed.

Maybe it was already building more.

These maybes brought up questions, especially the questions of whether Midlandis should learn to build Weapons too, and— if both sides were to have them— of which countries would ally with which, should there ever come a day when opposing powers, each with a finger hooked into the delicate, menacing detonator pin of its respective Weapon, faced off and threatened to end this earth.

Questions, maybes. But no one dared to *do* anything. That is, until His Highness, Prince Malfred of Castramars, stepped forward.

Prince Malfred was a new player on the international stage. He had not been born into the royal House, but had become King Enrick's brother as the result of a decree. Up till the moment the King pressed his ring into the document's golden seal, saying "I hereby adopt you Fred hmm just a moment I'm not sure that's really a word let me ask Margadet. Sweetheart is *hereby* a word? Really? All right Fred all right I'll get on with it I hereby adopt you as my brother, born the same day I was. Ha ha that makes us twins, Fred, we both turn thirty-six next month. Da would have liked this. Oh don't squeeze me so hard Fred. Don't pound my back like that. Margadet make him stop it ouch hold on Fred I still have to say *'and now let it be so'*"— up until the moment His Majesty uttered those words, Prince Malfred had been Malfred Murd, a commoner who as a boy had been brought to serve as the young King's personal Fool.

But the looming Weapon had put an end to Malfred's jesting career. He had turned deadly serious, organizing a diplomatic conference which he named *The League For Peace.*

True, Fred suspected that the Kingdom's pompous scholars, overstuffed petty nobles and imperious wielders of wealth listened to him only out of curiosity regarding "the Trickster Prince", as he quickly came to be known. But the idea did catch on. First among the countries of Midlandis, and then worldwide. From the Strait of Swez to the Herb Islands and beyond, word spread. Envoys were appointed. The League For Peace became a fragile reality, and a date was set for its first meeting.

The closer the date drew, the harder Fred studied.

In boyhood he'd learned to read and write; now he plunged into an ocean of information. Each of the world's nations had to be respected, reassured, afforded dignity. He meant to learn everything about every one of them. The head that once had worn a jingle-bell hat now throbbed with a constant headache; the stout peasant limbs and broad commoner's back which once had performed athletic feats with the greatest of ease now felt creaky with disuse. By the eve of the League's inaugural session, Fred's orbit had been reduced to his study and the bath-chamber adjoining it. He ate at his desk, slept in his chair, and dreamed of—well, peace, he supposed. A future where the storytale of Midlandis and Abode ended with *and they lived happily until always.*

The question of where his own story led was, to Fred, far less appealing. Better not to worry about it. Because who was he, anyway? Nobody. And besides— with the Weapon hanging over his head, what kind of fool thought of himself?

CHAPTER 3

THE TRICKSTER PRINCE HAD A major-domo, who gently opened the heavy, paneled door of his master's study, threaded his way among stacks of clamp-binders that had been ransacked from their shelves, stepped over mounds of notes tamped down by crystal paperweights and empty mugs, and reached three massive roll-top desks pushed together to form a makeshift island, with their backs facing the doorway and their tops littered with wyrmlight lamps, oil lamps, and burned-out candles. He stood up as tall as he could make himself and tried sending a discreet whisper over the mess.

"Your Highness?"

No reply.

The Trickster Prince also had a valet, who slipped into the room after the major-domo and tried it his own way.

"Not like that! He hates whispering. Do like this. Ahem! Your Highness!"

Still nothing.

The Trickster Prince had a Chief of Household Guards, who pushed the men aside with a growl of "Aw, the both of you lemme at him" and banged one desk with her knuckles; he had a cook who insisted the smell of some food would get the job done; he had, in fact, a long train of servants who all tried, and failed, to get His Highness's attention. But at last, with a profusion of apologies, they all withdrew and left the Lady to announce herself.

A bumping and scratching sounded from the footwell of the furthest desk.

"Are they gone? Ye Gods, I wish they'd leave me alone. I've got just one night left to bone up on details. Take 'em all home with you, Dok."

"There's this thing about servants, Fred: you can just order them to go away."

"I'm not ordering anyone anything. You know that! I'm trying to get rid of that whole mentality, where people jump just because some purebred hound with a 'de' this or a 'House of' that commands them to. I'm putting a stop to that. I'm—"

"What you *are* is invited to a theater premiere tonight. Very, very strongly invited. Dame Irona put her invitation in the form of an interpretive dance— I'll leave you to imagine that. And Donn Felip is worried about you. He says if you don't take it easy, you'll sprain your cerebrum. He swears it happens to some scholar at least two or three times a year."

"Oh, scabflaps, Dok. Did *you* ever see it happen? When you were at The Bureau, working your brain ten times harder than he ever did? Give me a break."

"That's it! That's exactly what I want to give you! Come on out here."

Fred sighed. He'd stepped right into that one.

He emerged from behind the desks, an odd figure indeed. Though his clothing was pitifully rumpled, it was stylish and well tailored; his hair, though badly out of place, showed the lines of a precision cut; and his face, though neatly shaved and patted with norrange-blossom water and at first glance seemingly decisive enough, was— well.

When he wasn't busy performing, Malfred Murd had always been aggressively unmemorable. The more anyone looked upon his features, the less any of them stood out. This was one of the qualities which had brought him to The Bureau's attention: without

it, he might never have been chosen to visit Abode as a secret agent—
Dok's agent. But now, as she bent down to press a series of kisses
across his forehead, saying "Even Controllers used to take breaks,
Fred. Even when I had a dozen Operations running at once…" he
was sorry he'd brought the topic of The Bureau up.

"Dok, don't take this the wrong way but I wish you'd never
mention Operations or Controllers ever again. Those days are gone,
hear me? You're *free.* You can go around having emotions… and
letting people recognize you… and, well, just doing whatever you
please. No more hiding your light! The Bureau can kiss my— *mmph.*"
Her lips found his and squashed the words away.

For a moment there was silence. But then Dok was on to
something worse than mentioning The Bureau.

"Look here, Fred, I've brought you one of those books you need.
This isn't from the Public Stacks at Brewel Hall, it's from Donn
Felip's own private collection. He says if it's not the right edition,
he'd be happy to place an RCD call to Mitsa-Konig… they could send
a different one by the next stagecoach, or…"

"Gods' guts, Dok! You spent your morning crawling through
some deep-damned library?"

"Why not? I want to help you."

"But I don't *want* you wanting to help me."

"No? So you're saying I'm not free to not want you wanting me
to not want—"

"Stop it!" cried Fred. "We've been over this!"

From the little table where Dok had set it down, the book
seemed to mock them both. Gingerly Fred poked its sea-green
rayskin cover, as though testing to see if it were dead. When he
looked up at Dok she was expressing emotion, all right. Plenty of
emotion. Fred's heart felt like something was jabbing into it.

"Uh, see, the thing is, I'm through consulting books. I'm only going over my notes now. So thanks, but I don't need this, all right? Take it back. And don't rush! Drive slow. Stop in a café, visit some shops. Get yourself whatever you like and charge it to me— just show 'em the— hoy, Dok, keep it." She was slipping the ring off her pinky, taking Fred's hand, pushing the red and yellow enameled lump of gold back into its place on his left index finger. When that was done she wrapped her long, strong arms around him and then she was rocking him, enfolding him, pulling him close to her... he closed his eyes. Gods, she felt good. He was tempted, so very tempted, to take the break she was offering...

Her arms fell away. She reached for the book. "So you're sure you don't need this?"

"Positive."

"If I take it back, will you do me a favor?"

"Name it."

"Will you *please* pry yourself out of here and come to the show tonight? I know I won't be seeing you for the next few weeks— believe me, I understand why security has to be tight. But I thought—"

A sound like a barrow full of bricks rolled into the room. "Hoy, Fred!" chirped a bright, angular voice. "Hocka, bocka, dominaka. Look what I've conjured up for you!"

It was Corvinalias Elsternom e Rokonoma IV, the Count of Upper Cloudyblue. Corvinalias was an accomplished young noble, and a pioneer: as Isladorro University's recently appointed Prophessor of Abodean Studies, he was not only the first member of a brand-new department, but also the very first scholar at any Midlandic institution to be of a species other than the one his people— that is to say, magpies— referred to as "Uman-beings".

At the magpie's chirp Fred's eyes, closed in exhaustion, flew open. Dok turned around. Both found themselves looking at Corvinalias, perched atop a cart pushed by a big, strong serving wench. The cart was heaped high with books and more books.

Corvinalias spread his wings, thinly feathered but still very dapper in black and white and iridescent blue. "Ta-daa! It's all those books you asked for! Well, all but one. Your coachmaid drove me all over town, but for some reason— *there* it is." He hopped across to the volume Dok had brought and began pecking at it. "Oooh, look at that binding. So shiny."

If Fred had felt a jab in his heart before, what struck him now was an absolute flurry of slashes, as though he were a broadspear target. He almost couldn't bear to look up at Dok and see her... smiling.

"Pretty, isn't it?" she said to Corvinalias. "Well, I'll see you fellows around. You know where I live." Her smile grew brighter; her whole face glowed. And before Fred could say another word, she'd reached the door and disappeared.

Dok's smile had been contagious. It had drawn matching expressions from the serving wench and even from Corvinalias, inasmuch as the leathery corners of his beak could bow upward and the whiskers around his nostrils could twitch. But not from Fred. Fred looked
utterly miserable.

Dok's smile had cut him to the quick. Because it was warm, and charming, and radiant— and symmetrical.

Fake, fake, fake.

CHAPTER 4

A SHIP SPED ACROSS THE BRANDY-BLACK Midland Sea.
The *Yuliyo Advance* was the world's most modern
vessel and moved more swiftly than any wind, any oars, any team
of Cloud Whales. She was powered by something known as an
Alkemikal Drive, and had been tasked with carrying Abode's envoy
to the League For Peace.

The *Yuliyo Advance* was, to be sure, emphatically not an
Abodean ship, though her design had begun as such. By contrast
with the filthy and dangerous Abodean warship which had wrecked
in Coastwall Harbor, leaving Midlandic engineering Prophessors
free to examine it, this version of the Alkemikal Drive was safe and
clean; it was what the Abodean warship might have been, if that
country's Dictator had not imagined himself to be a learned man
and shown such a fondness for meddling in Laboratoriums.

The Tekology of the *Yuliyo Advance* even extended to its
navigation. Gone was any need for a specialist who knew the stars,
or the swells, or whatever the local method was. Instead, the ship
itself showed the way: sensitive instruments aimed at a gleaming
shard of Iyolite crystal could detect changes in its color which
corresponded to positions on the globe. So between CrystlNav
(a trademark of Yuliyodyne Systems, formerly the Del Yuliyo
Shipbuilding Concern) and the Alkemikal Drive, a modern craft
such as the *Yuliyo Advance* had no need for any but the very barest
skeleton crew.

Under the hand of a single skipper and her mate, such a ship
could theoretically soar unchecked across the Peaceful Ocean,
thread its way among the Herb Islands, and fly from the Warm

Ocean through the verdant Straits of Swez without the slightest concern for wind or tide; and once in the brandy-black Midland Sea it could flash past the great delta of the Ni'il, pass the Milestone, the Isle of Gold, and finally the Perdoffino Light, and at last come gliding into Coastwall Harbor without ever having slowed down, let alone stopped anywhere.

Theoretically.

But scholars the world over know, only too well, that theory and practice are never quite the same.

Circumstances arise.

Eventualities occur.

In other words, things *do* go wrong.

CHAPTER 5

COASTWALL'S NEWEST PLAYGROUND, THE DABROO Center, was a massive entertainment complex built upon the site of a former farm and donated to the city by anonymous benefactors.

Why there had ever been a farm deep in the guts of what used to be the Brewel Country's most filthy and felonious district was a mystery, but there it was; now it was home to a marketplace, a dining hall, a tournament arena and a theater, and the whole neighborhood had become most startlingly chic. Visitors could lose their money not to pickpockets, grabby brats and knife-wielding bravos but to overpriced boutiques, and find themselves stumbling not over the grimy bodies of sailors too drunken to locate the harbor, but into long conversations with dimly remembered but undeniably fashionable acquaintances.

Beneath the glitter of street lamps, one of the carriages making its way toward the Dabroo Center was plain gleaming black, discreetly ornamented with hair-thin pinstripes of red and yellow. Its leather top and glass door panels were raised against the chill and inside it, Fred was saying "But seriously. That was rotten of me. I—"

Dok shook her head. "That's enough. I forgive you. Let's talk about something else."

"Like what?"

She smoothed the crisp tiny pleats on the breast of his shirt, straightened his dark woolen overcloak, twisted a curl into a bit of his hair. "Like maybe the party after the show."

"Oh, no. I didn't sign on for any party! I only said I'd watch this thing of the de Brewels' because they want my honest opinion. Afterward I'm going straight home. I've got a few more hours left to

read about how maritime treaties functioned in the early years of…
what do you have there?"

Dok had bent down to a calfskin valise lying at her feet and
unbuckled its flap. She pulled out a wad of cheap pulp pages.

"Something a lot more amusing than maritime treaties."

They were that afternoon's news bulletins. The first one,
labeled *MULTI-EXTRA!!!*, consisted of nothing but a striking sketch
of Dok's eyes behind her sun goggles. Fred couldn't help smiling at it.

"Look at you. Nobody would ever guess that last year you were a
faceless spymaster."

"Mm. Now I'm a nameless lady. Much more glamorous." Dok
showed him a second sheet, featuring the speeding power carriage
under the headline *NAMELESS LADYS HI TEK RIDE*. Fred smiled at
this one, too— the country from which the carriage originated was
dear to him, and its ruler was the closest thing he had to a mother.

"That's a nice one. Let's send it to Dame Elsebet," he said.
Despite himself, he was warming up to the news sheets. At least they
didn't call him any silly names. Or mention him at all, in fact.

The third sheet, however, was a great big close-up of the
Castramars ring on Dok's as-yet-untattooed hand. *STILL NO
WEDDING INK?* pouted its headline. Dok scowled and jammed it
back into the valise, beside some object packed in a velvet bag.

"Pocks to those busybodies! Forget that one. Here, try another."

The next page she held up for Fred's inspection was not
illustrated, but its headline, *XCLUSIV GLIMPS OF THE TRXSTR
PRINCE*, was as enormous as it was badly spelled.

"Oh, no," groaned Fred.

"Oh, yes!" exclaimed Dok. "Now, this one's a little racy so ignore
the first part, all right? In fact, ignore pretty much all of it up to…"

Fred's eyes were round. "*What* did I just read about my *what?*"

"I told you, ignore that part. See where I'm pointing? This is where they mention the League For Peace. Go ahead, start reading right here."

Fred didn't read anything. Suddenly he felt clammy and ill. Had he eaten an undercooked eel roll? Caught some sort of bird illness from Corvinalias? Abruptly he recognized the feeling as flop sweat. It was the first time he'd ever dreaded attention, feared getting a laugh.

"Uh, Dok, this Patrons' Box where we'll be sitting. It's not up front or anything, is it?"

"Of *course* it's up front, Fred— that's the whole point. You've been hiding away all month. People want to see you."

"You mean *glimpse* me. Glimpse the Trickster Prince. Which, by the way, is three hells of a tongue twister."

"And what's wrong with them wanting to... gl... all right, that *does* sound weird. But what's wrong with a few minutes in the public eye?"

"I don't know." He slumped against the cold window glass. "They say any attention is good attention. But all of a sudden I don't think so."

Fred stared past his reflection, remembering the reflected curtain of Phantactive poison that had oozed from behind the Abodean warship as he and his friends chased it across the globe... desperately, abortively, finally failing in their mission to keep the Weapon from entering the heart of Midlandis...

"I can't be a joke. Tricks and laughs can't be all I'm known for. The League can't be just the pet project of some deep-damned former Fool."

Dok, too, had seen what the Weapon could do. "You're right," she whispered, and said no more.

The traffic crawled onward.

At last their carriage arrived in front of the theater, and a series of thumps and bumps from the roof signified its footmaids climbing down from their places.

Dok lifted the calfskin valise to her lap, pulled out the velvet bag. Fred had assumed she was returning Donn Felip's sea-green book, but no.

She'd brought his coronet.

Unlike the ring, which had its daily uses, this was a piece of regalia Fred hadn't laid eyes on since his investiture ceremony. It wasn't something he ever felt the need to wear. But of course, what was his was Dok's, including keys to the safe where the jewels were kept.

There was just enough time for him to yelp "Oh, no!" before the heavy golden hoop was resting on his head and the door of the carriage was opening.

CHAPTER 6

ALL THE WAY TO THE Patrons' Box, Fred felt pressure: a thousand grains' weight of gold on his brow, ten thousand eyes on his every step. He kept expecting some witty oik to cry out "Why, if it isn't the Kingdom's clowning glory!" or "Tip us a folly, Your Ma-*jest*-ee!". But they did no such thing, even though beneath the heat of all the chandeliers blazing down upon him, he felt sure he smelled tablet wax. If there were news hounds in the audience, they were keeping themselves on a leash. Huh. Maybe this would be all right.

"Look, sweetheart!" came a yell. "Lady Dok *did* convince Brother Malfred to join us! Over here!"

Dame Irona de Brewel was waving at them, as tall and hale as ever, and all the more imposing as she was standing upon her chair. By contrast, her sedate and scholarly husband Donn Felip greeted them with a bow.

"Good evening, Your Highness and Lady..."

"Yipes, Fred, don't sit on me!"

This last remark issued from Corvinalias, who was camouflaged against the black and white of a cushion.

Fred, Dok and Corvinalias took their places beside the couple who thought of themselves as good old down-to-earth Buddy and Ro-Ro Dabroo. Never mind that Buddy and Ro-Ro were probably the richest nobles in Midlandis— or would have been, had they not recently begun the practice of giving most of it away.

"And have your brother and his family arrived in town yet?" Donn Felip asked Fred. "Mesir Corvinalias and I have been talking about Alkemikal Drives— in a few years I'm sure all ships will have them, but till then, travelers must count on the winds. I hope they were favorable for the Royal yacht."

"I think so. I got a note from Enrick saying they're settled into the Royal Suite at the Nautilus. He sends you his particular regards."

Donn Felip beamed. "It's extraordinary, Your H... I mean, Malfred. Just extraordinary how, after so many years of completely misguided enmity, His Majesty and I finally meet and... well, I suppose that's an example of what you're doing on a larger scale with the League For Peace."

"Excuse me," interrupted Dame Irona, "but did I hear the word '*league*'? And '*peace*'? Also, '*for*'? I'm not a thinker like Buddy, but after hearing those words I feel sure you're talking about The League For Peace. Are you? Because—"

"Ro-Ro, honey. Shh. It's starting."

Chimes sounded, the lights dimmed, and the show the de Brewels had most recently financed began its premiere.

Fred hadn't been sure what to expect. But to his great relief, this was a winner.

It was a humorous variety act, led by a young master of ceremonies who, in his opinion, was destined for stardom: he had the moves, the gab, the magnetism. For well over an hour, the crowd was firmly in his hands as he moved them skillfully through an array of pleasant emotions... till alas, far too soon, the show began winding to a conclusion.

Its star was about to impart some touching and important final message. The business on stage fell to a hush. The audience leaned forward and

Rrring

From somewhere offstage shrilled the metallic jangling of a handbell. Thousands of heads turned this way and that, looking for

Rrrring

A growl of annoyance oozed from the audience. The show continued, but the spell was broken.

Rrrrring

"RCD," someone said, and the comment set off a ripple of indignation. Remote Conversation Devices were still a brand-new and very expensive Tekology. A government office, or a University, or a luxurious hotel like the Nautilus, might offer the use of RCD booths, but to own a private one, portable no less, and bring it to the theater…

Rrrrrrring

"Rich blister!"

"Imagine thinking you're so important!"

Dok's eyes were enormous, for she recognized the source of the noise, and with a sick jolt so did Fred. It was coming from the pocket inside his sleeve.

Rrrrrringgg

"Uh, sorry!" he yelped, leaping to his feet. He meant to escape out the fire safety doors, but his coronet caught the spotlight and the crowd put two and two together. A volcano from the Peaceful Islands could not have erupted more forcefully than did the laughter directed at Fred.

"Look at that crown. It's the Trickster Prince!"

"Gods afar, he got me!"

"Best joke in the show!"

"What a wag! I hear he was the King's own Fool for over twenty years."

"I hear he still is!"

Rrrrrrinnnggg

All the way down the aisle, the bell rang and rang. Fred thought the sea-green carpeting would swallow him whole before he reached the exit. But he made it. Choking down embarrassment, he heard

the thick door slam behind him as he stepped in a puddle of...
whatever puddles in Coastwall alleys. He pressed his back against
the slimy wall of the building opposite and dug into his sleeve.

From it he extracted a pewter tankard, dull with use, no
different in appearance from any drinking can used in any tavern for
the past two hundred years. It was empty, of course— except for the
noise of a bell ringing from inside it.

"Hello," said Fred into the mouth of the can. The ringing
stopped. He held it up to his ear.

The voice that answered him had the unmistakable accent of
the poor and flinty Alpine country known as Yondstone.

"Malfred? You hearin' me?"

"I hear you fine, Alvert. Where are you?"

Alvert Dragonsson had been a spy with Fred in Abode— among
other things. His wife Ata Maroo had also been a spy with Fred.
Among other things.

"...up at Whellengood Hall. I'm a-callin' you from the talk booth
Dame Elsebet had put in. What a fascinatin' modern age we're
a-livin' in, ain't it..."

Fred couldn't get a reply in. Alvert wasn't always the chattiest
fellow, but just now his flow of speech was unstoppable.

"... so you're about to set your big project a-runnin'... you
must have a long list o' last-minute what-not to look after... like
ree-ceptions, ain't that what you call them get-togethers where you
shake hands wi' them foreign dignitarians..."

His babble was remarkably free from any actual message and
the longer Fred listened, the more certain he became that something
unhappy was lurking beneath it.

"...healing Doktors all said I ought to create a sportive virament
for Maroo, so that's why we're a-goin' up to Lorenz Whellen's ranch
tomorrow. Don't know if you've met Mesir Lorenz, Malfred, but

that's Dame Elsebet's brother... bought up a good fair bit o' Maroo's cattle herd when she sold the..."

Fred kicked away a rat that was sniffing his boot. "Uh, Alvert. Is anything wrong?"

The drinking can fell silent. Finally it said "... you can tell, can't you..."

"Tell? Tell what?"

"...that somethin' wi' me, is off, like..."

"*Is* something off? With you? Like?"

Another stretch of quiet, during which a nervous fluttering struck at Fred's belly from within. Then Alvert blurted:

"It's Maroo. She's dead..."

An icy wave of misery flooded Fred's mind before it registered the rest of what Alvert was saying.

"...dead set against gettin' any better, Malfred! It's like she's built herself a stumblin' block. Some days she hardly even stands up out o' her chair-cart..."

Fred inhaled a huge, ragged breath with which to shout *don't scare me like that, you sky-high thin-sliced golden-coated goat juggler!* But at that moment, the can emitted the most frightful ear-splitting squawk.

He yelled in pain and dropped it into another puddle of he knew not what. It was making even worse noises now, as though an oboe were forcibly impaling a set of bagpipes, and just as Fred bent down to hook a finger gingerly into its handle the whole can vibrated to a long, flat, metallic buzz. A stranger's voice leaped out at him: twice as loud as Alvert's, harsh and gritty, growling in Abodean.

Fred nearly dropped the can again. His visit to Abode still held enough evil memories to make the back of his neck crawl. Ata Maroo's terrible illness, the stunted state of Corvinalias's feathers, the Weapon oh ye gods the Weapon— all of these and more were the work of Abode. Abode still had the other tankard, the counterpart of this one: the Twin Cans had been the original RCD devices, back when they were unexplainable spellbound objects, before their Tekology was understood. Fred and Dok had used them to communicate across the globe when they were spies, trying to find a way to stop Abode. Just like he was trying to stop them now.

Trying how? He thought. By going to variety shows?

No, worse. By playing the fool and running out into alleys and standing around dying of worry while stray dogs slinked by, stopping to lick at him.

The can had gone dead. Fred shoved it back into his sleeve and chose a direction to walk in. Time to go home. He still had a few hours...

The fire door slammed. Boots rang on the alley cobbles, running to catch him.

"Wait, Fred! Wait!" cried Dok.

"Forget it. I'm not going back in there."

"No, of course not! But please. Please come to—"

"Or going to any deep-damned party, either."

Dok's jaw tightened. "Pocks to parties! I have somewhere else in mind. Please. Come with me."

CHAPTER 7

THE ISLE OF GOLD, A hundred leagues from Coastwall across the brandy-black Midland Sea, is the dwelling place of the royal family.

At this point it should be mentioned that Uman-beings also have a royal family, which happens also to live upon the very same Isle. Many of their behaviors are similar to those of magpies—similar enough, in fact, that the Scientific Institute has launched a long-term study of Umans, with the intention of confirming whether they possess actual intelligence.

But back to the Royals' island stronghold.

The magpie nobility who do fealty to the Throne all have their fiefs on the southeastern coast. Many of these holdings are pines: best known of them is Highbough, whose triangular pinnacle juts above that of the rounder, more stately Broadbough. Others are whitewoods, such as Ku-Pre-Sah, ancient and twisted like the lineage of its masters, or oaks, like Whispercorn with its thick, soft bark. Some fiefs stand alone, and some share a trunk, as do Upper and Lower Cloudyblue.

At dawn the serfs of these great holdings arise to work the boughs. They prune, they shape; they harvest fruit or nuts in season; they carry out trade and fight away invaders. It's only later on, at about noon or so, that the nobles come forth and go about their business.

Though their business is far less strenuous than that of the serfs, there is always plenty of it, and magpie nobles are rarely at a loss for something with which to fill their days. In fact, they often end by dining at midnight, as did the Duke of Lower Cloudyblue on the night when a Uman ship was forced to make an emergency landing on the Isle of Gold.

"I say, Peep," the Duke was saying to one of his servants. "Will you crush another firefly into the lamp, there? Very good, well done. This last batch of flies is substandard, what? It's really becoming most intolerable. Tomorrow I'll scratch a very strong letter."

His Grace was old and more than a little deaf; he didn't hear Peep commenting on the fact that a Uman watercraft was approaching. But he saw it. His eyes were still sharp— far sharper, certainly, than those of the Umans, who seemed to have forgotten something.

Closer and closer came the ship. Between bites of pickled lizard, the Duke dabbed his beak on his wing, wiped his wing on the border of his black and white vest, and remarked: "Humph, Peep. Those Umans there have neglected to fit a cloth to their vehicle, what? Silly fritter-minded animals. Can't focus, you know. Short attention span."

And here he thought the business was over. Uman-beings did not particularly interest His Grace, although among magpies there *were* plenty of Uman-fanciers— his great-nephew Corvinalias, for one. Young Vinnie was so besotted with the bally creatures that he'd gone off to the mainland to live among them. Well, he could keep his Umans. They were trouble— always poking at something with their busy, meaty ape fingers.

The Duke ate part of a sun-dried mouse, followed by a nice crisp locust leg, and by the time he looked up from his meal the situation had changed dramatically. The ship had beached itself like a dyspeptic whale.

"I say, Peep. Looks like the Umans are in trouble, what?"

And the nature of the trouble soon was revealed.

"Look at this, Peep! Have you ever seen a male Uman fighting like that? The female simply doesn't know what to do with him! Aha, he's got hold of something shiny... now he's getting out of the boat... running up the beach... she's caught him... no! He's loose again!"

The Duke hopped up from his perch with the agility of a fledgling. "And now here comes a second female! I say, this is capital amusement— and *noteworthy,* what? Fetch me a chip of bark, Peep. I feel I should jot this down. The Scientific Institute will surely commend me... I'll show them I'm a scholar as well as a patron... but where's the *needle*, Peep? How can I scratch anything without one? You know how brittle my old fingernails are! Hurry! Oh, bother. They have him."

As the two larger Umans maidhandled their captive back the way he'd come, the Duke of Lower Cloudyblue had the pleasure of predicting that their unattended vessel would get caught in a rip current and float away without them. But no such thing occurred. Without further incident the Umans departed, uttering their calls which really are so very much like language.

"Bother it all. If only Vinnie could have seen this!"

The Duke threw away the chip upon which he had planned to scratch his notes. It fell down, down, down through the darkness and landed on an outer twig. Before you could say "waste not", some serfs had scuttled out and grabbed it.

They didn't see the twig below them bow downward and bounce back up as someone took flight from it. Someone chasing the Uman ship, as it continued toward Midlandis.

CHAPTER 8

T HIN, SILVERY MORNING LIGHT SPREAD through the quiet friendliness of Dok's house. She kept no servants, so there was no wake-up bustle and clang. Instead there was Fred, wearing only his diagonally striped silk underbreeches, squaring off at one end of a hallway and, after a little preparatory bounce on his toes, performing a tumbling pass of three... four... six flamboyant flips and something known as a Tanley Twist.

True, at the end of it he collided very lightly with the wall. But still he felt he'd earned the right to whisper *yes!* to himself— he hadn't pulled off that combination since his fourth level Fools' Guild exam. Filled with satisfaction, he strode into the kitchen.

Fred jabbed the fire in the stove to life and put on a kettle of water. As it boiled he yawned, stretched side to side, scratched his chest; he plucked Dok's favorite cup from a hook on the wall and set it under a tinware cone filled with the roasted and crushed makings of an energizing black drink, imported from the Peaceful Ocean, that was becoming very popular among the smart set. He poured hot water into the cone and while the black drink brewed, he strolled out to the dining room.

On the floor, near a corner, lay a serving tray; he picked this up and went in search of a napkin, which he found dangling from the corner of a picture frame, and a plate, which he found lying quite unbroken on the seat of a chair. He had to look around a bit for a spoon, but soon discovered several of them beneath an overturned vase and chose the prettiest one. With the tray thus assembled, he carried it into the kitchen and added a bread roll, a slice of ham, some butter and jam and... after a glance back at the dining table, Fred decided to skip the fruit. The basket was upside down and its precious hothouse-grown contents had all been thoroughly squashed into the tablecloth. Instead he added a flower, conveniently found in the remnants of the vase.

On the way back up the corridor, Fred caught his big toe on something. It turned out to be his handsome pin-pleated shirt and he thought of putting it on, but after a look at it, changed his mind—those fruit stains all over the back were never coming out.

The door of Dok's bedchamber opened silently, and Fred stole in unheard. He'd planned to set the breakfast beside her, but at the sight of Dok, sunk deep among a mass of thick square pillows surmounted by the sunburst of her hair, his heartbeat rose to such a powerful crescendo that he feared he might spill the whole deep-damned tray. So instead he put it on a table and slipped into the warm hollow waiting for him at her side.

One corner of Dok's mouth curved; her eyes opened. "Good morning, Your Highness."

"Good morning, Your Brilliance. I brought you breakfast."

"It can wait. Get back here and— mmm, yes. Like that."

Though they both knew what the upcoming day held, neither was in a hurry. They twined together as the sun climbed the clouds. By the time Dok finally rolled to the edge of the bed and reached for her favorite cup, the black drink she sipped from it was ice cold. She, however, felt thoroughly warm inside and out.

Fred squirmed over to fill in the Dok-shaped, Dok-scented space she'd vacated. "Did you hear something just now?" he murmured into the pillows. "A kind of bump? Knock at the door, maybe?"

"Probably one of your servants, bringing your morning messages over here. I'll go have a look in a minute." She put the cup down. "So now the big question: how are you feeling?"

"I think you might have a *just* a little inside knowledge regarding that subject."

Dok laughed. "I mean about today. The League. Everything." Her face turned serious. "Will you be all right?"

"You know what, Dok, I finally think I will."

Before she went to fetch the messages, she turned back to kiss him: a long, slow, sweetly caressing kiss that somehow tasted like triumph.

A few minutes later she was back. She plunked down cross-legged on top of the covers, leafing through a bunch of papers in a canvas bag.

"Here. Most of these are just silly news rags and advertising. But you'll want to read this one."

The letter she handed Fred sported a notable complexity of interlocking security folds, which meant it could only have come from the de Vonn family. Rulers of the Vonn Country. Parents of the Queen. He broke the seal— a drop of wax the same pink as the famous de Vonn sapphires, stamped with a seven-pointed star— and started unfolding. And unfolding. And unfolding some more.

"Must be some big secret," remarked Dok, who as a former Bureau Controller knew everything there was to know about paperwork, secret and otherwise.

"I imagine they want me to be the first to know who they've appointed as their country's envoy to the League For Peace. But holy hells, did they ever wait till the last minute! Game starts at noon, you know. I was worried they'd... oh, for the love of boils. Listen to this: 'We regret that we will be unable to attend the bruncheon celebrating Mesir Murd's investiture as Prince'. *Will be?* That was last year!"

Fred turned the letter this way and that, looking for a date; finding none, he sighed. "Well, they probably just forgot to send it till now. They must have a lot on their minds. I hear their court's got more intrigues than... *huh.*" He had been lounging against some pillows. Now he lounged no longer: he sat bolt upright.

There was a thread of anxiety in Dok's voice. "What is it?"

"They mention something that happened last week. Which means this letter isn't old at all." Fred narrowed his eyes at it. "How can they write this stuff with a straight face? Oh, wait. They didn't. They were laughing up their sleeves! Their armored sleeves. Encrusted with pink sapphires and old Vonnish lace and the blood of their enemies." He scowled and began flipping the letter's numerous pages. "Well, what do I care if they snubbed my bruncheon? I just want to know who their envoy is going to be. Know whose hand I'll be shaking. Get the place cards right."

Dok sat, picking nervously at the bedspread, as Fred flipped pages faster and faster, his expression becoming ever more irate. When he reached the last page he clenched his jaw. "And that's it. No mention of any envoy. In fact, no mention of the League at all. It's like they're snubbing it, too."

In what she thought of as a no-nonsense tone, Dok said, "Well then, you'll just have to proceed as though the Vonn Country were not part of the Kingdom."

Unfortunately, Fred thought it very much nonsense. "Not part of the Kingdom? How? Their daughter's the deep-damned Queen!"

"Well, that *is* ironic. But—"

"But nothing! What message does it send, if I can't get my own sister-in-law's family to include their country in, you know, this little thing I threw together to keep the world from plunging into Symmetric Destruction?"

Dok knew she was making a mistake but it slipped out. "If you'd let me help—"

"Help? Sure! Here's what I need. I'm going to need Kharl and Hizabel de mumping Vonn to become kindly protectors of the common good, ready to put themselves out, just the *tiniest* little bit, for the rest of humanity. Can you do that for me?"

"I—"

"Oh! Right! You can't. Because they're cold-blooded mercenary reptiles!"

The subject of the de Vonns had touched off something in Fred, set a corrosive reaction bubbling up from the bottom of his soul, an Alkemikal cascade Dok was powerless to reverse.

"Did you know they didn't even come to Margadet's wedding? It's true! I was there! Instead they sent some kind of secretary, with a ledger, as if their own daughter were a... a shipment of something... or more like *payment* for something..."

"Easy, now—"

"Here you go, old man Castramars! How about we trade you this brat of ours for a hand in running the show once you've kicked the tub? She's ever so slightly blind, but *your* brat is ever so slightly odd, so that works out!"

"Fred! Please!"

He could see Dok's hands reaching out to him, kneading his shoulders and stroking his chest, but he felt nothing as he continued:

"Because that's the good old Vonn Country way, isn't it? Why keep a brat around unless it's *worth* something? I mean, if it's no good, obviously you just pitch it over the fence to a bunch of monks"— here he dismissed himself with a gesture— "but if it's a keeper, well then, you're in business! Guess it's no surprise they don't need my little international debating club. They've still got Margie's sister and she's the prime product! Not damaged at all! Wonder what they're saving *her* up to buy? Maybe some... hoy, Dok, what are you doing?"

Dok had sprung to her feet. From the floor she grabbed her robe and pulled it on, knotting its undersash with a vigorous jerk. She kicked a pair of boots upright and slipped her bare feet into them. Fred scrambled to free himself from the quilts and pillows, but before he could reach her, she was already at the door.

"Where are you going?"

"I don't know. Someplace!"

"Someplace where?"

"Someplace where I don't have to stand back and watch you putting yourself through all this, this..."

For a moment she seemed at a loss; then her eyes caught a target and flashed with hatred. She lunged back toward Fred.

From his fingertips she snatched the letter, crushed it in her fist and sent the poisonous ball of it whipping across the room into a trash basket.

Her accuracy was perfect, of course. Dok knew everything there was to know about paperwork.

CHAPTER 9

O N A CORNER A FEW streets southwest of the Kingdom's most luxurious hotel stood a long-suffering baslin tree.

As a piece of vegetation, it wasn't much. Its leaves were shapely but few, its bark was scraped and scratched with a vast catalog of rude images, and the protective fence around it had collapsed over the years from the weight of loiterers. But to those who plied the news crier's trade, that tree was nothing short of legendary.

For some reason, the crowds that gathered around it were extraordinarily free with their coins. Admittedly these were mostly brass, now and then livened up with silver; but the crowds were huge and, probably by reason of its proximity to the elegant Nautilus, on that corner bits of luscious gold found their way into the pay bowl with surprising regularity. Therefore the right to stand beneath that meager tree, delivering an audible compilation of that day's printed bulletins, was awarded to the very best man in the Criers' Guild.

A weedy little fellow carrying a scroll drifted into place under the tree. He loosened his collar, lifted his chin, and a voice as deep as the bellow of a bull aurochs— yet somehow touched with sassy glitter, besides being smoother than vintage Sherry Lorosso— rolled forth to fill the air.

"Good to see you, Coastwall! It's noon. Hear now your announcements for Tinsday, first day of the Month of Asparagus!"

The fellow unrolled a few feet of notes and locked eyes with the insufficiently disguised Guild inspector stationed in the crowd. *Just you try and put anyone else here,* thought the crier. It's my corner every day for a reason.

"...a word from our partner, deCoastwel Bank. Find it unpleasant to walk like a peasant? Stop trudging and start riding! You can finance your new sedan chair with no money down— come in today and find out how, at the Kingdom's biggest bank. Safe and strong, you can't go wrong when you keep your coins at deCoastwel.

"All right, everyone. Ready for some good news? Let's go!

"The hottest ticket in town is one you can get for free: *Oh, Honey* premiered last night to huge acclaim. Critics are praising its crowd-pleasing comedy, such as a hilariously disruptive bit featuring the Trickster Prince. Tickets are offered on a first come, first served basis. Apply for yours at the Brewel Hall Public Library."

That warmed the crowd up nicely. The crier had a bit of discretion as to the order in which he read the announcements; he liked to hook them with something light, then get his claws in deeper with something frightening.

"City officers advise caution tonight as notorious blade-for-hire Vernadet Speng remains at large. Speng, who has made no secret of her clash with Coastwall's infamous crime boss Granny Almantree..."

Among the listeners was a fat strongarm wench, who elbowed her scrawny friend. "Hah. Hear that? Speng. Granny's gonna get her yet. You'll see."

"Well, that's hobbious. Ya hear me arguin?"

"...breakthrough for Tekology, researchers at Mitsa-Konig University have announced the discovery of a Phantactive variant that will revolutionize..."

A sedan chair hovering at the rear of the crowd raised its curtain long enough for a servant brat to pop out, golden coin in hand, and run toward the pay bowl.

"...your lottery numbers are..."

At the front of the crowd, a scribe's apprentice who hoped
to make a career change threw his last brass penny into the bowl,
trying his utmost to make eye contact with the crier.

"...the month might be named for Asparagus but this week it's
the plum that reigns supreme, with special celebrations around the
clock during the season's beloved Plum Blossom Festival... shop
late, dine early, and dance the night away! The famous party barge
moored at Holiday Street features music by..."

The crier's eyes and voice flowed along as smoothly as the
tide in the Denna, but his mind was on the Guild observer, whose
hands seemed to rest casually in the pocket at the seam of his shirt.
Anyone who'd been on the job longer than five minutes knew that
inside the pocket there was sure to be a counting clicker, with the
observer's thumb on its ratchet going ten leagues to the glass. *Well,
let it,* thought the crier— the crowd under the tree was even bigger
than usual, and he had them all hanging on his every word.

But then:

"...Today marks a historic moment in the emerging field
of world diplomacy, with the inaugural meeting of The League
For Peace..."

Aw, pus! Crowds hated this kind of thing.

"...a six-week conference intended to unite the world against
the ever-present new threat of Phantactive warfare. Envoys from
nations across the globe assemble at the renowned Nautilus..."

No, *no!* This bit went on far too long. His eyes raced ahead,
scouring the scroll for the little stars which indicated a change
of subject.

"...slated to include talks on border control procedure...
proposed new regulations regarding..."

The crier knew he was losing them.

"You know what, people? Let's skip ahead! Import of materials classified under... uh..."

He began to panic, frantically unwinding the scroll.

"Wait! How would you like to hear about the latest lurid crimes? Tips for healthy living? A highcat that was recently heard to ask its mistress for a cheese sandwich?"

The observer's hand, the crier was horrified to note, was no longer in his pocket. Worse: he was yawning. Worse yet— he was leaving.

"Hoy!" yelped the crier. "Here's how you can make up to ten silver bits a week without heavy lifting! Or how about this fellow: he lost six inches of unsightly muscle in only a month... healers hate him! Or... or... listen, everyone! To prevent the marthambles, just do this one weird thing!"

CHAPTER 10

THE NAUTILUS WAS A HOTEL, if one were determined to apply such a simple word to the home-away-from-home of those who could live anywhere and anyhow they wished. It was immaculately luxurious, as deeply tufted and lacquered as the palace of any noble, and staffed with serving folk who seemed able to read minds. From the standpoint of comfort, even the de Brewels— who back in their less enlightened days had lived a life whose opulence knew no limits— could not but approve of The Nautilus.

But it was also something more than a hotel, for in hidden lower levels beneath its red porphyry, white marble and plush velvet zigzagged the maze of the Central Agency for Intelligence, formerly known as The Bureau. In its day The Bureau had been the secret force guiding and protecting the Federated Kingdom of Midlandis, but its current iteration was not so very secret as all that; the Central Agency for Intelligence was slowly becoming an acknowledged tool of government. The Nautilus had even opened up some of The Bureau's former meeting rooms— at least, the ones that were ideally suited for hosting welcome receptions.

As Fred waited for the envoys of the world to come filing in, he was racked with pangs of empathy for those who are not typically in the spotlight. Though he held Fools' Guild certifications in jesting, clowning, tumbling, juggling, general acrobatics, funambulism, comedic monologue, poetry recital, poetry composition, play-acting, classical dance, tableau vivant, and miscellaneous amusements not specified, in this situation none of those were apropos. If it weren't for Corvinalias, who was perched on his shoulder making encouraging remarks, he didn't know what he would have done with himself. The waiting was killing him.

From across the deep, soft red carpet of the meeting room a pair of nearly identical wenches were fast approaching. Technically they were not envoys, but in a way they did represent Abode: they were its two highest-ranking generals, and after bringing the Weapon to Midlandis, they had seen the error of their ways, thrown down their hand-bombards and defected.

"Fred," whispered Corvinalias. "I think I've figured out which one of these two is which. That is, unless they've traded wardrobes again."

The pair now expressed allegiance to their new homeland by wearing aggressively partisan uniforms— not military ones, but those of the Brewel Country Seahorses and the Oldmarsh Beavers, two throwball teams whose rivalry had re-arranged the interior of many a tavern. No one could persuade them that this mode of dress was anything but appropriate for every occasion; they were wearing it even now.

Closer and closer they strode, in their martial Abodean gait, without expressions on their distinctively Abodean faces. The leftmost general was wearing a cap embroidered with the words *SEAHORSE NATION*, so new that the merchant's price ticket still adhered to its rigid brim, and she strode up so close to Fred that it nearly knocked the coronet from his head. Her loud, guttural speech was a form of Midlandic that could best be described as sparse.

"Greet. Party good."

The other general, wearing an oversized brown and green tunic that proclaimed *DAM STRAIGHT BEAVERS WIN AGAIN!*, said nothing, but made the inexplicable decision to salute Corvinalias.

Fortunately, Corvinalias knew Abodean; instead of taxing the generals' linguistic powers he began speaking to them in their native tongue, using a voice that sounded authentically full of barley and yakbok hair.

His facility for mimicking speech had never failed to impress Fred, though Corvinalias did protest modestly that Uman languages were ridiculously easy to pick up. They were hatchling peeps, he said, compared to Bat, with its extreme pitch, or Whale, with its complex chordal tones— and don't get him started on the language of moths, which he was fascinated by but could *not* speak, as it was completely olfactory.

At last Corvinalias put his beak to Fred's ear. "They say they're looking forward to the arrival of the envoy from their— well, when they say 'former homeland' they use what's known as the pejorative register. That's insults, basically. The things they call Abode, whew— they are, uhh, pungent. However. When they talk about the envoy himself, they use the laudative register: that's praise, high praise. They say the gentleman is not only very intelligent, but also very well connected and..."

The two were now obviously discussing the envoy's physical charms, making gestures it didn't take an interpreter to understand. Corvinalias felt Fred's ear turn hot and pink.

Abruptly the general wearing Seahorses gear looked down at the Prince and the Count and, in perhaps the most grammatical Midlandic sentence she had ever uttered, exclaimed "Envoy good. Not like Dictator, Marshal Fo."

"Fo *bad*," agreed the Beavers fan. "Bad like... self-goal Beavers!"

"*So* bad! Like penalty one Seahorses!"

"If I Abode again? See Fo? Face, bam!"

"I Agree! Foot! Beans! Bam!"

The generals' gestures re-ignited, this time in ardent pantomime of what they'd do if they ever again encountered their former commanding officer.

"Jab fat middle!"

"Mustache pull!"

"Neck, twist!"

"Beans again— bam bam bam!"

Fred angled his head discreetly toward Corvinalias. "I'm really glad I took your advice not to put any liquor in the punch bowl."

"I had a feeling. Anyway, you can always break it out later. I hear there's an excellent selection of Lorosso waiting in a pantry somewhere."

The magpie stretched his wings. They looked functional enough, but Fred knew they were still recovering from the incident which had left them not quite up to the task of flying. "Hoy," said Corvinalias, "I might regret this, but will you lift me over to one of these goodwives' shoulders? I'll entertain them. You should go help your brother— he's getting swarmed."

King Enrick was indeed the center of a rapidly increasing crowd. The envoys were arriving.

The envoy from Swez, a gentleman with a great woolen cloak pulled up around a kind, old, sun-leathered copper face, bowed to His Majesty; behind him his entourage formed a wall as silent as the cliffs guarding the eastern mouth of the Midland Sea. The envoy from the Herb Islands was jolly, deep brown and angular, surprisingly young for one representing such vast old wealth and power. The envoy from the Ocean Empire happened to be a relative of Ata Maroo's; she had many, and most of them in high places. One after the next, the King and the Prince received this fascinating collection of people; and though it was most gratifying to see the folkwear and customs he'd only read about in books come to life, for Fred the most astonishing thing in the room was the King himself.

How smoothly he moved. How naturally he spoke. How easily his eyes met each new acquaintance's, held them just long enough, moved cheerfully on. Fred glanced at Enrick's feet, standing rock solid in their black eelskin slippers, not fidgeting in the slightest. And then back to his face, where, framed in a natty little pointed blue-black beard, there was an actual smile.

Could this possibly be the same weird wet towel of a kid he'd been dragged to the Isle of Gold to serve, twenty-three years earlier? Could life really have been so kind? A prayer of gratitude, left over from Fred's boyhood as a failed novice monk, floated up from the depths of his brain:

> *Joy, that all which might have been*
> *has left me this, which is.*

And then came the sweetest, the most unbelievable part of all, the part where a door opened from somewhere across the room and in came a handmaid, guiding Queen Margadet de Vonn.

Despite her family, despite their handicaps, they had a beautiful love. She and Enrick had been married for, what, five years now? And still Fred couldn't look at them together without feeling as though— against all odds— there really *were* hope for the world.

"Sorry to be late!" Though Margadet's eyes were as motionless as a portrait's, there was a lively flush of exertion in her cheeks. "It's just that little Neddie had *such* a burst of energy. He went clog dancing, clippity-clop, all up and down the corridor, and wouldn't let me leave till I'd listened to him. He said 'I'm practicing to show Uncle Fred'— but I told him that would have to wait till tomorrow. I know this will be a busy day. Who are we meeting right now?"

The King didn't miss a beat. "Margadet I am putting your hand into the hand of this gentleman who is the envoy from... oh I am so sorry Your Excellency. I did not hear you say which country you represent. Will you please repeat it as I present you to Her Majesty?"

Amazing. Simply amazing. Fred marveled at the two of them, and the knots of worry inside him began to loosen. *Everything's going to be fine,* he thought. Maybe I *will* invite Dok to the big gala dinner tomorrow.

More envoys, more greetings. More servants in the red and white uniforms of the Nautilus, replenishing the buffet tables at the back of the room and adding more harmless punch to the bowl.

Fred's apprehension had just about faded away when a steward came in walking very, very fast, with a look on his face and three message cards on a tray. "Your Highness. These are for you."

The first one read: *The Yuliyo Advance, bearing the envoy from Abode, is approaching Coastwall Harbor. It flies a message indicating apology for delay.*

The second one read: *Yuliyo Advance has docked. Again apologizes for delay, and for disruption at harbor.*

The third one was blank. Unless you count a scrawl which looked like the pen had been knocked sideways, ending with signs of an ink spill.

The doors at the back of the meeting room burst open and in surged a sedan chair.

Its own bearers looked alarmed at their predicament. The chair was covered in road dust, its curtains were rippling, and a maniacal jumble of noises issued from within: monkeys shrieking, goats bleating, some kind of bird... from among the noises Fred recognized Abodean words, uttered in a snarling basso.

The curtain of the chair flew open and the Abodean generals, serving themselves some punch, turned to look. When they saw who was in the chair, they threw down their cups and yelled.

"FO!"

The generals rushed the vehicle. Something black and white popped out of it to attack them.

Corvinalias, left perching on the lip of the punch bowl, toppled backward into it having chirped out a single, horrified word.

As pandemonium swept the room, Fred had just enough time to wonder whether that word was Abodean, or Oceanic, or what. He'd never heard it before.

What did it mean— *'rooki'*?

CHAPTER 11

And now for some facts about Marshal Fo, the Dictator of Abode.

As far as his people were concerned, Fo's was the strong hand grasping the halter of the yakbok which, in this metaphor, was their country. It was he who guided them through the snows of adversity to fields of bounteous barley; it was he who did various other metaphorical things, all having to do with yakboks. The yakbok, it should be mentioned, is a stubborn, durable and largely uncomplaining creature. And that is well, because in Abode, complaints lead only to places like Healthful Hard Labor In the Cold Wind Camp and But Your Relatives Don't *Want* to Come Home Ever Again Camp.

So if the people of Abode suspected that Fo really didn't know one end of a yakbok from the other— that he was no more than a shadow puppet, held up to the light by powers greater than he, they refrained from saying so. Abodean shadow puppets, it should be mentioned, are made from yakbok hide, so this plays into the metaphor.

Yes, if the people had such suspicions they refrained from airing them. They looked away from the growing chaos emanating from the Sublime Palace of the Citizens of Abode, and ignored rumblings— sometimes literal— from the nameless University where Alkemikal Energy Research had ground to a halt. They paid no heed to rumors that Marshal Fo had run afoul of his puppeteer, and was doing his Dictating from house arrest; in short they followed the Abodean saying, older than Dictators or whoever handles them, which runs: *The ice storm blows; the yakbok grazes on.*

Then something most astounding happened— Marshal Fo escaped. And here the yakbok metaphor must end, for no yakbok had ever yet managed to reach the coastal country which Abode had long been bribing to build it a navy, and there go aboard a modern, Alkemikally driven ship. No yakbok had ever let the two mariners in charge of such a ship assume he was their rightful passenger. No yakbok had ever spent seven days prostrate with seasickness, then abruptly snapped out of it and spent the next four nearly destroying the ship which, it should be mentioned, was the *Yuliyo Advance,* chartered to carry an envoy to a peace conference in Midlandis.

The glittering dome located at the front of the boat reminded Fo of things he'd seen in his researchers' Laboratoriums and he did his best to try and examine it, just the way he often tried to examine the things he saw in his researchers' Laboratoriums. Breaking the dome open, and plucking out the shard of crystal that flashed beneath it, caused a lot of excitement. It was as though the sailors— two wenches who spent all their time shouting at him in some language— didn't *want* him to break open the dome and examine the shard of crystal.

Maybe the part where the boat did a lot of zigzagging, and came close to turning upside down, and ended up running up onto a beach somewhere, had something to do with the crystal. Fo didn't really know— the wenches wouldn't let him keep it. When he tried running away along the beach, they grabbed him and took the crystal and pushed him back into the boat. They locked him in a room, just the way his third general had locked him in a room back in Abode. Always the rooms.

Fo looked out the round window of his new room and saw a bird; he opened the window and let the bird in.

That, Fo now thought, might have been a mistake.

EVER SINCE THE SAILOR WENCHES had pushed Marshal Fo off the boat and into a curtained box, the bird had kept up a continuous shrieking and shouting. The shouts sounded something like the local language, but Fo couldn't understand them, so he paid attention only to the shrieks— which were so annoying that pretty soon he stopped paying attention to those, too.

The curtained box had taken him somewhere and when its curtains opened he'd been attacked by two of his generals who, he suddenly seemed to recall, had been missing from Abode for quite some time. It took a lot of guards to pull them away from him and then after all of that, Fo was *not* surprised to be taken away and locked into another room.

The bird was left outside the room. It scratched at the lock and shrieked some more while Marshal Fo looked around.

This latest room was rather nice.

In fact it was a whole series of rooms.

The floor was covered with rugs, as soft as the one in the Citizens' Supreme Chamber of the Sublime Palace of the Citizens of Abode. Except these rugs went all the way into every corner, so there probably weren't any bugs or mice under them. Fo decided that if he ever tired of this room and escaped it, he would cut off a good chunk of rug and take it with him. The one back in the Supreme Chamber had cost a lot of money.

In the lamps overhead there were artificial light jars, like the ones made in Abodean Laboratoriums. Except these were more like globes, and were a pretty color, and didn't stink. A few of the light globes would fit nicely in his pockets, if he decided to escape.

There was a truly gigantic bed. Fo sat on this for a few minutes and it occurred to him that these rooms must be a dormitory. In that case, he made a mental note to demand that the other families assigned to this bed be sent away. He wanted it for himself.

There was washbasin big enough to lie down in. Again, whoever was sharing this would have to go.

There was a squat bucket, but a really nice one, which Fo at first thought was some kind of storage cabinet. All his, only his.

And then came the very best part: a table with food on it. Fo crammed handfuls of it lustily into his mouth, on the theory that it was better to eat it now than see it taken away and given to someone else.

And so here he was. What his next move would be, Fo had not yet completely decided. But this dormitory was really quite the best place he'd ever been. Much nicer than the Supreme Palace of the Citizens of Abode. Fo wanted to stay forever.

Where, exactly, was he?

CHAPTER 12

THE GREAT MEAT MARKET OF Coastwall *wants* to be sanitary. It truly does. It tries.

Time and again citizens have enacted measures to ensure that filth and ordure, noise and mess are banned from that shambles of covered streets, crammed end to end with stinking stalls, from which Coastwall emits its hams and sausages, ribs and racks and shanks. Donn Felip de Brewel himself had recently made an inspection tour, before which he downed a very large gulp of plum brandy and said "right, let's see what we're up against"; the result had been practically a whole book of new laws. And sometimes the laws do work— for the creatures to be eaten, at least. A hog in Coastwall today has a very fine chance of perishing in a swift and painless manner. Not so for the crooks of Coastwall, should they have the misfortune of running afoul of Granny Almantree.

One of the places where Granny holds her roving court is at the meat market. Her audience chamber there is literally underground, in one of the great cellars lined with blocks of ice and sawdust where flesh awaits its fate.

"Na then, me benny wenches," she crackled to the thugs peeping out at her from among hanging sides of mutton, beef and pork. "I hear news as one of yez brung me a giftie. Out with it. Yer Granny feels a slim sliver unwell this afternoon."

Here she coughed up a lump of something and spat it across the pool of lamplight in which she stood; the lump had a distinct smell of maidenroot but none of Granny's underlings dared to wonder why she still chewed the stuff. If the ancient empress of Coastwall crime wanted to think of herself as still young enough to whelp a brat— or pretty enough to appeal to anything with a set of beans— she was welcome.

Silently a thug came forward and handed her a box.

Under the butcher's-paper lid of the box lay a slab of ice and upon it two thumbs.

"Heh, heh! Well brung! These is most clearly the correct set a grippers."

Granny plucked one from its bed of ice and held it up in the oil light. It was bloodless and waxen, but its skin was decorated with a network of green, blue and purple flowers: one-tenth the wedding ink of Vernadet Speng.

"Ha! She won't throw any knives at Granny ever again. And she'd a got worse, but for her luck in husbands. If her man weren't such a benny ratmouth, that mally moll wouldn't just be wearin' Coastwall mittens— she'd be a barrel o' flumbers' flesh!"

The crooks in the meat locker muttered amongst themselves. They all knew about the man Vernadet Speng had married: he had gone off to live in Spireburgh, a city four hours away, and from there spy for Granny, giving her an inside look at the gang run by her only rival, a literate male crimelord who, with his inkhorn crime syndicate, had lately begun cutting into Granny's profitability.

She raised her head, which was an amorphous ovoid encased in a greasy wrap, just like the rest of her. "Which a yez can I thank for this matched set?"

The thug who had handed her the box glanced back toward the sides of meat. In the shadows among them hid a small, scrupulously clean, somehow mannish-looking wench dressed in the red and white uniform of the Nautilus. She raised one hand, unconsciously keeping its thumb tucked back.

Granny bared her dirty teeth at the mannish wench. "Ah! So it's Bessy the Boy who snooped Speng's hideout! Care to tell yer Granny how? O' course thez na got ta say."

Bessy the Boy felt she *did* have to say. "I... followed her husband. He led me right to her."

Granny growled. "Did tha? So he was in Coastwall?"

Bessy the Boy was unsure what Granny wanted to hear. She liked her thumbs and so said nothing.

Granny pressed her. "Was Speng's little sweetheart here in person? Physicalwise? Not sendin' word to his wife by way a mediaries?"

"Y-yes, Granny."

Out flashed Granny's withered hand. From it flew something small and metallic— a penny, perhaps? Yes, but a penny with a razor-sharpened edge, which embedded itself in a hanging side of mutton.

"Thick weeping pusboils!" roared Granny Almantree.

Fearful murmurs raced through the troop of crooks in the great dim locker. A nastier than usual smell had entered among them and its source soon became evident: the slit the sharpened penny had left in the mutton was rapidly turning an ugly color, emitting an ugly stink.

Granny was no longer a hushed and motionless lump. She was shouting, striding about.

"Hamel scab-flappin' Fliss *never* lets his men step an inch from Spireburgh! If Speng's sweetheart was here, then he's been gave the boot from Fliss's gang. His use to Granny is finished!"

When Granny thrust the shadowy cowl of her head right up to Bessy the Boy's face, Bessy didn't flinch. Granny's dirty-green eyes glowed approval.

"Yez a tough lil brute. If only yez really *were* a man— what use I'd make a that! If I had more weepers a-watchin' from inside Fliss's gang I could work it like a puppet. That soft dangling sack a paper-scratchers! All they do is inkhorn wheezes— fakery and forgery! Fliss his own self can't even point a little steel finger."

The fingers Granny pointed were usually darts, tipped with poison. Whatever had been on the penny was clearly one of her worst concoctions: the slit in the mutton was now the bull's eye of a gritty gray circle, which had begun not only to stink, but to smoke. As the reeking ring of ash grew and grew, there was silence among the crew of crooks. They seemed as frozen as the brown ice all around them. But then Bessy the Boy spoke up.

"Why not go bigger?"

The fact of someone speaking to her out of turn so surprised Granny that, by way of reply, she could only utter a gurgling noise; possessed by some reckless bravado, Bessy the Boy went on.

"Working a puppet's a fine thing, Granny, but why limit yourself to the Fliss gang? Let them have Spireburgh. *This* is the capital. If you were behind someone at Brewel Hall, you could work the whole country." She took a breath and brought out a handsome phrase. "After all, the bigger the puppet, the bigger the show."

The glow of Granny Almantree's eyes cooled from admiration to envy.

Very deliberately she raised her hand a few inches, pointed it at Bessy the Boy's red and white uniformed heart, and was rewarded with seeing her cringe.

"An how dez tha know I ain't got someone there already, me brave little mannish wise-wench? Clap yer gape shut before you give away my game! I collect yappers, as well as grippers!"

She meant tongues, as well as thumbs.

The crooks hid themselves deeper in the maze of meat.

Bessy the Boy liked her tongue and so— again— said nothing.

"Out with yez! All a thez!"

The crooks were only too glad to comply, and swarmed for the door with alacrity. An oddly colored light had begun to creep up the hanging side of mutton.

Granny Almantree was left alone to watch the slab of flesh go up in what were not precisely flames.

Up until Bessy made her remark, Granny had enjoyed the simple pleasure of imagining her target as Hamel Fliss— but she couldn't go back to such callow yearnings anymore. Now her head was filled with rage that she'd never thought to raise her sights any higher.

Bessy the Boy was right, damn her deep and burn her black.

The bigger the puppet, the bigger the show.

But who would it be?

What puppet could be big enough for Granny?

CHAPTER 13

I N A SERVING PANTRY JUST off the meeting room, Corvinalias lay on a counter wrapped in a tea towel. "I'm... all right," he coughed, and a bit of citron peel flew out of his beak along with more punch.

Fred hunched over him feeling as though he really ought to do more. "Should I hold you upside down? Should I shake you? Just a little, I mean."

"No, no..." More coughing, but at least no more citron peel; Corvinalias gulped and gasped for a few moments, and then squirmed upright. "I'm not going back out there, Fred. Not until she's gone. Why in the hells' hind hoofprints is she even *here*? Never mind! I know!"

"Well then, you know more than I do. Who's this *she* and why are you more worried about her than about Marshal mumping *Fo?*"

In answer, Corvinalias retreated into the towel. From inside its folds sounded a mixture of growl, whine and whisper: "*She* is Rookapella Elsternom-Elsternom. Rooki."

Rooki. Fred took a deep breath. Now it made sense.

The towel shivered. "She's the one my family keeps nagging me to marry. Well, I won't do it!"

Fred suppressed a sudden urge to run up the wall of cabinets. "No offense, Corv, but how is a tiff with some relatives a hundred leagues away more important than having a peace conference crashed by an unhinged Dictator?"

"If you knew Rooki you wouldn't ask. *She's* an unhinged dictator! She'd yell at the sun for rising wrong— I'm not kidding, Fred, I've heard her do it."

"Well, I appreciate that, Corv, but—"

"She's the worst shrew this world's ever seen— and I should know, I've seen the world! You'd think my Great-Uncle Jey and my Auntie Chakta and everyone else would realize what a shrew she is. And they do. They *do!* They don't recommend any of *their* nestlings marry her, do they? Of course not! Make *me* take the brunt, that's their way of thinking. They couldn't care less whether I'm a Prophessor now or have any important projects or still hope to have more adventures. Oh no, they just want to see eggs! Keep the bloodline going! As if Rooki hasn't got boughs and boughs full of *other* fifth cousins who'd work just as well! I suppose it's because she's clashed with them all. She does every hobby, joins every society, pushes herself in everywhere. There's not a soul in Upper Cloudyblue, or Lower Cloudyblue, or anywhere on the Isle, who hasn't got scorch marks from her tongue! I wouldn't last a day with her as my— no. I won't even say it. With my luck, there's still a wish left in me and it might happen, Ye Gods forbid."

"But Marshal Fo..."

"Oh, how I wish Rooki would get the deep-damned scabby flux away from here! Anywhere, as long as it's far from me! And take Fo with her!"

Fred began pacing the pantry. Back and forth along the space between its red lacquered shelves, all filled with red and white porcelain, lit not by globes but by long, sleek tubes. A nice, neat, narrow place, without room for error. Maybe he and Corvinalias could stay in it forever.

The door opened a few inches to admit a soft voice with a honey-sweet Vonnish accent. "It's me. Are you two in here?"

Before he could reply, the Queen had slipped into the pantry with them. She began speaking into a shelf full of soup tureens, but the complex metallic quality of their echo told her she'd missed her aim. Quickly she turned to face Fred.

"Enrick told me you rescued Corvinalias from drowning in punch, and that there was a brawl at the reception. He says I'd have liked the brawl, that it turned into a real demonstration of the combative arts. He says I could probably have taken on both the Abodean generals at once— isn't that sweet of him to say?— and that with my skills, I could easily have torn them away from, well, he wasn't clear about who they were fighting."

"Margie, listen. I don't want this to spread, all right? But instead of the envoy Abode was supposed to send, we have a substitute…"

"Rookapella damned Elsternom-Elsternom!" wailed Corvinalias.

Blind or no, the Queen could not have looked more blank. Fred pinched the magpie's beak gently shut and explained: "One of our guests is, uh, someone who should *not* be here. But. Ah. Well. Let's not worry. Nobody panic. I'll figure it out. I'll come up with a plan. I'll deal with it."

"Is that your foot making that noise? Goodness, you're tapping it faster than Enrick ever used to. Calm, now. Breathe from *here*." The Queen's strong and motherly young hands, grown stronger still from her practice of combative grappling, settled on Fred's solar plexus. They did calm him down, but not by much. "Do you need more time? Let's postpone the opening ceremony. The envoys can wait, I'm sure."

"*No!* No. I mean, inconveniencing them really should be our very last resort, understand? They've come from across the world. Months and months, some of them took getting here. Even the *Yuliyo Advance* takes a week and a half to make the trip."

"So what's a little longer? My mother once made an envoy from the Pashma Country wait so long that he fell in love with the knight guarding his chamber, caused her a brat, and brought that little one to the meeting with him. Oh, now, I can hear you clenching your fists! Your knuckles crack." The Queen drew a deep and resolute breath of her own. "You know what? I'm sorry I even remembered that stupid story. There are things my family does that I've always hated— in fact, a lot of times I find myself guided by a wish to be as *un*like them as I possibly can. So don't worry. I understand. I'll make sure no one hears about this."

Fred squeezed her hand. "Thanks. Now. I saw some guards taking this gentleman..."

"You mean Lady," interjected Corvinalias. "She's a baroness."

The Queen was confused. "Who is?"

"Don't mind him, Margie. Just tell Enrick to keep making the guests feel at home. He's doing great. Meanwhile I'll go check on this, this person."

"Excellent plan. Do you need more help? I'll send for Dok."

"No! *No!*"

Corvinalias snorted. "Way to go, Fred. Shout louder. Her Majesty's ears aren't sensitive at *all*."

"Pocks, I'm sorry."

As the Queen massaged her ear, she said "Fine. I won't send for Dok. But are you sure you won't need anyone else?"

"Positive. Now that I think about it, we're all right. This probably looks worse than it is— maybe Fo *does* know enough about Abode's, ah, situation to be able to speak for them. At any rate he can't do much harm, can he, locked up in his suite? Of course he can't. So. Deep breath for me, and thanks again for listening, Margie. I'll go check on Fo after the ceremony."

Corvinalias scrambled free of the towel and opened his beak, about to say something; but he corrected it to one last cough, which included a fragment of clovespice. Fred was already agitated enough. He didn't have to know that, to the list of her myriad hobbies,

Rookapella Elsternom-Elsternom had recently added the art of picking locks.

CHAPTER 14

OOKAPELLA ELSTERNOM-ELSTERNOM ALWAYS KNEW
WHAT to do.

This was her absolute conviction. If any misguided soul
happened to suggest that she was wrong about something, Rooki
would tell them where they might store their suggestion: loudly,
with great emphasis, and at length. In crushing her opponents, she
liked to be thorough. The world didn't hold back; why should she?

And so she was determined to show everyone that they were
wrong, absolutely wrong, when they said no one could ever fully
tame a Uman.

Rooki was sure it could be done. Corvinalias Elsternom e
Rokonoma had very nearly succeeded at it, and in Rooki's opinion
had gone wrong only in his choice of animal: Vinnie's Uman was
flashy and entertaining, but it was far too young. There hadn't been
more than three or four gray hairs in the coat under its jingle-bell
hat— it was probably in its low thirties, and thus reaching the peak
of wildness. A foolish choice. This Uman of Rooki's, however, was
older and mellower and she had the very highest hopes for it.

For one thing, it seemed very familiar with the concept of being
told what to do. Rooki couldn't speak its language quite yet, but
she had worked out a way to issue commands by means of properly
timed and located jabs of the beak. Using this method she had
managed to keep her pet well under control, though other Umans
did seem a bit threatened by him. That didn't matter, as long as *he*
was a bit threatened by Rooki.

Just give me a few months, she thought. I'll put this fine
strapping beast aboard another Uman ship headed back to the Isle,

and enter him in the Lower Cloudyblue Agricultural Exposition. Or maybe an art show like the Ku-Pre-Sah Biennial. Or rent him to a circus. There were endless possibilities. The world was going to marvel at Lucky— that was what she'd named her Uman.

"All right, boy, I'm back!"

Rooki's wings were a black and white blur as she fluttered down to perch on the latch of Lucky's cage. She perched one-handed, while inserting a Uman hatpin into the keyhole. "This fancy twig I found will do the job. Yes...yes... almost... ah!"

The lock clicked open. That was Umans for you: always inventing some puzzle. But you couldn't blame them. Nature made them want to exercise their busy, meaty ape fingers.

"Lucky! Oh, Lucky! I'm here! So this is the cage they put you in, is it? Well, I tried to stop them. I *told* them you were a free-range Uman and that being locked up is bad for your mental development... but did they listen, those rotten, thieving wet hens? And they have the nerve to say *we* steal! All right, let's see what they gave you for feed and bedding."

Rooki had to admit that her pet was being held in a very impressive trap. Most wild Umans lived in tiny structures with only one or two chambers to them, but this was a proper hive— it compared very favorably with the Uman hive back on the Isle, the one where Vinnie had found *his* pet.

That hive had been built of golden sandstone, and contained countless fascinating nooks full of objects, many of which were red and yellow and sported pictures of magpies. Its chambers were designated variously for feeding, sleeping, grooming and so forth: Umans lived in their hives almost exactly the way magpies lived on boughs, and it was truly fascinating the way the creatures had evolved characteristics so very similar to those of people. When she'd joined the Scientific Institute, Rooki had attended a lecture series on the topic of convergent traits, and had enjoyed it greatly, although the speaker *had* been wrong about many things and she'd spared no effort to tell him so.

However, as she soared through the lushly appointed rooms of Fo's suite, Rooki found herself approving of all she saw. This was a very rare position for her.

"Hmm. Good lighting, good ventilation… Lucky! Where are you? *There* you are! Oh, now *look* at that feeding station. Have you been a gweedy widdle monster? Who's going to have a tummy ache? Did you go poo in the special corner? Good boy!"

However. The longer Rooki considered the comfortable qualities of this hive, the more convinced she became that they spelled trouble. If Lucky got used to this place, he would never want to leave it. She'd seen it happen: the Umans in the sandstone hive almost never came out. It had been fortunate indeed for Vinnie that his pet had been rejected by its littermates and forced to leave— otherwise it would never have amounted to anything. Well, Rooki would be damned if she let herself fail so early in the game. Like it or not, Lucky was going to live where and how *she* told him to.

MARSHAL FO HAD BEEN ENJOYING a nice leisurely lounge on a soft bench near the food when the bird flew at him. He threw his arms up in defense: that thing liked to go for the face.

It cawed and crowed and twittered on and on. Gradually Fo began to figure out what made it stop, or at least slow down a bit. Standing up seemed to help. Walking was better. He threw a sad glance back at the food table, but if leaving it behind meant this bird pecked him less, it was a trade-off worth making. A rarely-used corner of Fo's mind glowed gently, showing him an image of the general who had recently taken to ordering him about, back in Abode. The image changed to a feeling: the feeling of a hand-bombard, pushing into his back as he stepped out onto the balcony to address his Citizens. This feeling, and the feeling of the bird pecking him, shimmered on the verge of making some sort of connection, but the mental effort was too great so instead Fo reached into his pocket after one of the pastries he had stashed there.

He munched the pastry and walked. Sometimes he turned in a direction that made the bird angry; with the instinct common to even the most rudimentary organisms, he then avoided these directions. Not long afterward, he was surprised to find himself passing through the door of his dormitory and out into a corridor— and once there the bird did a remarkable thing. It pressed its feathery crest against his cheek and burbled a few notes of song.

Once again, somewhere in the foggy jumble of Fo's consciousness, an image presented itself: a gigantic, friendly woman, connected somehow with food and the idea of being lifted up. The image lasted only a moment but it was nice. Being here in the corridor was nice. Fo was glad to be in the corridor.

He continued onward, away from the bird's pecking and toward its other, kindlier action, and was just getting the hang of it when the bird went crazy. It started pecking him wildly, hitting him with its wings, clawing. Fo gave a little shout and that made it worse so he held his tongue and fled from the bird through a little door he saw standing open.

Whew! whistled Rooki. She was perched on the upper edge of an open door: a safe place because, in her experience, Umans rarely looked up. And besides that, she knew their eyesight to be extremely dull. Magpies could see all kinds of things Umans couldn't: for example, a reflection in the handle of a samovar at the end of this corridor, clearly showing a troop of females on the way. How very fortunate for her pet that— Rooki looked back over her shoulder into the little room where he was hiding— that this pantry had been left open for him to duck into. He was lucky indeed.

The approaching female Umans weren't visible yet, but they would be around the corner in a few seconds— oh, no! Rooki remembered the door of Lucky's cage. He'd left it open! They'd notice he was missing!

Rooki leaped from her perch and hurried to fix his mistake. She swooped to the keyhole, hooked her fingernails into it and hurled herself against the weight of the door. It didn't move. She did it again and again. Still wasn't moving, damn it! And the soft carpet made it hard to hear how close the females were getting!

Rooki's heart was racing leagues to the minute. At last the momentum of her attempts built up to a tipping point and the door swung easily on its well-crafted and thoroughly oiled hinges. With a soft thump and click it pulled shut just as the female Umans arrived.

Rooki pressed herself against the intricately carved doorframe, praying that the animals' feeble senses wouldn't register her. And they did not. It was unbelievable how Umans could look directly at something without seeing it.

In their mainland dialects the animals communicated to one another about how someone would be back later to check on Lucky. Then they went away.

The racing of Rooki's heart suddenly felt good. Excitement: isn't that the point? Avoiding excitement was like avoiding conflict— it made for a vegetative life, really no life at all. What kind of blockhead wanted a world that was nothing but peaceful?

WHEN SHE REACHED LUCKY AGAIN, he was drinking from a bottle he'd found in the pantry.

Uh-oh. Rooki knew this drink: it was an intoxicating liquor. How much of it had he downed already? Oh, no! And all the pecking in the world couldn't stop him from finishing the rest.

Never in his life had Marshal Fo tasted something so delicious as this, whatever this was. The bottle it came in was heavy and looked like diamonds, so the drink inside it must be valuable, but in Abode even the most valuable drink was throat-searing, nose-watering poison compared to this. Again and again Fo slurped it, relishing how every draft brought gustatory memories forth and set them dancing upon his tongue. Among other things, this drink tasted like truffles, and leather, and sugar, and smoke, and walnuts, and butter, and raisins, and oh so many of the other delicious imported flavors he had enjoyed as Dictator of Abode. The best thing about this drink was how it didn't taste anything at all like barley, which is what most of the food in Abode tasted like, being made from barley as most of it was.

Fo tipped the Stewen crystal decanter up to his mouth and let its last drops of Sherry Lorosso delight him. Then he put it down with a much harder thump than he'd been meaning to, collided with the door frame somewhat and went off in search of more.

The bird. For a moment he'd forgotten the bird. It was there again, pecking. Well, let it peck. Fo's face felt most wonderfully immune. He swayed leisurely down the corridor, now and then impinging on the wall to no great effect. The flavor of the drink stayed with him, unfolding into newer and deeper iterations, like— like this pretty flower, which had fallen out of a fancy pot when Fo rammed into the little shelf it had been sitting on. He tried to put the pot back but it really wouldn't go so he let it fall to the soft floor, contemplating the flower, which had layers like the flavor of the *ow!* The flower was sharp! He threw it down in anger just as he hit the edge of something waist high and tumbled forward over it into a bunch of soft stuff.

Fo pulled the soft stuff closer in great armfuls, buried himself in it. Through a gap he could see a woman in a red and white uniform. She was hovering over him somehow, moving with him, carrying him... the memory of the friendly giant was back and he heard himself whisper "Mumma?"

Rooki clung to the side of the laundry cart, glad the maid pushing it down the corridor hadn't spotted Lucky buried in its pile of towels and bedsheets. It was amazing how much Umans simply couldn't see. Rooki supposed they were like highcats, mostly noticing motion. Well, Lucky certainly wasn't moving now.

She took a deep breath and prepared for the arduous work of rousting him from the cart, once it reached its destination. Getting her pet out of this hive would take a power of pecking, but she was up to the challenge. Challenge was her element. Rookapella Elsternom-Elsternom always knew what to do.

CHAPTER 15

"Tʜᴀᴛ's ɪᴛ, Lᴜᴄᴋʏ! Gᴏᴏᴅ ʙᴏʏ! Good!"

Of course Rooki only *said* that. Her pet really wasn't doing well at all.

She praised him because it seemed to help him stumble down the street outside the Nautilus, but she had grave doubts about how far he would get. One of his paws was still wrapped up to the knee in a pillowcase, and with every lurching step he nearly tripped over it. Again and again Rooki tried to pluck it away, but each time she only risked a kick.

"Whoa now, Lucky," she sang, trying her best to keep the melody sweet. "Careful, careful— *whoa!* I said whoa! No, Lucky! Look where you're going! *Stop!*"

On a corner where a boulevard lined with baslin trees met another one lined with flowering plums, hired carriages and sedan chairs stood waiting for passengers. A big four-seater chair had just opened its doors to admit a party of fashionable ladies and gentlemen; the door on Marshal Fo's side was directly in his path and so, like it or not, it also admitted him.

The gentlemen screamed. The ladies roared. Fo clawed through the chair like a meldragore clawing through a honey hive, with his arms and legs jutting and jabbing and his cylindrical face void of any awareness that he'd just pushed one fist into a gentleman's eye, stepped on a lady's foot, upset the chair's refreshment caddy and knocked a tower of shopping out its opposite door as he tumbled through. At least the pillowcase finally came off.

The chair bearers dared to say some very unkind things to Lucky's back as he continued along the boulevard.

"You stay out of this, you two-legged jenny asses!" Rooki shrilled back at them. "*I'll* discipline my own pet, *if* he needs it!"

But who was she kidding? He needed it.

She really had to concentrate in order to follow Lucky. For some reason the streets were packed, though it wasn't a holiday— or at least, it wasn't a magpie holiday: not First-Bud, or Equinox, or the Feast of the Fatted Beetle. It was true that half the Umans Rooki saw were gazing up at the flowering plum trees, pointing at them, buying pictures of plum blossoms from street artists' barrows and eating pastries decorated with pink and white sugar, in the shape of plum blossoms. But who knew what that might signify? Umans did a lot of outlandish things.

Noise of a scuffle brought Rooki's attention back to her pet. Some other male Uman had rolled into him with a two-wheeled object of some kind. Umans had invented many interesting variations on that ingenious toy, the wheel, but most of them only led to trouble— this was a case in point. The Uman with the rolling two-wheeled thing was shouting abuse at Lucky and why? Just because Lucky was in the creature's way? That wasn't Lucky's fault! Well, now Lucky was shouting back and trying to take the thing. Maybe that *was* Lucky's fault.

Rooki swooped in to seize control. "Bad— no fighting! Leave it— no stealing! Hoy— you don't know how to— stop! Come back here with that thing!"

In imitation of the fellow whose hurry-horse he'd stolen, Marshal Fo had thrown his leg over the vehicle and now his stultified face flared with expression as he rolled away.

Fo's hurry-horse began picking up speed. The boulevard's fashionable ladies and gentlemen didn't deign to acknowledge a fat old news jotter; they only stepped out of the way and let him barrel downhill, flashing past one pink tower of plum blossoms after another, as fast as Rooki could fly. Faster. He was getting away from her.

"Stop it! *Whoa!* Just put your paws on the ground, Lucky! Do you hear me?"

Fo ran out of plum trees. He ran out of boulevard. With his normally narrow Abodean eyes peeled wide open and his typically surly slot of a mouth grimacing in a mixture of terror and delight, he swerved onto a dirtier, more common street. Here the going got rougher. The hurry-horse bounced over the cobbles, its wheels scattering street rubbish behind it.

Directly in Fo's path stood an ingenious attempt at selling the allure of the plum blossom festival to the lower classes: the owner of one of the street's grimy taverns had stuck a broom, brush end up, into a bucket of gravel and glued paper plum blossoms to it. The wights and wenches swilling rum as they sat in folding chairs around this makeshift tree scattered like more street rubbish as Fo rolled into their midst. But to prevent theft of the chairs, the tavern owner had chained them together; Fo caught and dragged one chair and then two and then ten and then all of a sudden the hurry-horse was upside down in a mass of legs and seats and Fo was upside-down under it all, moaning and... Rooki swooped down, heart pounding and wings weak. Was Lucky laughing?

"You can't lie here giggling!" shouted Rooki, pecking harder than she'd ever pecked before. "The owner's coming! That's her! Get up, Lucky, *up!* Run!"

Where she found the energy to drive him on, she didn't know. Pet ownership unlocks a lot of emotions.

He did escape from the tavern owner, who decided to keep the hurry-horse and go back to checking on her chairs.

After that, Lucky ran down streets that got uglier and narrower and dimmer until he couldn't run anymore. At last he staggered to a halt, drooping forward at the waist and gasping for breath through his mouth, possibly about to regurgitate. Rooki now found herself in a new difficulty, for she didn't have enough beaks to peck away all the street brats who emerged from the shadows to grab at Lucky's shinies.

Oh yes, Lucky had lots and lots of shinies. Rooki didn't like to think about them *too* much— she preferred to tell herself she'd taken to Lucky strictly for his own qualities— but of course the shinies had been a big factor. He had rows and rows of them, round and rectangular and shaped like various stars, mostly dangling from ribbons, and they clicked and clanked on the breast of Lucky's black woolen garment in the most irresistible manner. Street brats fairly swarmed after him and even if their little fingers hadn't been alarmingly precocious in the ways of crime they would certainly have managed to snatch a few. There were simply too many to keep track of— brats and shinies both.

"Get away from him! Give that back! Hoy, Lucky, peel off your coat. Hurry up! *Both* sleeves off! Turn it inside out— I *saw* that, you sticky-fingered little filcher!"

With his shinies hidden behind the inside-out coat, Marshal Fo was now better able to withstand the street brats' incursions. He dealt one of them a solid kick to her tiny pantaloons; Rooki decided to allow it.

So. Where were they?

The sun was sinking and the early spring day, never terribly warm to begin with, was growing cold. The neighborhood around them looked most unsavory. Rooki pecked and screeched and goaded Lucky on, back along grubby trash-strewn lanes and under collapsing sandstone archways, seeking a place where a still somewhat intoxicated Uman could den up for the evening. She tried to find a balance between staying close enough to keep him safe, and flying high enough to get a bearing, but it wasn't easy— and on top of that, Lucky's shinies were obviously starting to irritate him. He scratched at his coat as though he had fleas. He took it off.

"Careful, Lucky, you'll catch cold!"

EVEN IF FO HAD UNDERSTOOD Rooki, he'd have disagreed with her. Abode was far colder than Midlandis, and he didn't feel particularly uncomfortable. But just the same, the bird seemed to have another one of its plans. Fo didn't know what it was saying to the rag-seller who'd approached him; he didn't know why it was plucking one of his medals loose and trading it for some kind of blanket; he didn't know why it was making him stuff his old coat into some kind of bag that came with the blanket and bundle himself up in the... hmm. Marshal Fo had to admit this thing felt nice. It was colorful, too. How very pleasant. He walked on, now happier to obey the bird.

ROOKI WAS PROUD OF HERSELF. The rag-picker had been trying to sell an academic robe, and that was exactly what Lucky needed. Its thick folds would keep him warm; its great capacious Doktoral hood doubled as a carrying bag. Everything about it was perfect, and she could tell that Lucky found it particularly cozy turned velvet side in, lining side out.

Rooki was familiar only with the scholars of Isladorro University, back on the Isle of Gold; she didn't recognize the garment's pattern of sapphire-pink stars and mellow green lorro leaves. But Lucky liked it, and it helped hide his cache of shinies, and all in all it was a brilliant stroke of resourcefulness for which Rooki congratulated herself thoroughly. She allowed herself a deep, deep breath of satisfaction. Doubts about her own superiority vanished. *Yes*, thought she, in life you have to take the lumpy with the flat. You fight your way through adversity; you emerge victorious…

Huh. After their long and winding walk Rooki found they *had* emerged. Into someplace. She settled on her pet's colorful satin shoulder and preened herself as she surveyed a clean, pretty plaza which was reassuringly full of Umans, dotted with vendors' barrows and ringed by shops. She must have found this place by instinct— unsurprising, really. Great trainers have great instincts.

The plaza she and Fo had reached was the home of the Judge's Jaws.

It is an ancient stone fountain in the form of a mask, and though it no longer emits a flow of water, it receives a steady flow of visitors. A folk belief states that those brave enough to put their hands into the mouth of the fountain, and ask for its judgment on any matter, will receive it— in the form of either a blessing or a curse, though there is no way to tell which one was given, short of waiting to see.

Oh, and it is also said that, in very dire cases where a curse might not be enough, the Judge's Jaws will bite.

A queue of festival revelers had formed for the purpose of putting their questions to the famous fountain. They stood sipping from flasks of plum wine and plum brandy, and munching plum pastries, and Marshal Fo was intrigued.

All these people seemed to be trying to dig something out of that hole in the crumbling bit of wall. Whatever was in the hole must be very valuable, for so many of them to keep reaching in after it like that. He lurched up to the queue, pushed away the fellow at its head, and thrust his hand into the great snarling mouth of the fountain.

The fellow he'd pushed started telling Lucky off; Rooki flew from his shoulder, claws out.

"No, *you* go away! Lucky's *not* a selfish mumping oik! He's a good boy! Aren't you, Lucky? *Who's* a good boy? Are *you* a good boy? *Are* you?"

There was one more thing about The Judge's Jaws: street brats sometimes jammed stolen loot deep into its mouth for safekeeping. At that particular moment, it contained a brooch— whose pin jabbed Fo right in the finger.

With a scream he snatched back his hand.

Everyone in line saw the blood.

Everyone screamed. Everyone fled.

The Judge's Jaws had spoken.

CHAPTER 16

SUNSET, AND GINO V. DOAK, the Grand Constable of Law and Order in the City of Coastwall, had two skulls' worth of a headache.

He pulled off the peaked cap of his uniform and clawed furrows in his hair. Like his mustachio, this was gray but dense: the Grand Constable might no longer have been young, but he was still an objectively handsome man. Under a kelp-green uniform his frame was slim, under thoughtful brows his eyes were piercing, and beneath his mustachio not too many teeth had been lost to the brawls he'd once been plunged into, back when he was not yet the Grand Constable but only a simple thief-taker.

Back then, as a young fellow earning his bread in the private business of outwitting criminals, he'd struck his blows against wrongdoing with no more than a pair of manacles and the knowledge of a few reliable wrestling holds— *and you know what*, he thought, back then I think I did this town more good. Now he was forever stuck in the Station House, with his desk so shingled with paperwork he could hardly see its sea-green painted top. He dropped his hands from his hair and ground the heels of them into his eyes. Oh, to get out in the alleys again, to swing a truncheon, to clap a miscreant into the rowdy-bracelets! Might as well wish on a nullicorn.

"Want me to bring you a medicine bolus?" asked the officer who strode through the door with still more papers for the desk. "We've got some that'll knock that headache of yours right out."

The Grand Constable shook his head. "Boluses knock *me* right out. I'd rather have some fresh air. Could you...?"

"Sure thing, boss." The officer unlatched the windowpane, swung it open and left the Grand Constable alone.

A cool breeze rushed in, carrying the jingle and boom of a music-barrel that someone was busy cranking. A cool breeze, a fresh breeze— too much breeze. The Grand Constable threw himself over the desktop just in time to stop stacks of papers blowing away.

Damn it deep, he'd forgotten what fresh air *was*.

From a drawer that stuck and scraped, he brought out a selection of paperweights. Most of them were cheap pressed glass bearing slogans such as "I Find Coastwall Agreeable" and "Whatever Occurs in Oldmarsh, Remains in Oldmarsh". Some were no more than stones or chunks of broken brick. But one of them was beautiful: a Stewen crystal seahorse, engraved with the words "Thank you for finding my shoe — Irona de Brewel". The Grand Constable arranged them carefully, then got up to open the windowpane a little wider. The fragrance of the plum blossoms stole in, lilting above a bed of grime and river water.

Plum blossoms can kiss my skull-duster, thought the Grand Constable, reaching to his belt to clutch the truncheon that hung there.

Every year it was like this: the moment the foggy chill of winter loosened its grip enough to let a flower poke out of a bud, people let themselves go wild. They wanted an excuse to kick up Dizzy Dan, to swill wine and brandy in honor of spring; and really, no one could blame them for that. But adding hundreds— perhaps thousands— of Public Disturbance cases onto the workload was a crime in and of itself. Every instance of liquor-fueled misbehavior drew precious resources away from the pursuit of actual crime. Crooks knew this, and ramped up their activities accordingly; it was a vicious loop, made even worse this year because so many of Coastwall's peacekeeping officers were off protecting diplomats at this new thing, this League For Peace conference.

"The League For Peace can kiss my skull-duster too," thought the Grand Constable, and was alarmed to realize he'd said it out loud. The headache must be playing all hells with his brain. Maybe taking a bolus wasn't such a bad idea.

In the hallway outside, the officer was arguing with a bailiff who had lost her patience and punched the squirming prisoner she was escorting to the cells in the basement.

"Aw come on. It's only Quickfinger Maggie," insisted the bailiff, twisting the prisoner's arm.

"The law is clear about mistreating those in custody—"

"Custody, my flaps! That law's still so new the paint ain't dry. Just lemme— see? She's doin' it again!"

The Grand Constable took two sugar-coated lumps from the pottery dish on the officer's smaller, less cluttered desk and popped them into his mouth. "I'm going out. Who'd you say made these?"

"Doktor Matchrun."

The Grand Constable spat out the second bolus before it slipped down his throat— that particular healer was well known for having a generous hand with the redflower sap.

"Relax, they're just willow bark!" the officer called after him, but he was already on his way through the great bronze front doors of the Station House.

Headache or no, festival or no, standing on the portico under the inscription "HERE DWELLS JUSTICE" never failed to thrill the Grand Constable's heart. While it was true that most of the city couldn't read— he himself had only learned the skill later in life— still there was an undeniable power in the words. They named sweet Lady Justice, his one and only love, the one he would sometimes forget the depth of his feelings for and then, in passionate apology, fly back to time and again. The intake papers could wait. He'd go out for an hour or two and cop a few crooks just to show Justice he was as still as quick-witted as ever. Well, and then after that go inspect the officers at that deep-damned League For Peace.

As the Grand Constable jogged down the long sandstone staircase which ended in the plaza which sloped downhill to the streets which zigzagged to the Harbor which fanned out into the brandy-black Midland Sea and thus touched the whole wide world, something colorful caught his eye in the waning glow of sunset.

Something colorful— and shameful. It appeared to be a Prophessor, a Vonn University Prophessor if he was seeing correctly, with his robe turned inside out and his hood slung over his shoulder and a magpie perched on his frowzy drunken head. The fellow was lying face-down on the staircase, dead to the world.

The sight of a learned man so forgetting his privilege was disgusting and besides that, it was another instance of Public Disturbance. But Gino V. Doak, the Grand Constable of Law and Order in the City of Coastwall, couldn't bear to go back into the Station House and face his desk again. So he allowed himself a single insult to sweet Lady Justice.

He told himself one of his underlings would bring the fellow in. And then he turned away.

CHAPTER 17

FRED HAD NEVER BEEN BLESSED with the ability to enjoy sitting still, but what he felt now was well-nigh intolerable. The urge to flee from the conference room-turned-theater in which the opening ceremony of the League For Peace was taking place, to go instead and check on Marshal Fo, was possibly one of the strongest forces in nature. Fred felt he would explode like the Weapon, searing a vast jagged black chasm in reality itself and releasing who knew what kind of strange new materials.

Why had he listened to those who said there needed to be an opening ceremony at all? Why had he agreed it would do honor and dignity to the assembled envoys of the world, that they would be entertained by it and thus put in a good frame of mind for the negotiations ahead? Why had he let Dame Irona write the pocking songs, build the pocking set, design the pocking costumes?

Oh, Honey had been terrific, but this performance marked a return to her typical form. To begin with, the stage was crammed with winsome little boys and girls, each wearing a rectangular canvas configuration, like a portable painting. The paintings showed vistas from foreign countries and would have been all right, except for the unsettling tiny faces and hands protruding from them. And even worse was the song. Ye gods, the *song*.

"Brats of the world, join hands, unite," sang the animated foreign vistas. "Peace to the world, let's never fight. There's a lot for us to share…"

A view of Coastwall Harbor, with a little boy's face peering from the top of the Lantern, stepped forward and, in a gap-toothed warble so drenched in sweetness that it made Fred want to wipe

his tongue with his bare hands, piped "...we'll get along if we
dare to care..."

Fred clenched his teeth and breathed deeply.

"...let's make our future bright," sang the rest of the paintings.
"Brats of the world, unite!"

The last word was marked by a bit in which the floors slid apart,
sweeping most of the brats offstage and leaving behind only ten,
who turned around to form the image of a sunrise overlaid by letters
reading WRLOD PEECA.

Fred was on his feet and moving for the door even as he heard
the master of ceremonies saying "And now, opening remarks by His
Highness, Prince Malfred of Castramars."

Gods afar! Fred scrambled to the stage, grabbed the megaphone
and said, "I've got to make this fast. So. Anyone here from
out of town?"

THE PLUSH CORRIDORS OF THE Nautilus had never seemed
longer to Fred, or more full of random irrelevant frills. Flower
arrangements, catering carts, city officers in full dress uniform— he
passed them all at nearly a jog, so focused on his goal that he didn't
even notice that Mesir Doak, the Grand Constable of Law and Order
in the City of Coastwall, had joined him and was keeping pace at
his elbow.

"Ahem. Your Highness. If it's not an inopportune moment..."

"It is."

"Of course. Well, nice event you've got here, Your Highness.
My security officers seem to be in order. If Your Highness should
need any..."

Fred wanted to shout *not now, and quit Highnessing me!* but
gritted his teeth and decided to take pity on the Grand Constable.

Sure, he was being an unmitigated toady— but Fred supposed he'd do the same, if some wight he'd once brushed off and let go to the gallows ended up transforming into a Prince. Living down that sort of wee embarrassment might take some doing. But for pocks' sakes, *not now...*

Knock knock knock went Fred's knuckles on the door of Fo's suite.

No, no, no reply. Not even after several attempts.

At last Fred turned to the Grand Constable and allowed that there *was* something he could do, after all.

When officers opened the suite to find no one in it, Fred had to take a seat, most abruptly, on a red and white velvet divan.

He let the Grand Constable bring him a glass of water. He listened as the Grand Constable ordered his officers to go find— please describe the gentleman again, Your Highness— do you hear that, men? You're looking for a gentleman of about sixty, Eastern-style foreign face, with sharp-cornered eyes and a wisp of a mustachio, wearing a dark woolen military-style suit covered with lots and lots of medals— got it? And keep it discreet, for pocks' sakes. Go.

Fred watched the officers rushing away. He listened to the Grand Constable's reassurance that it would be brats' games to track an old gent who'd never before been to Coastwall. Why, it would be surprising if Fo even found his way out of the Nautilus.

"But he's got a magpie with him!" Fred protested, although the Grand Constable seemed not to appreciate the relevance of this. "You hear me? He's got a magpie!"

"I do hear you, Your Highness. That's a very important identification detail. I— ah— damn it deep, your mentioning magpies reminds me of something but— well, never mind. Oh, this headache. I wish I'd taken that second bolus."

CHAPTER 18

THE PARTS OF COASTWALL THAT have plum trees, and street lamps, and places for festival-goers to go, were bright and bustling. There were vendors, and music barrels, and Fools; it might almost have looked like a typical evening in the Whellen Country. But the Whellen Country this was not. There still was a class divide.

The de Brewels were certainly doing their best to bring modern conveniences such as wyrmlight globes, ox-drawn railways and cable ferries to their people. But the Brewel Country had no Heart of Stone; Tekological machinery had not yet generally taken the place of muscle power. So the Brewel Country still thronged with old-fashioned laboring types— and though a peasant wight may dress up in his once-a-year finery and travel to Coastwall for the Plum Blossom revels, his muscular figure is still easy to tell apart from that of an easeful Gentleman; a peasant wench, however tall and hale she might be, and how decorated with the latest fashions, walks not with the regal stride of a Lady shouldering her weapon but with the stoop of one who wheels a barrow or breaks rocks. Upbringing always tells.

But this cuts both ways— for example, the upper classes' use of slang rarely rings true. So if a young Lady who happens to idolize popular street musicians were to pull aside the curtain of her sedan chair, turn to her maidservant and utter the words "Peek *this* old cully with the flashy rags, bee! He must be kookalooloo!" the maidservant would probably suppress a sigh.

The Lady in the chair, however, was determined to use the idiom of the streets. "What's with the sigh, bee? Don't you agree he's straight-down dumped his pumpkin? I mean, look at that coat.

Last time I peeked such a rowdy rag-stack was... well, maybe I *did* see something similar at Fashion Preview Week. Hmm. What do you think— would I look good in that? Oh, for the heavens' sakes, stop sighing."

The cully with the flashy rags felt eyes on him.

Long years as Dictator of Abode had caused Marshal Fo's natural streak of vanity to expand into a great, distinctive stripe. He raised his chin and met the sedan chair Lady's stare of delight. It had to be delight— she couldn't possibly find him unsatisfactory. That would earn her a very quick ticket to Now Move Those Rocks Back Again Camp.

Or would it? A dart of horror jabbed Fo in a long-untouched place as he realized there might not be such camps in this country: it might really have been *that* kind of stare. He felt the evening somehow turn very, very hot. He swatted away the cloud of pickpocket brats clawing at his bag of medals and darted into the anonymity of the crowd.

It took Rooki a bit of effort to find him.

"Bad Lucky! *Bad!* I leave you for one minute and you run away! Here. I brought you a plum cookie."

Fo grabbed the cookie and wolfed it down. The barbels of hair at the corners of his mouth became clogged with jammy, buttery crumbs. He belched and tried to remember why he had a vague bad feeling about himself; the feeling was receding fast and would have vanished completely had he not been standing directly before a barbershop. A mirror was propped in the window, and what he saw in it made him put his hands to his cheeks and utter that sound Rooki recognized as distinctive of an unhappy Uman.

Some researchers at the Scientific Institute assert that Umans can understand mirrors. Rooki wasn't so sure of that, but her pet did seem genuinely distressed.

"What's wrong, boy? Hoy, you're pawing at your whiskers... you can tell that Uman in the mirror is you! Wait till I scratch a paper about *this*! Even Corvinalias Elsternom e Rokonoma will be impressed." Rooki had an insight. "And I know what you want!"

Uman males often engaged in behavior meant to change the configuration of their whiskers and crests. In fact they set up shops specifically for that purpose— shops like this one, right here. Rooki hopped from Fo's shoulder to the bells hanging on the barbershop door. She plucked at them till they jangled; a few moments later the door opened and a woman leaned out, holding a hairpin in the corner of her mouth.

"Zat you, fella? Hoy, that's some sad case a mange you've got. Slide in here and lemme getcha quiffed. "

The shop smelled of soap and tonic. In the corner stood a silent music barrel. Though the place was very different from that of an Abodean barber— they usually shear yakboks alongside their owners— Fo understood what was happening as the woman guided him to a chair, loosened his collar and swept a cape around his neck. He shot her a grunt of approval.

She rattled soap and water in a cup, brushed a foamy cloud all over his face, laid a heated towel over his eyes. He grunted some more.

"You said it, bee. Feels good, don't it?" The barber rapped a three-minute sandglass sharply on a side table. "Right, lemme go crank the firkin." A grinding sound, and then a tinkling of music. "Like that? It's the latest from Slum Slim and the Fops. Ain't nobody else got this firky-plug yet, bee— it's an exclusive. My sister books the bands on the Holiday Street party barge. Right, lemme go tune my ax."

As the barber stropped her razor, Rooki, who had slipped into the shop along with Fo, watched and listened to the proceedings

with great interest. Truth to tell, she *had* been just the tiniest bit
ashamed of her pet's shabbiness. Well, no more.

With a deft pair of strokes, the barber swept Marshal Fo's sparse
Abodean mustachio into oblivion, along with whatever small stubble
had managed to grow on the rest of his face. When the glass had
run out and she lifted the towel from Fo's eyes, the first thing they
fell upon— besides his own reflection— was a poster of a handsome,
clean-shaven young man. He compared himself to it, then smiled
in smug approval. An image of the Lady in the sedan chair floated
through his mind, accompanied by a delicious feeling of revenge.

But what was *this?*

The mirror included a folding section which allowed Fo to
see the back of his own head. At first he was unable to identify it
as belonging to him, for it had been years since he'd looked at it,
especially without the cover of his cylindrical uniform hat. But once
he acknowledged ownership, there was no denying the ugly sight:
there, in the black-and-gray field of his hair, a definite gap existed.
Quite a large one, in fact. The barber immediately understood
how he felt about it: she was a professional and well attuned to her
customers' body language.

"Hate to drag you to sadland, bee— it's a straight-down cryer,
but time don't stop for no one. Although..." the barber turned Fo's
chair so as to aim his line of sight directly at a display of wigs.

Fashions in wigs, as they do in clothing, tend to change from
year to year; but being, as they are, the exclusive purview of the
servant classes, wigs have another property as well: certain styles are
associated with certain lines of work. For example, if a scribe wore
the wig of a valet he would surely be considered eccentric, and a
loaf baker who wiped the sweat from her brow and exited her shop
putting on the wig of a pastry-cook would certainly be regarded
as giving herself airs. But of course Rooki, hidden among pots of

pomade and jars full of combs marinating in distilled spirits, didn't know this. When she looked at the display of wigs, all she saw was that one of them would make the perfect hiding-place for a magpie.

"I want the one with the black and white curls at the back," she said, in the sort of gritty rumble she imagined as Lucky's speaking voice.

The barber, absorbed in sizing up Fo's bald spot, was surprised. "Huh. You a musician?"

The way she said it made Rooki think she ought to play along. "I am. Listen!"

Rooki mimicked a Uman instrument known as a fiddle. The tune she chose was the Elsternom family anthem, *From Boughs on High we Hail to Thee*, and it clashed terribly with Slum Slim and the Fops, still playing from the music barrel; but the barber was impressed.

"That's straight-down kookalooloo, bee! Like nothin' I've ever heard! And can you ever imitate those strings! Almost don't sound like they're comin' from you. Right, yer headgear— given yer, ah, needs I say we go with the long-term installation. Right, lemme clear the street."

And before Marshal Fo could so much as squirm, the barber brushed foam onto the crown of his head and shaved it bare.

He yelped in horror but she was unfazed. "Not done yet, bee." The barber pressed him back into the chair with one practiced hand, reached for a glue pot with the other, smeared a thick brushful across his bare scalp and twisted the wig into place. Fo froze, staring at the mirror in wonderment.

"Hot, right? Thirty years, gone just like that! Or twenty, anyhow." She tried to snap her fingers, but the handle of the glue brush had been sticky. "One second— lemme go kype a wipe."

As the barber went in search of a rag with which to clean her hands, Rooki hid herself in Fo's copious new curls.

"Can you hear me, Lucky? Can you feel *this?*"

She spoke softly, but pecked Fo's ear hard. And though he winced, he accepted her presence as a matter of course.

The barber was back. "Now lemme ask you somethin', bee. Spot this: my sister's party barge on the Denna is a real burnin' scene. I'm about to close up shop and slope down there— what if I brung you with me, had you play a set? Your sound is swang dang, bee, no lag." She paused and, just in case her new discovery was so rectangular as not to understand, translated: "Everyone would *love* to hear your music. Tell you what. No charge for the wig— call it an advance payment."

During the barber's search for the cleaning rag, Fo had been watching her back, and had found something undeniably enjoyable about the view; the whole time she was sweeping the floor, setting the sandglass back in its place, pulling the bumpy cylinder of Slum Slim and the Fops out of the music barrel, he kept watching her and his interest grew. So when the barber finally unwound her work smock to reveal a colorful, interesting, surprisingly tight and low-cut robe, Fo was more than ready to follow her, despite having not the slightest idea where or why.

CHAPTER 19

FO STRAIGHTENED HIS VELVET-LINED GARMENT and clutched his makeshift bag of medals tight as he and the barber arrived at the stone embankment at the very end of Holiday Street. Just beyond a series of sea-green bollards, a gangway led down to the Denna where a big, flat barge was moored: a barge strung with oil lamps, thronged with people and throbbing with music.

"Lotta pigs out tonight," remarked the barber as they went aboard.

Rooki dared to poke her head from among Fo's curls for a better look around: she knew 'pigs' was Uman slang for officers of the watch. Magpies had them, too, though their slang term was 'owls'.

"What's going on?" she grumbled in the Lucky voice.

"Just the usual hassarassle, bee— a lot of the pups here have a past, spot me? Well, I'm clean. And if you've got any bones in your locker I don't want to know— like they say, 'no word's the good word'. Right, lemme show you to my sister."

As her pet followed its new friend, Rooki scanned the crowd surrounding him. Magpies could see all kinds of things Umans couldn't, and Rooki noticed that, despite the music, and the dancing, and the intoxicating liquors being served from a bar, some of the guests at this floating festival didn't appear to be having fun. One of them in particular— the one with the dense gray hair, matching mustachio and thoughtful brows— seemed most unhappy. Even though he was wearing a festive shirt covered with block-printed plum blossoms and stood at a little table sipping from a tall, cool, dew-beaded can of punch with a little paper parasol stuck in it, he looked like a ball of nerves.

Got to be an owl, that one.

Rooki wondered who he was looking for.

THE GRAND CONSTABLE ALLOWED HIMSELF one sip from the drink in front of him. The overpriced chunk of ice floating in it was rapidly ruining the already flavorless mess, but he wanted to make the drink last, not to mention keep his wits about him.

He hadn't expected the missing Abodean dignitary to be so tricky to find. Given His Highness's description, the gentleman seemed unlikely to blend in among the locals, and besides that, the bird he had with him should have been an easy giveaway. But the night had grown late, and no officer had found the gentleman, and at last the Grand Constable had gone back to the Station House to dress in festival-goer's plainclothes and try for himself.

At first the prospect had been exciting: out on the street, with a pair of rowdy-bracelets hidden in a pocket at the seam of his shirt, he'd felt young again. But no more had come of it. He'd walked leagues of boulevards, streets and alleys, visited what felt like every celebration in town, bought trinkets from vendors while scanning the crowd, and asked what he thought were the right questions in the right places, all for nothing. So here he was at the last place he could think of— aboard the Holiday Street party barge— where he had to ignore at least two laws that were being broken right there in front of him. He wasn't looking for watered-down drinks or instances of pickpocketing. He was looking for... huh.

Directly beside him stood a fellow in a musician's wig, wearing a Vonn University robe turned inside-out. Just like the drunken Prophessor from the Station House steps. That must not have been a Prophessor at all, decided the Grand Constable. It was just some new fashion. He gazed sadly at the sleeve of his plum-blossom shirt, aware that it was at least ten years out of date— *now* who was unlikely to blend in among the locals?

He was startled by an unseen hand stroking his dense gray hair.

"Easy there, bee! Didn't mean to give you the jumps."

The hand led to a well-built woman, who had been walking with the musician. She raised an eyebrow and said "I crop tops for a living, and I've got to say— I like a cully with frost on the meadow. Plus a sense of humor— peep that shirt! Lemme just get this fiddler situated, and I'll buy you and me the first of many."

THE BARBER PUSHED MARSHAL FO through the crowd and up onto the stage. The moment he was there she disappeared, but this didn't bother him very much, as there was another woman onstage who strongly resembled her.

The new woman was talking to him in the local language, loud and fast, and making gestures— holding her hands in the air beside her head, sawing one of them back and forth while twiddling the fingers of the other. Fo couldn't figure it out. He ignored her and focused instead on a passing barmaid and the big platter of snacks she carried.

From the back of her pet's wig, Rooki took stock.

One of the lectures she'd attended at the Scientific Institute had been about Uman music. The rhythmic clanging, banging, and twanging the creatures set up with the help of various mechanical devices was primitive, but Umans really seemed to enjoy both making their din and listening to it. On the stage Rooki spied plenty of devices she recognized from the lecture: a dulcimer-drum, a flute, some kitars... the musical Umans were picking them up... one of them pushed a fiddle into Lucky's paws and another snapped out the words "One, two-and three, four!"

The music hit Fo like a squall. Compared to the recording in the barrel at the barbershop, let alone anything he'd ever heard in Abode, it was lustrous, pulsating, overwhelmingly alive. He really didn't know how to react, other than to close his eyes, raise his arms and flail about. These objects he'd been given— one seemed to be a very narrow hunting bow strung with lots of hair and the other a wooden frying pan— were good for flailing. Everyone seemed very excited to watch him do that.

But after a while, as the gusts of music intensified, something seemed expected of him. The wench who'd made the sawing, twiddling gestures repeated them. Fo swiveled his head this way and that, looking for clues as to what he was supposed to do.

"Whatcha waitin' for?" demanded the fellow playing a kitar. At the unintelligible foreign question, Fo's sharp-cornered, multicolored eyes filled with confusion.

The fellow with the flute stopped blowing it. "Go on, bee— start gettin' busy!"

Fo still didn't understand, but he couldn't resist the pressure to act. Even though his hands were full of the wooden frying pan and the narrow bow, he brought them together and tried imitating the wench's sawing, twiddling gestures.

A wailing noise exploded from between the pan and the bow, sending a wave of pure energy into the crowd. They caught it, expanded it, sent it echoing back.

Fo had never felt anything like this, not even from the war-queen who had been his mistress. He whooped with delight. The wench who looked like the barber crossed her arms and nodded, holding back a smile.

Fo brought the bow and frying pan together for another noise. For a split second the crowd hesitated, then reacted even more powerfully. Fo was elated. He could tell they were ready for a third noise. He dragged the bow across the pan with great eagerness, but now something must have been wrong because no one seemed quite as pleased. A fourth attempt proved the magic was gone: the wench uncrossed her arms. The fifth, sixth and seventh noises were received in progressively worse fashion and the eighth one brought an expression to her face that Fo recognized from his mistress's darker moods.

In desperation he tried making the noises louder, but the tide had turned against him. The wench was up on the stage now. Fo panicked and threw the bow at her like a javelin.

The crowd went wild, but not in a musically appreciative way—more like a crowd which dislikes the outcome of a match between the Brewel Country Seahorses and the Oldmarsh Beavers.

Back near the bar, the barber untwined her arm from that of the Grand Constable and spilled her drink down his sleeve in the process. "What the triple-whipping pock? That pup can't saw the spruce at all, bee! He straight-down tricked me!" And like her sister, she rushed at Fo.

Neither of them had been raised as Ladies; they had no compunctions about hitting a man. The barber was pushing up her sleeve and her sister was brandishing the bow when the most kookalooloo thing happened: a bird jumped out of the pocking wight's wig!

"You leave Lucky alone!" it screamed, pecking and clawing anyone within reach. "Get your filthy paws off him, you damned dirty Umans!"

A few of the damned dirty Umans must have felt sorry for Lucky, because they took his side; others sided with the sisters; most must simply have been looking for an excuse to fight because within seconds, the whole party was in an uproar. Tankards flew. Tables flipped. In the pandemonium Lucky came face to face with the

Grand Constable, who under normal circumstances would probably have taken note of this fellow's unusually shaped, somehow multicolored eyes, and recalled Prince Malfred's description of Marshal Fo. But the night had worn on the Grand Constable, and his instinct for courting sweet Lady Justice sprang forth in a most illogical fashion.

"Hoy, fellow! You're no fiddler! Want to tell me you didn't cheat on your Guild exam?" he growled, and reached into the hidden pocket of his shirt for…

"No fair using *these!*"

The bird had beat him to the pocket and now soared up into the web of lights strung back and forth across the barge, a black-and-white silhouette carrying what was clearly a set of manacles.

Many of the guests did indeed have criminal histories. Upon seeing the manacles they sent up cries of "Lawman!" and "Leg it!".

The barge listed alarmingly as the crooks surged for the gangplank. Perhaps this interfered with the Grand Constable's balance as he sought to use one of his reliable wrestling holds. However it happened, Fo found just enough room and won just enough time to raise the fiddle high and bring it smashing down on the Grand Constable's head of dense frosty hair.

With his opponent dazed, Fo didn't need Rooki's wild pecking and shrieking as encouragement to jump overboard. He did that quite naturally, without stopping to recall the last time he'd tried to swim.

THE RIVER DENNA, WHICH BISECTS Coastwall with a stretch of water so wide it can only be crossed by ferry or by private craft, bears various well-known epithets.

Typical citizens find themselves referring to it as the broad brown Denna; singers croon about Old Mama River; poets name it Carrier of the World. But no one can think of the Denna without also thinking of Brewel Hall, for the ivory-tiled palace which hugs the eastern bank is as much a part of Old Mama River as the powerful tides that rinse the filth of the city from her mouth.

Something dark and lumpy floated through the crystalline, gold-and-white reflection of Brewel Hall. Something that twitched a little, and coughed, and flapped a pair of wings.

The cough and twitch came from a waterlogged man clinging to a dulcimer-drum. The wings belonged to the magpie perched on his gluey, shaven head.

"That was exciting!" pronounced the magpie.

The man made no reply beyond a kind of gurgling noise.

Some yards downstream, on the breast of the broad brown Denna, a wig drifted silently away.

CHAPTER 20

THE NAUTILUS CERTAINLY DID KNOW how to feed visitors.

At the back of the conference room where the League For Peace was having its very first session— a breakfast presentation by Prince Malfred of Castramars, titled "Whither Abode?"— a red-and-white porphyry table was set, and onto this table a maid laid out a selection of mini eel rolls and smoked mutton omelet bites en croute. Normally Fred had a decidedly hearty appetite, but this morning the very sight of food made him ill.

For the thousandth time he scanned the foreign faces aimed at him, wishing with all his might that, on the thousand and first scan, Marshal pocking Fo would appear among the envoys of the world, their translators and interpreters. Perhaps the fellow could slip discreetly in between the envoy from Northland and the one from Further Northland... oh hells, what did it matter if he were discreet? At this point Fred would have been fine with it if the Grand Constable had dragged Fo into the conference room in a laundry bag.

But no such bag had been dragged in. Instead His Highness was the center of attention, standing in front of a canvas sheet spread against the wall. With a pointy stick he jabbed at the words written on it.

"So as you see, there are *lots* of multilateral smart power protocols, both formal and informal, which we can leverage to create great synergy and generate an optimized outcome. But why? Good question! I've summarized the answer in fourteen simple points. Next sheet, please, Your Excellency."

Here Corvinalias, who was perched at the top of a ladder, tugged the knot from a piece of twine and another canvas sheet came flopping down in front of the baker's dozen already there.

The envoys of the world, along with their translators and interpreters, sighed.

Fred had never been at a loss for ways to capture attention. Starting with the first comedy stunt he'd ever performed— to an audience of exactly one monk who was trying to milk a sheep and not watch a small brat ride it around the barnyard— he'd had a keen sense of how to keep viewers engaged. Till now. Now he felt a sheen of dampness collecting in the roots of his neatly arranged hair. His underarms felt damp, too: maybe they'd stolen all the moisture that was supposed to be in his mouth.

If only it were appropriate to juggle the food, or do a dance, or declaim captivating improvised poetry about the very serious subject of Abode's place in the world of the future... he settled for twisting his ring around and around his finger till the knuckle was sore.

Eventually the thirty-minute sandglass gave up its final grains and the envoys of the world, along with their translators and interpreters, yawned and stretched and flung themselves upon the snacks. There would be a ten-minute break; then "Whither Abode?" would resume.

Fred slumped into a chair as Corvinalias fluttered toward him. "Pus buckets, Corv, this is terrible."

"You're not doing so bad. They liked the sheet with the pie on it."

"Only because they thought it was a breakfast menu."

"The trust-building activity where you had them tipping over backward and catching each other was fun."

"Not for the Northlander pygmy who had to catch that giant Peaceful Ocean fellow."

"Well, the question and answer session was a hit."

"I don't know, Corv. The only questions were 'where's the latrine?' and 'are we *sure* there won't be pie?'."

The last bite-sized ham soufflé disappeared from the table. A maid removing the empty tray happened to clang it against a samovar and the sound brought Fred a fragment of awful memory: the bell-like tone that had rung the sky just before the detonation of the Weapon. And then how everything had erupted with light... a light so bright he'd been able to see straight through his clenched eyelids, through his upraised hands, even through Dok, who only seconds before had been kissing him...

Though Fred willed himself to stop thinking of the Weapon, he couldn't stop thinking of Dok.

Gods, he hoped she'd spent a restful night in her comfortable house, slept through pleasant dreams. He hoped she was somewhere enjoying breakfast, or driving her power carriage, or still in bed having a late sleep in, or doing anything at all except ever again remembering that sound, that light, *that...*

Corvinalias cleared his throat and Fred was back in the conference room. "What, Corv? Sorry."

"I said if you don't mind, I'm going to hop out to the courtyard."

"Want me to carry you?"

"No thanks. I'll be fine. I'm getting stronger."

Once out in the corridor, Corvinalias risked a quick backward glance to see if Fred was following him. Even though the very first of the Rules— the code by which secret agents lived their lives— was "don't look back", he thought he might be allowed just one small peek.

It had been nearly a year since he'd worked with the Central Agency for Intelligence. But he was still on the books as a Bureau operative, and the Nautilus was still a Bureau front, and though the maid who had taken away the empty tray might fool Umans,

Corvinalias knew she was no maid at all but a Bureau man in disguise. Fred might want this whole thing to be above the board— no Utmost Secret operations or shadow business— but Corvinalias felt the time for playing it straight was over. It was time to get proper help.

He zigzagged between the envoys' feet and caught a glimpse of the maid's red-and-white Nautilus uniform just as she— or he— rounded a corner. Onward he followed, further and further down softly carpeted passageways. It took all his energy to keep up. Before the maid vanished around a final corner, Corvinalias took a gamble and uttered a short but piercing whistle.

It worked. The maid stopped, turned. Panting with exertion, Corvinalias hopped the last few yards and said "Three one two."

The maid's face was a perfect blank. "What do you mean by that?"

"I mean we need help. I'd never use the emergency code unless it was, well, an emergency."

Scowling thoughtfully, the maid lowered the tray for him to climb onto.

Up close, Corvinalias was satisfied to note a whole cluster of sex-linked characteristics: the Bureau was good but they couldn't fool a seasoned Uman-fancier. For starters, the maid was no taller than Fred, and besides that sported a hairline that was thinning in a subtly diagnostic way; her eyebrows were thick and low; and at the front of her neck protruded a small example of that telltale lump so typical of males. The fellow *did* do an excellent job of sounding female, though. Very professional. "Emergency code, you say? There's an emergency?"

"That's right— the Grand Constable hasn't come through for us."

The maid's expression said: *tell me everything.*

So Agent Corvinalias did. He told the maid— the Bureau operative— all about how Fo had unexpectedly joined them, and how Rooki had done the same, and how she'd attached herself to him. He summed up what a dire situation this represented for Umanity: there was no telling what kind of ridiculous commands Rookapella Elsternom-Elsternom might give to the Dictator of the world's most pivotal country.

"What do you mean by 'pivotal'?"

"What I mean is— let's be honest. The whole League was really only formed to give the rest of the world a chance to form a united front against Abode. Because that general who's still back there running their show— I mean the third one, who seized power from Fo— she's an unknown quantity. And with Rooki in the mix, things might become even more unstable. We need top men on this immediately!"

The maid was thoughtful. "So a very important country is under the control of an upstart, who is using a familiar figure as a puppet?"

"To put it bluntly, yes. But that's nothing new— Abode hasn't had transparent leadership for the past forty years. What's new is that the puppet has left the stage."

"And he's come here."

"That's right."

"With a bird."

"Rooki's a magpie. Like me."

"I see. This is valuable information. I'll act on it immediately."

"What a relief! I can't thank you enough! Now you'll have to let me get back to helping His Highness."

The maid lowered the tray to the floor; as Corvinalias hopped down from it he winked and said "So glad you're on the case, Mesir."

He regretted the words as soon as they left his beak: they seemed to offend the fellow. *Hmm,* he thought, maybe I shouldn't have used the expression 'on the case'. Secret agents were probably sick to death of hearing it.

Meanwhile, the maid watched as the talking bird who repeated things from the Prince's important meeting hopped away down the corridor. The maid stripped off the red-and-white uniform smock of the Nautilus to reveal an indescribably drab garment that no one anywhere would bother looking twice at. The uniform went into a laundry cart. So did the tray.

For a moment, but only a very brief moment, temptation crossed the maid's mind. This important puppet man with the bird might be worth going after— a treasure worth having, a powerful tool.

But no.

Bessy the Boy liked being alive.

She'd be a good girl and tell Granny.

CHAPTER 21

I N A CERTAIN HULK, IN a certain ship-breaker's yard, a certain lower deck was rapidly filling with crooks and their offerings. Every one of Granny Almantree's minions eyed her neighbor with narrow-eyed suspicion. Each thought she had a chance at the reward: a fair benny shucklebox cram-full of silver bits, for the wench what brings Granny the old man and his bird.

The word had gone out fast, and thoroughly. Not a single bravo, bent operator or fingerwork specialist in Coastwall seemed to have missed it. The only hitch in Granny's announcement was that it failed to mention any consequences for bringing in the wrong merchandise— so here they were, by the squawking, chirping, honking dozen. Birds too.

"Give it up, why don't ya?" said a wench holding an aged gentleman by the waistband. The gentleman was very much confused, but clearly in possession of a chicken. "What you brung ain't gonna fly."

"Zat so?" replied someone who had brought her own toothless, unshaven dear old Da, along with a wicker cage containing a recently stolen dove. "Look who's talkin! Yours don't fly at all. Leastways not more than a couple feet."

"It ain't got to. Granny said bird— she didn't give no pockin stakes race conditions."

"Neither of yez got a chance," interjected a third wench. This one had heard about the need for not merely a bird, but specifically a magpie, which was a point in her favor. But perhaps her prisoner's magpie would not prove to be the right sort: the man was a dried-up old street Fool, complete with jingling bells on his shoes, a long, striped tassel at the tip of his conical hat, and on his hand a puppet made from a black and white woolen sock.

"Hocka, bocka, dominaka!" crowed the old Fool, thrusting his hand at a grizzled geezer's duck. "Ow!"

Just when it seemed the hulk couldn't hold one more set of applicants, a bulkhead door sprang open to reveal Granny herself. She was not pleased.

"What's it I see here?" she roared, kicking aside a goose, a turkey, and a crateful of bouncing, beeping finches. "A mally stack a oxshit, that's what! Out a me sight, all a thez! Next moll what brings me some old oik an his scabby feather mop will meet a dart as got sauce on it!"

The hulk emptied quickly. Soon only a startling variety of bird dung remained.

Among the disappointed crooks who filed out of the breaker's yard was a stout woman with a single eye, chewing on the stem of a clay pipe. It was a shame that Granny had missed meeting this one, for in addition to a red-cheeked drunkard of an old wight and a flamboyant peacock, she had brought with her a piece of information.

It seemed that at the edge of town, down near a part of the Harbor where ships from the Isle of Gold discharge their cargo, an ox-driver loading a pallet of books had struck up a very strange conversation. For a good ten minutes she'd chatted with a bald old man who, though he had no bird and thus unfortunately didn't meet Granny's criteria, was still worth mentioning for the fact that he had never once moved his lips.

It seemed the old man was a foreigner: he was dressed very oddly and had wanted to know what else there was to see and do in Midlandis. At one point he'd winced in pain, shaken something out of his boot and, discovering that it was a shiny brooch on a ribbon, had traded it to the ox-driver for a spot aboard the wagon.

The rest of the message, if Granny had only heard it, would have assured her that the ox-driver did not plan to keep all the money once she sold the brooch— and the books she'd managed to filch. Oh no, Granny would get her cut of those, per their agreement.

But back to this old man: such a strange talker must doubtless be some sort of crook, no? Granny ought to be made aware. That's why the ox-driver was sending word.

But thanks to Granny's fit of temper that word, like the birds, had flown away. Thus she failed to learn that Marshal Fo, with Rookapella Elsternom-Elsternom hidden in his rumpled sleeve, was on his way to the fair city of Spireburgh, home of Mitsa-Konig University— and of the scholarly crimelord Hamel Fliss.

CHAPTER 22

Though Spireburgh is known as the City of a Hundred Towers, in truth that name is a woeful understatement. Over the years the intrigues, rivalries and sheer vanity of its Esquires and Burgesses caused them to build one hundred sixty-one great pillars of brick and stone, which loom over the plazas of Spireburgh.

But lately another thing has been looming over Spireburgh: great, semi-rigid, oblong balloons full of the Phlogistical gas used in experiments at Mitsa-Konig University.

The balloons are massive. Some are as long as entire plazas. They make a gentle booming sound as they bump against one another; their curves catch the sunlight like the sails of ships; they cast shadows as clouds do. And like clouds, they are transitory— for by the time the season of thunderstorms reaches Spireburgh, the balloons will be gone, their gas used up in projects such as the race to develop the world's first self-piloting transport barge.

This was a literal race, as well as an intellectual one. Teams of students from Mitsa-Konig's new College of Tekology planned to launch their various entries from a garage on the Renno Canal; if all went well, the self-piloting barges would travel ninety leagues upriver, finally to arrive in the Whellen Country. There, an impartial set of Prophessors from the Whellen Institute of Tekology waited to award the prize.

The "Great Challenge", as it was known around MKU, was less than a week away and everyone from the loftiest Doktor Magistre to the lowliest first-year grind was filled with excitement about it. It was the biggest event on the University's calendar. Parties and rallies raged day and night.

Fo, however, knew nothing of this. Rooki, though she would never have admitted to such ignorance, knew nothing of it either. Even the ox-driver knew nothing beyond the fact that the wights at Em-Kay-You were at it again with the parties and such. She dumped the load of books— and her strange-talking passenger— unceremoniously outside the College of Letters' Library for Old Vonnish Studies and drove off in search of the wight as owed her for this shipment.

Fo was left alone. Well, not completely. Rooki peeked out of his sleeve and up at the great balloons, shaded pink and gold in the sunset.

"Huh. Pet clouds." She squinted. "They're so smooth— Umans must have sheared 'em." She hopped up onto Fo's shoulder and preened what was left of his hair. "Well, I'm against shearing. Any oaf can see it damages the coat. I hope this grows back in time for me to show you off when you're fully trained." She began an enticing singsong. "But who's a handsome boy? Who's hungry? Who wants me to go find him a yum yum?"

Umans are well known to be remarkably adaptable in their diet: they will eat almost anything, especially if it's been treated with fire. But it is a curious fact that many Umans don't know how to forage for themselves, or perform the fire treatment on their own feed. Therefore they tend to become very dependent upon those who bring them meals; among the pet-fanciers of the Isle of Gold it is a truism that he who feeds a Uman, leads a Uman.

For instance, Rooki knew that although Corvinalias Elsternom e Rokonoma had captured his exciting jingly pet by offering it shinies, he had kept it loyal to him by bringing it frogs, locusts, lizards and other such delicacies. She meant to do the same for Lucky— though once again she would never have admitted it, Rooki *was* ever so slightly worried that Lucky might be turning feral.

Popping a few delicious, crunchy beetles into his mouth would bring him back into line. All she had to do was find some safe nook to stow him in while she went out foraging.

But that plan soon came off its hinges.

At Mitsa-Konig as elsewhere, one of the mainstays of the student diet was the humble cheese-topped flatloaf. Entire bakeries were devoted to making nothing else; whenever students felt hunger pangs they would send word to these establishments, and delivery-maids would hurry fresh flatloaves hot from the ovens to the ravenous boys. And when just such a delivery-maid hurried past Lucky, carrying a folded paper tray from which floated a savory, salty, oily, impossibly alluring smell, his stomach snarled. Instinctively, he followed the smell— Rooki had no part in his decision.

"No, Lucky! Wait!"

The delivery wench moved easily through the flow of foot traffic along campus streets, through gates, under porticos. At every step the crush of students grew thicker; to Fo's credit he stayed with the maid remarkably well and to Rooki's, she didn't lose him until the very last moment. But lose him she did; she was left fluttering back and forth over the crowd, shouting at the top of her lungs.

"Lucky! Where are you? Get back here!"

He was nowhere to be seen.

"Excuse me. Have you seen a— pardon me. By any chance have you—"

In desperation, Rooki followed the crowd through the front door of a big residential building. The bustle there was worse than ever, but then she spotted Fo's sheared head among those of the younger Umans.

"*There* you are, you bad boy!"

She was swooping down to peck Lucky when...

"Hoy, a bird got in here! I'll get it!"

An arm holding a hat jutted up in front of her. Rooki failed to avoid it and flew directly into the hat's hairy-smelling depths.

Meanwhile Fo was hemmed into a mass of chattering, whooping, snorting and snickering scholars, many of whom had decided that liquor was a study aid. To them, the sight of eccentric behavior was nothing new— why *not* a foreign Prophessor with an inside-out robe, a half-shaved head, and an unstoppable urge to steal someone's flatloaf?

Fo had finally caught up to the delivery maid. He lunged for the delicious-smelling paper tray she carried and tore back its lid the way a meldragore tears open a sweet and golden hive— most appropriate, since the meldragore is the emblem of Mitsa-Konig University. He grabbed at the slices of flatloaf and began cramming them greedily into his mouth, as though he were a hungry student.

"Hoy! That's mine!" wailed the loaf's rightful owner. "I spent my last brass on that! You've got to pay me back!"

But his fellows found the situation hilarious.

"Think this wight can drink as fast as he eats?"

"Only one way to— hah! Guess he can do it *faster!*"

"Hoy, old fella, are you from Vonn U? Schpricky Vonsh?"

"Oh, be serious. No one speaks Old Vonnish anymore! Give him more mead."

"Fix his robe, though. It's inside out."

"Here ya go, old fella... oh, now he wants my sandwich!"

"Damn it deep, can he ever put away that grub."

In short order Fo found himself turned into the dormitory's mascot. Before he knew it, he was wearing a scarf shaped like a meldragore and an octagonal satin academic cap which had been left behind by a different visiting Prophessor. He also found himself in the presence of a music barrel, and was unable to resist shaking his bottom back and forth to the beat. That delighted the students no end.

"This wight's a kick! You know where I bet he'd have some fun? Up in Guffer's room. He's throwing a party."

"When's Guffer *not* throwing a party?"

"Guffer's the best."

"On to Guffer's!"

Up, up and up flight after flight of stairs they went, till they reached a room with a skylight, and incense burning, and a pair of doors thrown open onto a balcony.

The sun was now well and truly set. In the courtyard below, wyrmlight lamps blazed at full strength upward onto the bellies of the huge and stately Phlogistical balloons. Beneath the balcony a crowd had come together to chant the latest cheer:

"Paws and claws and four times four! Better catch that meldragore!"

Fo stepped to the railing of the balcony and looked down. His scarf slipped from his neck and fell into the crowd— which did indeed catch that meldragore. This filled them with glee; so much so, that they burst into a rendition of the grand old half-cheer, half-song *Mother Mitsa, Guide Us On*, with its wise and stirring final words "ooh, hah, ooh ha ya".

Fo was riveted. The energy was incredible. Tentatively he shouted down into the plaza.

"Ooh, hah, ooh ha ya!"

The crowd echoed him with such intensity that it caused his mind to make what was, for it, a vast and startling leap.

Back in Abode, he'd often stepped out onto the balcony of his chamber and gazed down at a vast tapestry of people. Then as now, he hadn't troubled himself thinking what to say to them; his mistress, or his Prefect of the Guards, or most recently the third general, would say something quietly, and Fo would repeat it loudly, and then the crowd would roar their approval of him. That was how it was and he'd always enjoyed it, till lately.

Lately the fun had been marred by the hand-bombard pressed into his back, which gave Fo a sense of bracing himself for something unknown but very bad. There was a tension about it, like the pressure on the little iron nubbin holding back the spring of a longwolf trap...

And here came the leap.

But that's over now! Thought Fo. *Life is good again!*

The spring had released. The danger was gone. And the good part, the sweet part, still was true: when he spoke, the crowd roared. They were his. He commanded their love.

CHAPTER 23

"**H**ERE, RICKY. FINISH THIS OFF. I've had more than my share." Fred guided the Stewen crystal bottle to the lip of King Enrick's glass and tipped it sharply upward. The Sherry Lorosso that dripped from it was the very last drop, rich with dregs, as fragrant as a feast.

He set the bottle down, very slowly and carefully, on a little round table. Then he set himself down— also slowly and carefully— in one of two big wicker chairs. He stared over the balcony railing at the dark, silent courtyard below the Royal Suite.

Other, smaller balconies also opened onto the courtyard; from one of them floated fragments of foreign music and from another, a fragment of foreign conversation; from the garden below wafted the scent of wet earth and among the strips of cloud above shone a pale silver moon.

The King drank the last drop and said, "Thank you Fred will you tell me why was Dok not at the dinner tonight? Margadet says these kinds of dinners are more than just meals they are important for other reasons she is right I listen to her Fred she is very smart. Dok is very smart too and Margadet really likes her and I was surprised Dok was not with us tonight. Where was she?"

Over the past twenty-three years Fred had learned it was futile to try and evade Enrick of Castramars. Still he couldn't help trying. Maybe it was the Lorosso.

"Hoy, Ricky, don't be shy— go on. Ask me a personal question. Really put me on the spot. Break the mood."

"I am doing those things already Fred you don't need to command me. I am not even sure you *can* command me. That paper might say we are twins now but I am King so whatever command you give me is only a suggestion."

"Can I command you to change the subject?"

"Yes but because it is only a suggestion I don't have to do it."

The brothers sat quietly for a while. Fred found he still had the stopper of the bottle in his hand: a red nautilus shell. He flipped it into the air and caught it neatly, again and again, until something in him untangled just enough to let him reply.

"All right— here's the thing. You know how you said I can't command you? Well, I also can't command Dok. And by can't, I mean won't."

"Are you changing the subject Fred?"

"I'm not. That's my answer. She wasn't at dinner because— who am I to tell her where she ought to be? She's *free*, damn it deep. Paid a big price for it, too." Fred flipped the crystal nautilus shell once more, but this time the throw was clumsy and he missed the catch and it vanished into the courtyard, glittering in the lamplight as it fell.

"So you didn't invite her?"

"That's right, I left her in peace. Ha! That's appropriate. Peace."

"But Fred what if she wanted to be at dinner?"

"She didn't."

"How do you know?"

"I just know!"

"Well Fred I am pretty bad at telling how people feel but whenever I see Dok with you it reminds me a lot of how Margadet is with me and I really think she loves you Fred I think she wanted to be at dinner."

Fred lurched to his feet. "So I'm wrong— what do you want to do about it? Grab a broadspear and chop off my head?"

The King was alarmed. One of his feet twitched, but he held it still. "Are you making one of your comedy jokes Fred? If so that one was horrible I laugh at a lot of things now but that is not one of them."

Fred hunched over the railing, stared down into the garden, felt his face turning as red as the fake seashell, lost someplace among the trees and flowers.

"Sorry about that. I don't know why I thought of it. I, ah, I'm not sure if you've heard, but I'm up against a great big problem."

"Now you see Fred this is why you need Dok if I were up against a great big problem I would tell it to Margadet so if *you* are up against a great big problem you could be telling it to—"

"Pock that. I'm not about to wreck Dok's life by forcing her to share mine."

"But Fred what if she wants to marry you?"

"She doesn't!"

"How do you know?"

Fred grabbed the bottle and threw it after the stopper. A faint shattering noise reached them, along with the startled yelp of a nightbird.

The King was perplexed. "I saw you drop the first thing by mistake but I don't understand why you had to throw the second one."

"Do I need a reason? People throw all kinds of things away, all the time! It's as natural as can be! They throw 'em away and just walk! You know what, Ricky, I'm tired. I'm going to my room."

"You haven't told me how you know—"

"Good night, Your Majesty."

King Enrick of Castramars was left alone. So he sat. Not tapping his feet, not swaying. Just sitting.

The Nautilus was quiet and comfortable and it was a place his late father— *their* late father— had enjoyed very much. Good things happened at the Nautilus. Because of what Fred was doing here, the whole world would soon be at peace.

But he *is not at peace,* thought the King. I don't know why, but from the very moment Da brought him to me, Fred has never been at peace.

An owl flew by. Then a bat. Then one of the moths known as a soulcomet, the most beautiful moth in the world.

After that, there was nothing but the moon. Finally the King stood up and left the balcony, thinking one final thought as he went.

I don't know if I can help Fred, thought the King. But I can try. I can make sure he knows that if ever he needs me, or Margadet, or even little Nedward, we're here.

CHAPTER 24

"WHICH OF YOU STEPPED ON my finger?"

This outcry came from the middle of a densely packed loaf of students, all crammed into a very tiny room whose folding door was made of pierced tin, like the cabinets in which bakers store bread. At Vonn University, earlier that week, twenty-one students had managed to cram themselves into an RCD booth— and Mitsa-Konig would not be outdone.

From other parts of the loaf, high and low, came a spate of replies.

"Oh, wah, your poor finger. Meanwhile about three of you cankerscabs are standing on my foot!"

"How about me? Someone's got his knee *way* too close to what we at the College of Healing refer to as The Goods."

"Ugh! Who ate bean stew?"

"Everyone just shut up! Count off. I think we're almost there."

One by one the boys called out their numbers. The one whose face was shoved against a metal dome— the part of an RCD booth from which sound emanates— heard a young voice, complete with a posh and honeyed Vonnish accent, asking "How many did I hea-ah? Eight-teen you say? Is that all?"

"We *said* twenty!" roared the boy closest to a ceramic cone— the part of a talk booth into which a user is supposed to speak.

"Did I hea-ah something?"

"You're about to hear your record crushed, that's what! There's twenty of us in here now and we're about to cram in the Schmargel brothers!"

This was a pair of extremely small twins; unfortunately, from somewhere deep in the mass of bodies, a voice said "Uh, no. We're already in."

"What? Then who's left?"

As there was no longer enough room for anyone to turn his head, all that turned were eyes. And when forty of them landed upon the only student remaining outside the booth, their owners' hopes died. There was no getting round it: those blisters at Vonn would gloat insufferably, and point out that *their* emblem was the Lorro leaf, symbol of victory— because there was no way Petir de Brewel would ever fit even one of his great big shoes into the booth now.

Petir de Brewel would have been a popular and well-liked young gentleman even if he had not been the son of Donn Felip de Brewel. By no word or action did he ever flaunt the fact that his family ruled the entire Brewel Country and were the University's largest donors— though admittedly under the name Anonymous. And now, because he was the instrument of dear old MKU's defeat, he let his friends berate him.

"Aw, Petey!"

"Where the hindmost hells were you when we were putting down the base layer?"

"Next time we'll just saw you in half."

The metal dome emitted the cruel sounds of someone singing. "Vonn, oh Vonn, thy victr'y grows, fair and evergreen…"

"Oh, shove it," grumbled one of the Schmargel brothers.

The dome was offended. "You, sir, are out of aw-dah! I say good day!" And then came a loud click, a long, flat, metallic buzz, and dead silence. Vonn University had cut the connection.

A completely free talk channel was a rare thing indeed. At Mitsa-Konig there were four RCD booths in the Student Center and seventeen others at the various Colleges, and since their installation not a single one of them had been out of action for more than a minute. Night and day, lines of young scholars waited for the use of this incredible new Tekology, mostly in order to taunt friends at other institutions, or inquire whether they happened to keep their Old Folks brand smokeweed in a jar; cramming bodily into RCD booths was a new fad, and perhaps not destined to last.

It took time for twenty boys to unfold themselves from the depths of the booth— at least half a minute. That gave someone, somewhere, an opportunity: the last boy was just shaking the feeling back into his numb and wobbly legs when the bell beside the metal dome began to vibrate.

"Answer it, will you, Petey?" said the boy, slumped miserably against the far wall. "I can't reach the pocking thing. I may never walk again."

Petir de Brewel lifted the ceramic cone from its hanger, pulled it to the end of its cord and held it to his rosy young lips under their bravely struggling infant mustachio. "The caller ahoy. This is RCD three, Mitsa-Konig Student Center."

"Thank Ye Gods! This channel has been busy for hours. I'd like to talk to Petir de Brewel," said the metal dome.

"You're in luck, then. That's me. Who is... wait a minute. Is that you, Mesir Dimachi?"

Following a huge donation by Anonymous, there had lately been a hundredfold increase in scholarship students; Petir would never do anything so crass as to address his family's major-domo by first name in front of students who might not have any servants at all.

"Yes! Yes, Your High Honor. It's Rhonso!" came the voice from the dome. Petir blushed as the voice continued: "Listen to me. Three, one, two. I repeat. Three, one, two. Acknowledge."

The boy slumped against the wall was puzzled. "What's with the numbers, Petey? I thought you were a Philology major."

"Your High Honor! Is someone listening to—"

Petir covered the metal dome with his big paw of a hand. "That's a fascinating solution, Prophessor Dimachi! I'd love to hear how you arrived at it. But this is a public booth. I'll call you from the College of Mathematics."

"You won't get in there," said the boy against the wall. "Guffer and his friends are taking shifts reading the entire Collected Works of Parafu to... hoy, Petey, did you hear me?"

Petir de Brewel was a young Gentleman, and as such had not been raised to exert himself physically. His running skills left much to be desired. As he lumbered out the front door of the Student Center and off across the pedestrian mall, the hurry-horse that rolled up beside him really was moving at no better than a crawl.

"What's the trouble, stubble?" asked his sister. "Something on fire?"

Out of respect for the young de Brewels' social position, no one ever mentioned how each of these two took after precisely the wrong one of their parents. But it was true. Kiki was boyishly slight and resembled Donn Felip as exactly as Petey was tall and sturdy and resembled Dame Irona. Life can be so unfair.

"Rhonso— called. He— said— three— one— two."

Kestrella's amber eyes opened wide. Her little feet in their hard-toed sculptor's workboots missed a step. "What's it about? Should I set up the..."

"Yes. I'll— meet—"

Before Petir could gasp out the word "you", Kestrella had given the ground three great kicks; her hurry-horse rolled away across the mall.

It was the best hurry-horse on the market, with wheel bearings of fine Whellen Country steel, and rolled very smoothly indeed. But as Kestrella passed behind a brightly painted fence that momentarily obscured her from view, she did one extra thing. With a delicate, paint-stained finger she pressed a switch hidden on the hollow frame of the hurry-horse.

Secret clockwork whirred to life. The machine bolted like a racing highcat. Kestrella tucked her feet up, put her head down, and within a minute she had crossed the entire campus; only a wish not to attract further attention stopped her from riding up the front steps of the dormitory and straight through its open door. But she mastered the impulse and by the time she was entering The Residences she had dismounted, and now looked like any other student walking a hurry-horse.

Well, not *any* other. Kestrella was in fact the very first female student in the history of the Federated Kingdom of Midlandis.

She had won her place fairly; the application wholeheartedly approved by the College of Art was under the pseudonym "N. D. Whorrell". And just as Petir never abused his social rank, so Kestrella was among the very hardest-working of the Art students who lugged cumbersome materials back and forth across campus and pulled frantic all-night studio sessions. The fact that boys' cheeks flared pink when she entered life drawing sessions was neither here nor there; real artists cared as little for the implications of nudity as did students at the College of Healing. But the University did make one exception for a female scholar: they gave her a private courtyard, in which to practice the sword, twinstaves and broadspear.

And in this courtyard was a shed.

And in this shed she kept a private Remote Conversation Device.

Because Petir and Kestrella de Brewel both were operatives of the Central Agency for Intelligence.

With trembling fingers, Kestrella set up the mechanism, a miniaturized RCD disguised as the last upon which a cobbler repairs boots. The emergency calls they'd made before had been only drills. But now, as she adjusted the foot of the last and listened to the tones issuing from its hollow shin— a horrible racket, like a goose fighting a bassoon to the death— she knew it was real. Her brother never ran anywhere.

He was just stepping through the door of the shed, sweaty and puffing, when the horrible noises focused into a single, clear chord.

"That's— our— channel!" panted Petir, who like many students of language had a keen musical ear. "Ring the— bell!"

Kestrella began hammering the toe of the last with a cobbler's mallet. After a moment in which she and Petir worried that they had called the wrong device, on came Agent Dimachi.

In this context he was no longer the staid, faithful servant who ran Brewel Hall, and the young nobles his masters. Now he was the senior operative and they were new recruits, zealous but untried, faced with the chance to prove they belonged in The Bureau, that theirs would be its new generation.

"You're being activated," he told them. "This is a manhunt."

CHAPTER 25

FRED SMOOTHED HIS CRUMPLED NOTES and stared out at the other desks around him. There were at least twenty, arranged in what was supposed to be an egalitarian array of semicircles, but the arrangement clearly had not worked its magic on the desks' squabbling occupants. He broke off staring, instead to press both hands to his face and rub it. Corvinalias, perched on the back of Fred's chair, counted that as the twelfth time he'd done so.

For a fleeting guilty moment, Corvinalias considered hiding his colossal blunder from Fred instead of telling him. But of course that was unthinkable. He'd always done right by his pet, starting when the fellow had been a poor, hungry, ragged vagabond— only then, thought Corvinalias, *then* I'd been good for him. I'd kept him fed on delicious mice and lizards and worms. Now what have I done? I might have doomed the world.

Fred lifted a cold paper cup of black drink and took a slurp. He cleared his throat and told the interpreter assigned to the Feud Islands: "Please tell the gentleman that I appreciate his point, but we need to move on."

The interpreter relayed this to his charge, a man whose long, curly, pale hair was studded with the shafts of terrible arrows, whose face was covered in fearsome geometric scars, and whose only concession to the fact that he was at a peace conference was not having worn the helmet of his armor. He nodded when the interpreter murmured into his heavily pierced and tattooed ear; but there were two such gentlemen at the desk, and the one who hadn't been murmured to raised an outcry.

It became intense enough to make the envoy from the Peaceful Ocean stand up.

"Ah yah, this waste time. We not here to make peace between faction of Feud Island— that as futile as closing Strait of Swez."

Upon hearing this, the envoy from Swez leaped to his feet, pushing his panicked interpreter back into his chair. "What? Close us? World economy dies then! It dies!"

Corvinalias noted the way Fred's fingers shook when he grabbed the edge of his desk. "Please, Your Excellency, be in order... nobody ever said anything about..."

"*He* do!"

"Ah yah, I only say..."

Now the interpreter for the Pashma Country stood up. "Why *not* peace in the Feud Islands? If I may remind all of you, we are working toward a unanimous agreement. Or have we decided that some of us are of lesser importance?"

"Lesser? Us? Without us, world economy *dies!*"

"Ah yah, he only say..."

While this was going on, one of the Feud Islanders turned his country's desk ninety degrees clockwise; this would not stand with his counterpart, who turned it one hundred eighty degrees the other way; and seizing upon the idea of adjusting the seating arrangement, the envoy from Pharrendolia stacked his chair on top of his own desk, scrambled up into it and looked down upon the rest of the world.

Amid the ruckus that burst forth, Fred put his head down and dug both hands into his hair. Corvinalias forced himself to hop from his perch to his pet's shoulder; once there, he had a lapse of self-control and pecked at the shiny Castramars ring on one of Prince Malfred's clenched fingers.

"Ow." Not even enough energy for a proper flinch. Oh, poor fellow...

"Fred. When this breaks up I have to talk to you."

"Talk now. We'll be here forever— we were supposed to be setting the morning agenda, remember?"

Corvinalias felt like flying away. But of course he couldn't do that. Not only because it was wrong but because of his feathers.

He drew a deep breath, positioned it in front of his lungs, pushed it through and took the plunge.

"All right. I did a bad thing. I disregarded your wishes. I told The Bureau about Fo being gone."

Corvinalias knew the pause felt longer than it really was. That didn't make it any more comfortable waiting until Fred said "Oh. Well."

"And, um, something happened."

Fred let go his hair and turned his head till Corvinalias saw the corner of his eye. "Please don't tell me they dragged Dok back into The Bureau."

"Um, no. They didn't do that. Wait, Fred, you're not going to smile when you hear this. I, ah, all right. Here it is. I told The Bureau about Fo being missing and talked to her about the importance of that and—"

"What do you mean, 'talked to her'? I thought you said Dok wasn't involved in this."

"She's not! I talked to a maid, I mean I *thought* it was a Bureau man disguised as a maid, but that was yesterday morning and I didn't see anything being done, so at lunch today I complained to Agents Moktabelli and Dimachi, saying hoy Nicolo, hoy Rhonso, listen, I'm not really what you'd call an active Agent anymore and I don't ask you for many favors but—"

"Just get to the point, Corv!"

Corvinalias clamped his wings to his sides, screwed his eyes shut and shrank to a lump. "They had no idea what I was talking about! That maid wasn't a Bureau man at all!"

"Well, who *was* she?"

"I don't know! The Bureau activated Petir and Kiki to hunt for Fo. And they opened a secondary investigation to hunt for the maid. All of which distracts you from this." A black claw pointed tentatively from the lump at the scene around them.

"Ah, yes," sighed Fred. "This."

The envoy from Pharrendolia was no longer sitting in his chair but standing on it, in order to be taller than the other envoys, as they had moved *their* chairs atop the desks; the envoy from Swez was roaring at one and all; several interpreters were taking surreptitious slugs from liquor flasks; and off in a corner the Feud Islanders had begun a vicious dance battle.

The lump stuck to its argument. "So it looks a little messy. It's still progress."

"Is it?"

"And I pocked it all up."

"Did you?"

The lump felt something nudging it. A single glittering eye opened from among its feathers. The nudging thing was Fred's hand, palm up, waiting. "Come on, Corv. You've seen the whole Universe, and you're trying to tell me that a mistake you made is the worst thing in it?"

"Well, something has to be."

"I doubt it's that. Go on, featherhead, hop in my hand. I'll carry you over to the refreshment table— there are a *few* things left on it, and nobody's listening to me anymore."

As the two of them picked through some bits of dessicated sandwich and shriveled ring-shaped bread, watching the envoys of the world engaging in their diplomacy, Corvinalias made one last try at explaining the depths of his blameworthiness.

"But Fred. I really feel like I opened a crate of eels. Rooki is— she's— well, I'll admit sometimes I do wish I could be more like her. You know how they say 'if only her powers could be harnessed for good'?"

"Maybe they can. After all, Alkemists have split the Mote."

"Hmm, maybe. But Phantactive substances are safe as milk compared to Rooki. Whoever *she* teams up with had better be ready for anything."

CHAPTER 26

The Varsity Versery was a sweet and cheerful little bookshop built of dark wooden beams and white plaster, with striped awnings over the windows and pots of red crushflowers flanking the door. It stood at one corner of a pentagonal brick plaza, leaning against Spireburgh's oldest and tallest tower as though the two of them were the very best of mismatched friends.

Inside there were books for sale, of course— the shop specialized in poetry— but also soaps and candles and scent bouquets, cozy little lap blankets, needlepoint pillows bearing slogans like "Stay Tranquil and Continue What You're Doing", and a corner where customers could sink into armchairs to read their purchases, sipping icy tea and devouring toasty-warm biscuits. The Varsity Versery stayed open late, and sold brandy while poets showed off their skill at Open Megaphone Night.

The owner was a gentleman named Humble Flowers. Mesir Flowers moved slowly, but he was an inspiration: he got on so well despite his speech impediment, his bad foot, and the slight paralysis affecting one of his hands. Such a gentleman would have been well within his rights to seat himself behind the counter of his shop and stay there, but Mesir Flowers was not one to sit about and watch the world pass by. He was constantly on the move, limping in and out through the sunshine-yellow door of his little office at the back of the shop, bringing an inexhaustible supply of personally chosen books to his customers. And he was never without a friendly smile on his ham-colored face.

But if one looked more closely at Humble Flowers, one would have seen... nothing at all to indicate that the speech impediment, the bad foot, and the paralysis were fake. Of course not. Hamel Fliss was a master of disguise.

The Varsity Versery, likewise, was masterfully disguised. After choosing it as his headquarters, Fliss had taken great care to murder everyone who knew its secret. Now he alone knew that the cheerful little shop had been built long ago by a rich book fancier with a passion for thievery, and that behind the sunshine-yellow office door was an office, obviously, but also a cabinet blocking a closet opening into a chamber containing a stairwell that led down into a vast labyrinth connecting every library at Mitsa-Konig University as well as several in private homes. From this nerve center the literate lord of Brewel Country crime ran his empire.

His network included bent Prophessors by the dozen, including many in the College of Geophilosophy; and besides that, he had invested many toilsome years digging subtle channels in Granny's mob, through which word of her doings might flow to him.

So he knew all about the League For Peace, and had heard all about Granny's abortive hunt for the man who could prove to be the key to the world.

A wight like that was such a benny prize that Fliss had been prepared to go back to Coastwall for him. Four hours' drive, who knew how many of Granny's goons to kill, probably some trouble with the big lawman in the capital, and the risk of a confrontation with Granny herself, would have been worth it. But an internal sense, born from long years remaining alive at his hazardous occupation, told Fliss there would be no need.

The Abodean was in Spireburgh. He simply knew it. The strange Visiting Prophessor who had harangued the crowds from a balcony the night before, who had appeared from nowhere and spoke no word of Midlandic, was he. All Fliss had to do was come up with a way to find him.

CHAPTER 27

By the time Rooki found Lucky again, she had learned more about Umans— well, at least about the young males— than anyone alive. If she hadn't been in such haste to find her pet, she would have found some material to scratch on and taken time to document the creatures' behavior.

She'd been particularly fascinated by the way they fought for dominance over one another using language, and by their reactions to the mating display of the few females who had ventured among them. Other aspects, however, were repellent, starting with the greasy hat she'd been trapped in and all the other filth littering the chambers of the animals' hive. The whole place could have used a good airing-out, and in fact that did end up happening. One of the young Umans had overturned an incense burner; a book had caught fire; someone had thrown open a window and Rooki had seen her chance to escape.

Out into the night she'd flown, zigzagging among the strange smooth curves of the sheared clouds. "Lucky!" she'd called, again and again, but the only reply she got was from a female Uman who, off behind a hedge with a male, had looked up at her and said "I know, right?".

It had been tedious, and for the longest time fruitless, except perhaps apart from the mental map she managed to build. All flying birds have what might be described as a storehouse of the brain, in which they capture location imagery; and though the Phlogistical balloons tethered all over the MKU campus prevented Rooki from flying at the optimal height for mapping, still her senses did their work and picture after picture began clicking together. One hundred sixty-one towers piercing the dark sky like spikes of deeper darkness. Eight big plazas and fifteen small ones radiating the warmth of the previous day's sun. One point one five square magpie leagues of dewy campus lawn. And a river, winding and natural, that bit by bit got bled and dammed and compressed into a series of canals. That was Spireburgh. But where, oh where in all of this, was Lucky?

The sun rose. The day wore on. Rooki was so exhausted she actually fell asleep gripping the branch of a rowan tree, her head against its trunk. She was so tired she couldn't even muster the energy to reply to whoever it was that perched overhead, telling her companion: "Look at that, right there in public. Disgusting. Just because the berries ferment, doesn't mean you have to eat them."

Rooki didn't sleep for long, though. She had a job to do. The urgency of it reached deep into her mind and woke her up so she could go on searching, dipping low and soaring high among the shadows of the great, oblong, smooth-sided clouds.

A rude part of her mind, perhaps piqued at having been woken, blurted: *What if he's dead?* The thought chilled her heart. What would Corvinalias Elsternom e Rokonoma say, if he heard Rooki had killed her pet? Not to mention how sad it would be about poor Lucky, of course. Rooki wondered if Umans understood death.

But wonder of wonders, at some point in the afternoon she happened to be double-checking a certain part of the largest canal—and she found him! In an open-sided shed around a dock!

"There you are!" she shouted, flashing to his side. "Bad boy, *bad!* You had me *so* worried!"

One of the students working in Tekology Laboratorium #1 turned to his lab partner. "Hoy, hear that magpie? Sounds like it's learned to imitate your Ma."

"*I'll* imitate your Ma."

"Ha ha. But really, there's a bird in here— see it? Behind the ESP-1 Phlogistical Fractionator? Oho, it's met our new friend."

"Good. Maybe now we can finish this in peace. *No, Mesir! Stop that! Hands to yourself, remember?*"

The last part was addressed to a visiting foreign Prophessor, who had stumbled into the Laboratorium and begun ransacking the place with an eager, destructive curiosity that reminded the students of the blue-arsed apes used in experiments at the College of Education. Again and again the students had had to stop him from twisting dials, pulling levers, and taking apart apparatus. Inquiries as to which Department he'd come from went nowhere and trying to force him out of the Laboratorium got an extremely aggressive reaction— the rage that flashed into the old gentleman's sharp-cornered, multicolored eyes actually frightened the students. Well, a bit. Enough to make them give him a few samples of inert Phantactive substance to play with, and push a few tables together to fence him into a relatively harmless corner.

These particular students had reached a critical juncture of their project: a few of the teams' self-piloting barges featured specially modified CrystlNav guidance units, made just for them by Yuliyodyne Systems. They were supposed to react not only to direction but to the busy traffic that would surely face the little barges on their route from Laboratorium #1, through the maze of Spireburgh's canals and ultimately to triumph. A big cash prize awaited whoever won the challenge, as well as publication in the new *Midlandis Journal of Tekology*, Kingdom-wide acclaim, and a year's worth of free flatloaf. But this particular CrystlNav unit wasn't going to install itself. The team was fighting to stay on schedule and had to manage the task today— why, oh why, did this foreign wight have to come in and turn everything upside down and sideways?

Marshal Fo liked this place. It reminded him very, very *very* much of all the fun he'd had with his men back in Abode, helping them build the Weapon. He had come up with the design for something called a safety gimbal, and had been proud of it right up until the moment when, he wasn't sure why, the stuff inside the little round thing at the center had suddenly become really hot and begun to squeal and Prophessor Okosh had grabbed it and thrown it and then oh the noise and the light and the glowing snow that had rained down everywhere! It was all people had talked about, at Prophessor Okosh's funeral. Marshal Fo poked his finger into the gray lump the students had given him and wondered whether anything so exciting would happen here.

A familiar noise told him the bird had come back. He lowered his head, narrowed his eyes and growled— there were a few painful scabs on his ear, from that bird. He would throw this lump of gray stuff at the bird.

But the bird dodged it and the boys who had given him the gray stuff in the first place set up a shouting and they rushed over to re-arrange some of the machinery that had got knocked down. What a lot of bother. Fo squeezed himself out from among the tables and wandered off to look at some rafts that were floating in the finger of water that extended into the middle of the room.

There was another lot of bother as a few things happened at once. First, the bird set up a scolding. Then, the boys seemed not to want him near the rafts. Then the door opened and two men came in, one in a scholar's robe and the other one, well— he was obviously a very rich man. His ham-colored face was unassuming and his clothes were simple, but an air of power hung about him.

"Good gods," gaped one of the students, whisking off his hat and bowing low. "It's Dru Karneke. Uh, good afternoon, Mesir! Thank you again for this wonderful opportunity to, uh, further cement Mitsa-Konig's reputation as not only a leader in traditional subjects but a pioneer in Tekology!"

Dru Karneke, the University's second-largest benefactor, smiled upon the students and their work. He was a reclusive man and few had ever seen him outside of news prints, but now, for whatever reason, he was in Laboratorium #1. The students were in awe. The Prophessor escorting him was in awe. It would all have been memorable enough, but then Mesir Karneke did a wonderful thing.

He said, "Boys. If you don't mind, I'd like a word with your visitor over there— he's a foreign Doktor Magistre who could prove very important to a deal I'm working on. I'd like to take him back to my estate."

"Please do!"

"Yes, go ahead, take him!"

"He doesn't seem to understand our language, though, Mesir."

"Oh, damn it deep, someone get rid of that bird! Sorry, Mesir! Did it hurt? Let me get you some ointment."

Dru Karneke rubbed the peck mark on his ham-colored forehead. "Would you boys be so kind as to leave me alone with the gentleman for a moment?"

No one questioned this. Who would question the gentleman who'd donated the entire College of Tekology? They hurried out of the Laboratorium and left Hamel Fliss alone with the object of his greed.

Fliss walked around Fo the way a highcat walks around an animal it's about to chase.

Rooki, perched on Fo's shoulder, shrilled, "Careful, Lucky! I don't like this wight!"

From his sleeve Fliss brought out a thick leather money wallet, drooping with its heavy load. "Come with me and I might not have to give you any of this," he said, and somehow, Rooki sensed that *this* didn't mean coins. That wallet was a weapon. Those coins must be slugs of lead.

"Get away from him!"

She plunged at Fliss, clawing wildly. He staggered back a few steps. She leaped to Fo and began pecking his ear for all she was worth. "Run, Lucky! He wants to hurt you!"

But Lucky didn't run. He only swatted at her. Of all the times for him to act up!

Rooki was forced to get rough. It took everything she had to make him go— damn it deep, he'd tripped and fallen off the dock onto one of these little boats.

Well, Rookapella Elsternom-Elsternom was one who could roll with the current. She leaped onto the cleat the little boat was moored to, and cast off its spring line. Wait, that wasn't the one! Rooki tried another cleat, then another. Lucky was in danger of drowning, that other man was grabbing a boat-hook... Success!

With the last line she released, the barge began to float away, swerving from one side of the slip to the other as though it were alive and searching for the exit. Which it found. Rooki flew aboard beside her pet just as the barge surged off down the— boils! Were they caught on something?

Behind her, the door of Laboratorium #1 burst open. A beautiful, amber-eyed small young Lady and a lanky oversized young Gentleman were pointing, shouting. They were jumping off the dock, onto one of the other barges Rooki had cast loose.

Kestrella and Petir felt something tumble onto the deck of the barge beside them.

"I'm so glad you youngsters arrived! I'm after that man too!"

Petir's jaw dropped open in shock. Rhonso had told them they were on the hunt for Marshal Fo of Abode, but not that Dru Karneke was involved. And as for Kestrella, she was shocked by something else entirely.

"Look!" she yelled, pointing up ahead.

Rooki had cast loose one of the lines mooring a Phlogistical balloon. This was what Fo's barge had tangled itself upon; now the great gas-filled behemoth was flying free, plucking the barge up out of the canal. The barge dangled vertically and Fo yelped as he clung to it, unaware that Rooki was at work saving him. She had seized a second line from the balloon and threaded it onto a winch at the aft end of the barge; up it came and then it was more or less stable, suspended from beneath the Phlogistical balloon as Fo scrambled into a seated position astride it. Higher and higher the odd rig climbed.

The world beneath Fo was small and getting smaller. It looked like a toy. Suddenly he was more excited than afraid. He pulled off his hat and waved it. "Whee-hah! *Drowa!*"

Petir and Kestrella stared at the great, buoyant, snowy curvature gliding by above them. The self-piloting barge, with the rotatory oar in its stern now pushing it through air instead of water, was dragging the balloon along as much as being carried by it.

Hamel Fliss stared too. His ticket to the world was drifting away.

The barge he and the de Brewels rode on had aimed itself and begun a self-piloting pursuit, but after only a few seconds he could tell it wasn't going to be fast enough. So he speared his boat-hook into the wall of the canal and gave a mighty push. "Come on, you kids," he snarled. "Get your hands in the water and start paddling! Never mind if something bites at them— are you soft little blisters afraid of honest work? Hurry up, I say! Get me closer to that thing!"

Oh, how annoying it was to have to deal with the actual, physical world. Fliss had become used to other kinds of action: a small movement of his fingers could lay down a little curl of ink that might spell doom for some unlucky wight. That was power. This sort of scrambling and striving was, well, beneath him. But it would be worth it. He had to keep reminding himself of that. Sometimes you had to go low to rise high.

CHAPTER 28

"**W**HAT AN INSPIRATION YOU ARE, Mesir," exclaimed Kestrella de Brewel. Despite his vast wealth, Dru Karneke was poling their barge with as much energy as the toughest oarmaid. "I can see what's made you such a success."

Petir agreed. "You are indeed driven by a most prodigious fire. What would you say is the secret of—"

"Cut the yap and paddle harder!"

This was not the most politely phrased motto, but the young de Brewels admired its rugged economy. So they obeyed Dru Karneke's words of wisdom and emulated his example. They put their hearts into the work.

It was fairly slow going. The canal was busy with other craft carrying building materials, trade goods and passengers, piloted by ordinary wenches in the ordinary fashion. But at the bow of the barge, a glass dome would flash gold, or purple, or cornflower blue; with every flash something would whirr, and the rudder would make whatever correction was required to avoid obstacles great or small.

Above them, the runaway Dictator moved through the sky in similar leisurely fashion. At every turn of the canal, the dangling barge from which he waved gleefully down at them would hover in place, then pivot, then move on.

"We're synchronized with it," said Petir. "Every team's entry has to trace the same route, inasmuch as there really isn't any other. After this next turn, we'll be out of the canals. See? Now we're in the main channel of the Renno. And from here it's two nautical leagues to the Etkar, and after that we'll—"

"What did I say about yapping?"

"Yes, Mesir."

Petir fell silent, thinking about advances in Tekology. He was a passionate admirer of the new College, even though a seventeen-legged meldragore was going to require extensive work in the way of updating the Mitsa-Konig emblem. Oh well, that was a problem for Kestrella's gang at the College of Art. For a moment he felt a species of longing which was the closest thing in his soul to envy: Kiki had already made a strong mark in Art's own form of Tekology, having invented an improved form of printing which allowed for the reproduction of shades of gray.

"I wish *I* could make a contribution to Tekology," mumbled Petir.

"Hoy, chattermouth. What did I say?"

Petir lowered his head in shame, having not only disobeyed Mesir Karneke, but betrayed the College of Letters. But he had reason to long for something better; the great work of his young life, a monograph on the Spiral-Striding Fakirs of Pharrendolia, had not exactly taken the academic world by storm. More depressing still, it had been published under his name alone, since the Prophessor who'd been his guiding light was in prison. *How sad,* thought Petir, the way criminals find their way into every situation.

As the Renno flowed on he, Kestrella and Hamel Fliss drew undeniably closer to their quarry. When they passed through the arches of the great brick-and-stone bridge which is the extension of Spireburgh's ancient outer wall, a rope dangling from the runaway Phlogistical balloon-barge draped itself over the bridge as though it were giving the city a farewell caress; its friction also had the effect of slowing the air-ship down. *Air-ship*— what a memorable, appealing new word that was. Petir was very proud of having coined it and wanted to tell it to his sister— *air-ship!*— but he was afraid to speak again.

She wasn't afraid to speak, though. Kiki was never afraid of anyone.

"Mesir Karneke! See that rope? We're almost close enough to grab it! Let me get up into the bow, here..."

"Careful," murmured Petir. Though he was perfectly aware that Ladies learned to swim as a matter of course, he was also aware that large and hungry creatures lurked in rivers.

"I've... almost..."

Kestrella's fingers were touching the rope when an alarming wave traveled down its length and whipped it from her grasp. Up in the air-ship the bird that was with the Dictator— for a foolish moment, Petir saw its black and white feathers and thought it might be Agent Corvinalias— was cawing, pecking, whipping at the man with its wings; the barge of the air-ship had begun twisting, tipping its nose upward and down, swinging perilously from side to side.

Rooki was in an absolute panic.

"Lucky! No! *No!* Put it back! *Put the shiny back!*"

Back when he and she were aboard the *Yuliyo Advance*, she too had been mesmerized by the colorfully flashing crystal under its glass dome. But unlike Lucky, she was an intelligent being; having surmised that the shiny was something to do with navigation, she had been able to control her urge to steal it. This poor creature was unable to do so. He was, of course, only following his instincts. But instincts be damned— if he fell from this height, the river would be as hard as road paving.

Fo, who had been sitting comfortably on what he thought of as a gentle wooden swing, was terrified by the violence of its motions. His hat fell off and landed in the water far, far below... did something just *eat* it?

That terrified him still more. He no longer cared about the pretty jewel he'd plucked out from its setting under a pivoting glass lid. When the bird pecked and clawed his fingers open, he really didn't care that he dropped the jewel. As the bird folded its wings and fell after it like a falcon, he wasn't even watching.

Petir and Kestrella gasped as they watched the shard of Iyolite fall. They gasped again as the magpie caught it, just inches above the river.

The bird hurried to claw the dome open and replace the crystal within, but the damage was done. By the time the crystal was back in its socket, the air-ship had completely changed course. Now it floated over dry land, headed for the Whellen Country by a route they could no longer follow—

—and Petir had a vision.

Before his mind's eye, his contribution to Tekology unfolded like the turning page of a great codex. He envisioned a transport network of the skies, where air-ships like this one, set free from any need to follow roads or rivers, blazed unobstructed trails by the thousands. Freight lines such as Ata Overland and Re International would expand upward as well as outward; between air-lines and the RCD network, great distances would be bridged, time would be saved, and the world would shrink. Smaller, denser, tighter, faster; nothing would ever again be the same. The down on the back of Petir's neck stood on end with the thrill of having seen the future.

But a wail of rage from Hamel Fliss dragged him back to the moment.

"Gods' guts! Where's that damned gas bag *going?*"

That brought Petir up short. He and Kestrella exchanged glances. She took the lead.

"Why do you ask, Mesir Karneke?"

"What?"

Her voice turned dangerously innocent. "Don't you know where it's going? You're the College of Tekology's greatest patron. You chose the destination."

Hamel Fliss was a literate crimelord and a well-informed one, as crimelords went. But there were things he hadn't been informed of.

"I— it sounds like you think something's changed. Forget before. Tell me where they're headed *now!*"

This evasion fooled nobody. Quite the opposite, in fact. In that moment, like two RCD terminals recognizing one another, the crimelord instinct of Hamel Fliss and the Bureau training of the young Agents locked into a common channel.

CHAPTER 29

HAMEL FLISS WAS NOT A mere thug. He prided himself on having some brains in his head, of operating on a level above the crude impulses which governed the actions of such as Granny Almantree. For him, violence was only a backup plan.

"I think we're on the same side, little Lady. Why don't we trade information?"

Kestrella's eyes clenched into two golden slivers. "All right, Mesir. But first tell me: how many socks does a meldragore have?"

Fliss knew this one. He'd heard about the new College of Tekology. "Why, seventeen, of course."

That answer was wrong— a Bureau operative would have replied to any numerical question with the three-digit code of the day. But it told Kestrella all she needed to know; likewise her little hand, thrust inside her sleeve, found what it was feeling for.

"Entirely correct, Mesir! So you know the man up there on the flying barge is... the thief who stole that priceless painting."

"Just so! I was sent to help you capture him. Tell me then, officer, where's he headed *now?*"

"There's no need to test me. I can keep a secret."

Though Fliss did pride himself on brains, a thuggish rage roiled his innards. Now he wished this *were* a Granny Almantree situation— the kind that could be solved with a whack of the boat-hook. Into his memory trickled his old boss and some of her pet phrases. "Me benny." "Me mally." "Thez na got to say."

Thez na got to say...

All at once it dawned on Fliss that this slip of a wench did not have to say. Irony of ironies, it was the young gentleman who'd given the game away: he'd said the barges were synchronized, set to reach the same destination. That meant there was no more need for Ke-scrawny de Brewel and her big bumptious brother— oh yes, Fliss had recognized them. The news in Coastwall would be sad, but river monsters were perfectly happy to eat nobles as well as commoners...

He raised the boat-hook high and swung it, but he was, as they say, a writer, not a fighter.

The smallest infant brat, without so much as a wooden blade yet fitted to her tiny broadspear, would have recognized the signs that he was about to employ a diagonal slash. Long before Fliss brought the improvised weapon down toward her, Kestrella's hands were gripping a pair of twinstaves and moving fast. Crack went the boat-hook, sent flying out into the river; whack whack whack went the twin bronze rods, ever so gently crushing Hamel Fliss in all sorts of non-lethal places.

Over his continuous agonized howling, Kestrella chirped to Petir: "Go tell 'em!"

She meant he ought to go back to their shed and call the Bureau. But traffic on the river was perversely thin: two scows loaded with bricks, a rowing dinghy full of town officers, a fishermaid's delivery launch— that's all there was, and each craft was too far away for Petir to jump aboard.

"I think we'll have to wait a bit," he said, watching a shadowy form with huge jaws flicker beneath the barge.

Kestrella crouched beside Fliss, twinstaves at the ready, and said: "Take your time. I've got this wight pretty well subdued. You, sir! Will you sit quietly, or do you want a few more crunchies for dessert?"

Rubbing his smarting fingers and toes, nursing his smarting pride, Hamel Fliss glared at his captors. He'd been in tough spots before— hells afar, he'd escaped from Granny herself. It never felt good to be pressed against the wall, but then again it never lasted long either. He, too, would wait a bit.

Ugly minutes passed. The barge propelled itself inexorably upstream, toward the confluence of the Renno and the Etkar; here there *was* plenty of traffic, and Fliss began to worry.

So he used his brains.

He watched everything. He watched the dip and sway of the buoys marking the channel. He watched how, for a better look at some approaching craft, Petir raised himself to his knees. Like the buoys, the barge tipped and bobbed. The moment was *now.*

Fliss turned his head sharply, as though he'd seen something, and said: "Is that *Kwaga*? I thought he was locked up!"

Doktor Magistre Delahaie Kwaga was Petir's former Prophessor. He also happened to be one of Fliss's underlings, and in truth he *was* locked up, in the Spireburgh Penitentiary. But instinctively Petir leaped to his feet for a look, and Fliss kicked those feet out from under him. Overboard he tumbled. And the girl— she did just as Fliss had hoped. In her sisterly concern, she turned her back on a crimelord.

"Petey!"

Fliss had his cosh out. He raised his arm to slap its lethal load of lead across the back of Kiki de Brewel's skull.

But in seconds it was over, and Fliss could only stare over the transom at the rapidly receding de Brewels, enraged at how Fate had snatched them away.

The big one clinging to a buoy. The little one hooked on the boom of a boat. And both alive, damn it deep. Who knew how long it would take them to get help but— gods' globby guts, the brats had escaped him.

CHAPTER 30

THE TRADE ROAD, THOUGH NOT as ancient as the stone-paved Ve Hamilia which runs from Spireburgh to Coastwall, is one of the vital arteries of Midlandis— a broad, well-engineered ribbon of clay and gravel, connecting the capital to the rest of the Brewel Country and beyond.

A pair of rails had recently been added to the Trade Road, along which freight wagons glided as easily as skates on ice; this railway and its wagons belonged to the Ata Overland company, whose new ownership had kept the name. The venture was a model of progress. Never before had the volume of shipping been so great, the transit times so short, the prices so low— but of course the price of progress was the loss of something romantic. Gone were the freighters' great overnight camps, with a hundred beasts or more picketed by the roadside while all around them cookfires smoked and fiddle music played; now, compact new wagons operated in shifts around the clock.

And so it was that a teamster, driving two yoke of oxen through the moon-touched darkness, had just exited the Coastwall municipal limit when she was startled by a thunder of hoofs coming up behind her rig. A warning bell clanged and someone roared "Out a me way wi' them cud-munchers!"

The oxen were not munching anything; only the teamster was, and she spat maidenroot down at the Trade Road as though meditating on life's injustice. Whoever this was could yell all she wanted; it's not as though a modern freight wagon was free to just pull off the railway. Besides, there was plenty of room for passing— the road was wide, and at this hour the only other traffic consisted of foot messengers pattering along at a soft jog and the odd sedan chair with its lanterns gleaming. The teamster stretched out one arm and made a "come on, then" motion.

The thing behind her hesitated, then with the crack of a whip and a strangled shout of "Yah!" it surged past: an ambulance. It banged against the freight wagon as it went, scraping a gouge through the neat brown-and-gold emblem painted on the side.

"Hoy!" wailed the teamster.

A pair of flyers— foot messengers carrying nothing but documents in bags around their necks, and wearing nothing but short knitted pantaloons, little knitted tunics and cleated goatskin shoes— bounced into the damaged wagon's orbit.

"Nice of 'er," said one of them, inclining her head toward the scrape.

"Aye," said the other. "It's like— learna drive, wench."

The teamster lifted her chin at the bright red lanterns shrinking into the night. "I remember when a Guild license used to mean something!"

"Aw, that sow ain't got no papers. We seen her a-comin' from them warehouses, you know the ones."

The second flyer agreed. "Aye— betcha brass penny there's no healer in that sickbox— nor patient neither— prolly fulla stolen goods."

"It's Oldmarsh up ahead. Ain't it procedure to tell someone?"

"Not me, sis— I'm behind a-ready— gotta make Silver Bit on the dub or boss'll kick my flaps. Won't make no account nohow— whatta they care in Oldmarsh, that someone stole a thing in Coastwall."

"True. See you, then."

"Aye." The flyer turned to the teamster. "Sorry bout yer incident, sis." She adjusted her bag, leaned into her gait and pulled away.

For some time the second flyer jogged along beside the wagon, in companionable silence, the way a highcat trots beside its owner's sedan chair. Eventually she felt she'd done all she could, and she too accelerated into the night.

The teamster sighed, spat another glob of maidenroot and reflected that it was a good thing the ambulance was fake. Anyone with such a terrible case of the marthambles, or the strong fives, or Ye Gods forbid the hockogrockle, or whatever— anyone needing a lift to the infirmary in the middle of the night shouldn't have to suffer the additional misfortune of being driven by a thumb-fisted oaf who might dump the whole rig in the next convenient ditch.

Her assessment of Granny Almantree's driving skill was sadly correct.

For decades Granny had been the one people came *to*, and therefore she had little need to travel; whenever it couldn't be avoided she was driven, or carried, or rowed, by an underling. So her skills at self-transportation had become somewhat rancid with disuse. But the business she was about now simply couldn't be trusted to anyone else.

Word had reached her from Spireburgh— and that meant it was already hours old, at least— about a panic in the workshops where University men built things. And more than that: the word included talk of a gas balloon on the loose and flying toward the Whellen Country, with some foreign Prophessor riding aboard like a statue on a festival float. None of it was very clear. Or rather, not clear to anyone but Granny. To Granny, the crux of it was as obvious as a curly-tailed dog's bunghole: somehow Hamel reeking Fliss had found out about the old foreign wight who held the key to the world.

Exactly how she knew this, she could not have said— she only knew that the hunches which had kept her at the ridge of the game all these years, benny and mally ones alike, were powerful things and not to be questioned. And if Fliss were after the same thing she was, then Granny would have to chase him and catch him, fight him and win; that was the front and back of it. Best to get on with the job.

CHAPTER 31

ALTHOUGH IT WAS A SEAT of high nobility, Whellengood Hall was not the kind of place where doors creaked open upon ancient hinges to reveal great solemn halls of timber and stone. Quite the opposite: it was the Kingdom's most innovative building, geometrical and modern, a faceted gem of soaring glass planes and gleaming steel pillars. There Dame Elsebet de Whellen, the Domina of the Whellen Country, greeted the dawn by rolling aside the pane of glass that was her bedroom door, and drawing a deep breath from her courtyard garden.

The breeze had not yet begun to blow; a hesitant warmth, scented with plum blossoms, hung in the air.

Dame Elsebet twisted her hair into a long, cool, white rope, which she let snake down the collar of her nightgown; then she stepped out onto the fine gravel walkway and listened— not for anything outside her, but for whispers from within.

All was quiet, however. So she went first.

It's your day again, she said to the ghosts.

Still quiet. So she went on.

Tradition tells me to put on my mourning clothes, visit the family plot, and spend the day in meditation, asking you to forgive me.

More than half a century had passed since the event that required forgiveness: twenty-year-old Dame Elsebet, having dragged her beloved father and dear new husband with her to a faraway forest in quest of adventure, had seen them converted to ghosthood in a gruesome fashion, mere yards from where she stood; afterward, the ghosts had vented their rage at her stupidity in such a tirelessly vivid way that she'd found it impossible to both listen to them and rule the Whellen Country. So her young brother Lorenz had ruled the Whellen Country for her, till after five years of expressing their opinion, the ghosts had receded far enough into the background to let Dame Elsebet get on with things.

Her country prospered, but of course it would naturally do that; she took no credit. The people of the Whellen Country were ingenious and hardworking, and the earth in its generosity had given them the Heart of Stone; they had harnessed its power and for three generations, going on four, it had done the very hardest work of life for them. The Heart of Stone let them lift their sights higher, and thrive.

It was true that a country called Abode had tried to steal control of the Heart, to conquer Midlandis. But they had failed, just as madness had failed to conquer Dame Elsebet.

So this year, she had some news for the ghosts.

Tradition says I should spend the day meditating on you, she told them. *But— have you been counting?*

Dame Elsebet was not much for counting. She considered herself a Lady of the old school, more at home with a broadspear than an abacus. However, she could count to fifty.

If you've been paying attention, she told the ghosts, then you know that I've given you the full number of years. In fact, I've even thrown in a few extra. So I believe we are, as they say, square. And now you will please— not forgive me, but excuse me.

The fine grains of the gravel walkway crunched under her slippers as she turned and strode back into her suite.

She had brushed her hair and put it up in a net before any of her maids even knocked on the door.

"Medame," said the oldest and bravest of them, "I beg you won't argue with us about your beauty routine this morning. Please, please let us apply just the tiniest dab of the sun cream. I know you'll say it's too late but—"

Dame Elsebet put a hand to one of her mahogany cheeks. "Very well. Perhaps you can make me look a *bit* less leathery."

This was a great surprise to the maids. And there was more to come.

As the oldest and bravest one spread protective cream on her mistress's face, she was astonished to hear the words: "And I wonder if maybe a little of that red paint might draw some attention to my smile. Make a contrast, you know. With the teeth."

Dame Elsebet's teeth were straight and numerous, and the maids had often exhorted her to show them off. Now they fell all over one another in their haste to apply maquillage to her lips. Once that mission was complete, the oldest and bravest maid braced herself.

"May we do your brows, Medame?"

Though she'd been prepared for the inevitable, she got the unbelievable.

"Well, all right. But don't make them look fake! Keep them a lighter brown than my eyes— maybe even a realistic gray— never mind what the fashion is."

"Yes, Medame!"

"Pocks to fashion."

"Yes, Medame!"

"One wants to present... what was that word... not a false, but an *optimal* version of oneself."

"Oh, indeed!"

"Yes, an optimal... not those boots, dear. Put those back. Bring out the pair with the rayskin tops— yes! Thank you. And the fawn-colored full seat breeches. And the new tunic. With a pin."

As they dressed Dame Elsebet the maids were fairly in raptures, especially when she reached across to the tub of ointment on the vanity table and began rubbing it into the backs of her hands. Of course no ointment could erase so many decades of wear and tear. But it could soften the wrinkles and bring out the beauty of the intricate ink that flowed from her fingertips to well beyond her wrists: birds and flowers, leaves and vines, drawn there in preparation for her wedding day, left to fade into a ruin, and recently renewed.

"Do you wish to wear gloves, Medame?" whispered the youngest maid. Or rather, the second-youngest. Dame Elsebet's youngest maid had recently taken on a pair of very similar wedding bracelets and left her service, having married Whellengood's chief engineer.

"No. I'm told that touch is one of the naturalist's great instruments. And now, my dears, I will be on my way."

Dame Elsebet rose to her feet with youthful ease— daily riding and combative training will do that— and strode out into the glass-and-steel corridor. Two archers, her habitual bodyguards, fell into place beside her as she traversed Whellengood Hall's gleaming spaces, some of them warmed pink and golden by the sunrise, others still a cool and shady blue. Out a door, into the breeze, off to the stableyard with its grassy and grainy smells, the snorting of horses, the morning bustle of grooms.

Dame Elsebet took the reins of her new filly, threw them over the animal's head and gathered them on the pommel of the saddle. She raised her left foot, set it into the stirrup and was just about to make the little spring that lifts a rider up, carries the right leg over, places her at the center of the world. But before she did, she turned to the archers, who were on the point of mounting their own horses.

"Ladies," she said, "Go find yourselves something to do. I will not be needing you today. I've been invited to view some plum blossoms."

CHAPTER 32

ON A GENTLE BUT DISTINCT hillside overlooking a point at the confluence of two rivers, the deep fragrance of springtime earth mixed with a wealth of strange and nameless higher-floating scents.

A score of small figures were at work on a great blank field, busily digging and hammering at its featureless gray expanse. Not one of them looked across the water and up the hillside, where an odd-looking elder gentleman sat perched upon a donkey.

Perhaps that was incorrectly put: the gentleman himself was not odd-looking, though indeed he had a foreigner's air about him; it was more that he sat oddly, with both legs on the same side of the donkey and his torso aimed far more in the direction of its tail than is customary. Had the beast been wearing a saddle, the gentleman would probably have noticed his mistake; but then again a saddle would have taken up precious room, room that was occupied by a number of neatly filled canvas foot messengers' bags, lashed and knotted together into a mass which the donkey bore with the same stolid patience it showed toward its rider.

When the gentleman saw Dame Elsebet riding toward him, he slid off the creature's back— it was difficult to tell if this maneuver was intentional or whether he simply made the best of it— cupped his hands to his mouth, and called out: "I'll tell you what..."

"How's that?" Even if the gentleman *had* told her what, Dame Elsebet was still too far away to hear it.

"I'll tell you what..."

"I can't hear you! Wait till I'm closer!"

Her filly trotted expertly down the hill, burdened only with its mistress and a small pair of saddlebags.

When she reached him, he was bubbling over with excitement. "I'll tell you what I found: a stand of *Pentofolium*. But with only three stripes in its leaves!"

Dame Elsebet dismounted and discreetly picked up the donkey's reins, a split pair which had been dragging on the ground. "You do surprise me. I remember you saying that fivegrass was the most uniform plant in the world."

Mesir Istivan Hawberry knew the world. Though Hawberry was a solid old Whellen Country name, the darkness of his complexion came not from the sun, as had Dame Elsebet's, but from his mother— the daughter of an Herb Islands spice planter, who had given her shockingly rich family a shock of her own by running off with a poor but adventurous Midlandic poet. Young Istivan Hawberry had grown up in a dozen countries, conversing in at least that many languages, fascinated with documenting nature; over seventy years he'd filled a whole library with his notes and publications. Literally, for he was a founder of the Worldwide Natural Society. And he had been a friend of the late, great polymath Leonn Atler, who was the father of Dok, who was that brilliant young woman so very perfect for Malfred. Chains of acquaintance led to so many beautiful and unexpected places...

"This, my dear, is something never seen before."

Mesir Hawberry was close beside Dame Elsebet, smelling of leaves and flowers. He pulled off his green spectacles, tucked them in one flap pocket of his slate-colored jacket, drew a handkerchief from another pocket and began unfolding it. "Common and uniform, sure, that is our friend the fivegrass. It grows in latitudes polar and equatorial, from desert to bog to snowpack — never varying in the slightest. But look." Inside the folds of cloth lay a specimen of the novel plant, just as described.

"How can you tell this one just hasn't somehow lost two of its stripes?"

"Why, surely to the heavens I picked many bags' worth." He gestured at the donkey. "I was hard put to stop *him* eating half of it! A new species, you may think. Threegrass. But I'm thinking it's not. I found it growing in a single, horizontal strip all across the hillside, as though all of it were a specific distance from..." and here his tone of excitement died. He lifted his eyes to Dame Elsebet's as if asking pardon for the thing he'd almost said.

She gazed over his shoulder at the point of land at the junction of the rivers. It was a glassy waste, flat and blank, though once it had been the New Capital of the Federated Kingdom of Midlandis. Utterly destroyed, all in one terrible moment: a circumstance Dame Elsebet knew only too well...

But no. There was more to this. Something had happened when the Weapon unleashed its fury— creation as well as destruction.

She'd been informed that the area now abounded in substances of extreme interest to scholars, and the men in the crater were chipping a hole in the crust, bringing out fragments of slag and scoria, busy as ants. A path had opened, leading to the future; so as Istivan Hawberry put away the specimen, Dame Elsebet felt it was all right to smile a little.

"You think the— the effects of the Weapon extended up this hillside?"

"Precisely, my dear! The humble fivegrass might help Alkemists finally unlock the secrets of transmutation. I'll take these bags down to your Institute of Tekology straight away."

"Oh, not *straight* away, I hope. What about our plum blossom viewing picnic?"

"Sure, I was mistaken to suggest it. There's not a single plum tree here at all."

"Don't worry," Dame Elsebet assured him. "I brought one."

She reached into her filly's saddlebag and brought out a blanket; when she unrolled it, there in the center lay a stoneware bottle. It was *linkapaa*, the plum brandy of Yondstone.

"This can do some pretty serious Alkemy," said Mesir Hawberry, handling the bottle with scientific tact. "I've seen it transmute a wedding into a brawl."

They spread out the blanket and sat. The donkey and the filly grazed in overlapping circles, as far around a picket pin as their halters and leads would allow. The saddlebags and message bags, now stacked beside the blanket, yielded up more treasures: a big smoked mutton sandwich. A pair of stoneware cups. A slate and stylus. A fiddle.

As Mesir Hawberry tuned the fiddle, he pointed to the bottle, standing by for duty beside the sandwich.

"In the land that our poison, there, comes from, I learned a little song I think is appropriate." Strumming the fiddle instead of bowing it, he sang:

> *"We're disagreein' an' ya set yer jaa—*
> *Time we should take a tot o' linkapaa.*
> *Said you were never gon-a sell that cow*
> *Let's have another! What d'you say now?"*

As his fingers twinkled through the musical figure connecting the verses, Dame Elsebet laughed. "Oh! I know this one!"

Her singing voice had never been very good; she had more of a hunting-field voice. But she wasn't shy of Mesir Hawberry. They tried for a harmony on the second verse.

"Look who's a-comin' but my son-in-laa—
Damned if he ain't a-bringin' linkapaa.
Oh, how I'm hopin' that accursed drink
don't make me tell 'im what I really think!"

They laughed some more. "One more verse," said Mesir Hawberry, "and I think I'll have worked up the nerve for a sip. Ready?

"Farm lad's a-puttin' up a heap o' straa—
Milkmaid approachin' wi' the linkapaa.
One thing another an' the straw gets flat
here come the honeymooners wi' their brat."

"Oh now, Stevie!" exclaimed Dame Elsebet, wiping tears of laughter from her eyes. "I'd forgotten all about that part. And if I recall, it gets worse from there!"

Mesir Hawberry put the fiddle away and reached for the dreaded bottle. "It does. I regret extremely that after that verse, the good ditty turns most profane, and as I am ill-disposed toward profanity in all its forms— would so much rather use scientific terms— I will not continue. Here is your tot. Down the pipe, Elsie!"

"Bottoms up!"

They drank. They winced. They spat out the fiery abomination, gasping.

"My dear. Would you mind terribly if I…"

"Not at all."

Mesir Hawberry flung the bottle as far from them as a learned old gentleman can fling anything.

He and Dame Elsebet flopped onto the blanket, giggling up at the sky, as the donkey and the filly raised their upper lips at the plummy reek rising from their owners. Clouds blew overhead. Elsebet and Istivan told one another what the clouds reminded them of— many and diverse things, drawn from two very different yet very compatible lives.

But then.

"*What* in the seeping, weeping, pus-pumping cankerboils is *that?*"

"Elsie! Language!"

"Pardon me, Stevie. But look— over here. Sit up. Look!"

Istivan Hawberry sat up. He looked. And looked again.

And then he whispered "Great God Almighty, that's around and within and between!"— which, though not profane, was far from scientific.

CHAPTER 33

D AME ELSEBET KNEW EVERY SIGHT in her country, and as for
Hawberry, he'd seen almost the whole natural world. But
whatever this was, making its way across the skies toward them, was
a thing unnatural and never before observed. At least not in the
Whellen Country.

"Quick, Elsie! Help me set up this tripod— that's it— now hand
me the spyglass. And my slate! I must document this!"

"But what *is* it?"

The circular frame of Hawberry's spyglass twisted into focus.
"Don't know. Looks like a starving jellyfish."

Sometime during the night, somewhere along the path it had
taken over the Brewel Country, the air-ship's Phlogistical balloon
had sprung a leak and now its ribbed sides were slack and bony;
it was sinking toward the ground. As Hawberry glanced back and
forth from spyglass to slate, drawing furiously, he added, "and
here's worse— it seems there's a small boat tangled in it. With a
bald-headed Eastern fellow aboard. Have a peek, now!"

Dame Elsebet bent to the eyepiece. The air-ship had slipped
out of view; she tipped the glass sharply down and saw engineers
gathered around a crane. They were gaping upward, mouths and
eyes as big as platters; into the frame loomed the air-ship. With a cry
of alarm Dame Elsebet pushed the spyglass back to Hawberry, who
scribbled and stared and wailed, "I can only *imagine* what they're
saying down there! Oh, the profanity!"

Down at the mining pit, the engineers were indeed shouting
every curse they knew. They had no protocols for this. No one had
ever imagined that a Phlogistical gas storage balloon would float

from the Brewel Country into proximity with a pit containing Phantactive materials. Before their horrified eyes, the great balloon hooked itself on the tip of the crane. A split began rending one of its sides; the barge hanging from it swung wildly.

An engineer pointed. "There's a man aboard!"

"I see him! I see him!" yelled the crane operator.

The crane was not the old-fashioned kind powered by a treadmill. It was a modern model, with an engine like the one in a power carriage, and the speed with which its operator acted saved Marshal Fo from falling to his death. The heroic crane operator managed not only to lower the dangling barge to the ground, but also to turn the crane and thus sweep aside the rapidly deflating balloon.

Well, almost. For as the engineers gathered around the fainting Fo and the frantic Rooki, the breeze shifted and a great strip of the balloon's canvas hide, suffused with gaseous residue, tore loose and blew into the mining pit.

A delicate hum filled the air. It was like, and yet unlike, the bell tone which had preceded the blast of the Weapon; in fact it reminded Dame Elsebet of the buzzing earth near the Heart of Stone, though she didn't consciously recognize it. She only knew she ought to grab Istivan Hawberry's hand, and hold it tight. Some deep and ancient instinct told her to.

And then the sky was alive and dancing, filled by an enormous spiral aurora.

"Elsie."

"Yes, Stevie?"

"Are we dead?"

"I don't think so."

"Ah, I'm glad of that— I'd hate to miss out on more life. I feel like just this morning, it became particularly interesting."

The aurora began a long, slow, beautiful display. It was a flower, it was a gem; it twisted and glittered; it changed its colors. From among its petals and facets it emitted deep, solid lights and slivers of translucent darkness.

Earlier, when they had been watching clouds, clouds had reminded Elsebet and Istivan of places and things, of events in life. But what now spread above them made them think of everything and nothing. They watched in contented silence, for in cases like these words failed, and in truth the senses failed too. This was more than a sight to behold. It was a wonder to be present for.

It was all, it was mighty.

Around, and within, and between.

CHAPTER 34

HAMEL FLISS HAD SPENT A miserable, hungry night aboard the self-piloting barge. He'd hardly slept on account of the navigation crystal under its dome, the glow of which had attracted a plague of flashbugs and soulcomets. The only good thing about being on the river was that it was one great big latrine.

Shimmying his breeches back into place, he set his mind to some figuring. The river he'd just used must be the Whellen; that meant the Dictator fellow must have reached his destination by now. This barge would catch up with him soon enough; what then? Fliss shaded his eyes and squinted upstream, his shadow stretching out before him, cool and thin... till it was obliterated by light.

IN ONE OF THE TOWNS punctuating the Trade Road, a wench in a nightgown, with the puffy face of a badly awakened sleeper, burst from a horse-dealers' inn.

"Thief!" she roared, legging it up the Trade Road in hot pursuit of a lumpy figure seated on a fast amble-gaited gelding. "Stop him! He just barged in and took my horse!"

For a short moment the wench was within grabbing distance of the thief's brown cape. But it didn't last. The stolen horse pulled away and left its owner panting in the middle of the road, hands on her knees.

"You see that?" she turned her puffy face up to glare at the town officer who of course had only appeared once it was too late.

The officer nodded, with a pitying expression. "I saw him, all right. A healer."

The wench drooped in defeat. "Oh. Ah."

"I don't suppose you noticed the ambulance he left in front of your inn— that mare of his was played out, couldn't have taken one more step." Not unkindly, the officer added, "Sorry this happened, but with luck his patient isn't far away. A healer on an emergency call has till the next bell to either bring your animal back or..."

"Yeh, yeh. I know the law."

"You *could* get a head start on the paperwork. Want to follow me to the Station House?"

"Eh, maybe I'll—"

At that moment the whole sky turned into one great big glowing swirl.

Up the road, seated on her freshly stolen remount, Granny missed the actual moment of the Phantactive aurora's unfolding. She was lost in thought, planning the sweet moment when she'd tap Hamel Fliss on the back with a little steel finger.

The finger would naturally be tipped with something from the healer's bag at her side— she'd brought plenty of remedies with her, remedies that would instantly cure her pesky case of him. And then she'd take charge of the benny birdy puppet-man, and be Boss of the world!

But where *were* her prizes? It had been a long, sleepless night. If only there could be some sign she was still on their trail...

The horse threw its head in the air and stopped dead in its tracks.

Granny collapsed over the animal's shoulder, saving herself from a crash only by grabbing its neck as her feet hit the cobbles. She was quite some time in sorting out her arms and legs and cape and mask, but at least the horse was no longer moving; its fast amble-gaited legs were planted in place and quaking.

And once Granny raised her dirty green gaze to whatever the mally nag was staring at, she quaked a little too.

A omen, this. A benny big omen indeed.

THE AURORA LASTED FOR MINUTES on end. In towns up and down the Trade Road, from Bog to Silver Bit, it brought traffic to a halt, though those who were indoors missed it.

Slowly the great colorful curls in the sky crumbled to glittering dust. The dust spun like a gentle cyclone. The turning cone shrank to a pillar, then to a rope, and finally to a single luminous thread; here the phenomenon reached an equilibrium, and apparently decided to stay. Hour after hour, the thread hung glowing in the heavens, as though pointing out some important location.

One from the road and one from the river, the two rival crimelords of Midlandis each saw an unmistakable signpost telling them exactly where to go.

CHAPTER 35

W HAT WERE ALL THESE *BABIES* doing at the Nautilus? That was Fred's immediate thought, upon seeing the bright-eyed, uncreased faces of the youths swarming in the corridors between the meeting rooms. A cluster of future diplomats from the Brewel Country Public Academy stole snacks from a table, wiped crumbs from their lips and fumbled with their writing slates. A knot of servingmaids' daughters slouched in a stairwell eyeing passers-by, leafing through news prints and whispering to one another.

All right, those visitors to the League For Peace were legitimately young. But even the second-tier guests— gentlemen in their twenties, with sashes reading NEWS SERVICE and THE COGWHEEL INSTITUTE and DE BREWEL FUND AGAINST POVERTY, who stalked the envoys and peppered them with questions— looked like mere brats to Fred. By contrast he felt one thousand and thirty-six years old. Had he ever, ever in life resembled any of these infants?

The break was ending. He turned to re-enter the meeting room for Part Two of a very important speech by... oh, he forgot who. He also forgot if it was Part Two of Four, or Part Two of Five.

Just as Fred put his hand on the door, one of the servingmaids' daughters wandered up to him and lisped through a collection of half-grown teeth. "Ethcu me. My friendth wanted to know. Anyone theen the printh?"

Fred noticed the jumble of pages in her big puppy paws. "News prints?"

She shook her head. "No, thilly. *Royal* printh. My frenz think if we thee him we can follow him and we might thee hith beautiful

Lady and ath her what ith like to be a beautiful Lady. Pluth" —and here the girl smirked at Fred as though it were a given he would agree with her on the lunacy of the very idea— "thumb people thay the Printh is han-them."

Fred was startled. "They do?"

"Thilly, right? But my mama thez... never mind. Anyway, have you theen him? We haven't, and we've been here *foreverrr*." The young find eternity so dull.

A chime sounded; the break was ending; a flock of envoys, pursued by baby-faced gentlemen in NEWS SERVICE sashes, pushed past Fred. When one of the envoys said "Pardon me, Your Highness," the lisping girl's head swiveled about as though she'd missed sight of a nullicorn.

"Hith Highneth! Where?"

Fred turned his Castramars ring inward so she couldn't see it, and gave her shoulder a cheerful little tap with his fingertip. "Tell you what, little Lady. I'm going in this room now to watch a show. If I see anyone who looks like a Prince, I'll come back out here and find you. Sound good?"

"All right. I'll loan you *thith*. To help." She pushed some kind of block into Fred's hand and darted back to her giggling gang.

––––––

THE SPEECH, HE SOON DISCOVERED, was part Two of Seven. Fred forced himself to listen to every word, but soon they started to blur; at last he knew it was futile. As unobtrusively as he could, he reached into one of his shirt's big pockets and brought out the thing the girl had given him. It was a thick pad of stiff pages sewn together at one end, and appeared to be blank.

What amusement could a girl brat find in a blank book? Fred flipped the pages idly with his thumb, looking for anything on any of them— and from one corner of one page, the picture of a young Fool skipped forth.

The animated Fool in the flip-book moved like a sassy, stocky, extremely expressive cat. Or perhaps a leaping monkey. Or maybe a gliding fish. He danced and tumbled; he was startlingly graceful; yet with hilariously inopportune timing the fellow constantly interrupted his own performance to adjust his jingle-bell hat.

Fred stopped riffling the pages. He knew this flip-book.

It was the record of his Second-Level Guild examination. Someone had managed to get their hands on it, copy it, sell it on the street. Though the Fool's face was too small to make out, the hat had been re-drawn; it was now obviously the Castramars coronet.

How in the world...

Rrring! Rrring!

The metallic handbell noise from Fred's other pocket filled the chamber. It was every bit as loud as it had been in the theater, but this time the second ring hadn't even died down before he was pulling out the Twin Can and racing for the door.

"Am I speaking to His Highness, Malfred of Castramars?"

"You are, Your High Honor— I mean yes, Medame— I mean this is Fred, Dame Elsebet. It's me."

"Hello, Malfred! You sound a bit breathless. Did I interrupt you at something? You weren't..." a shy pause... "with Dok, by any chance?"

"No, not at all. Dok's probably relaxing at home. Enjoying life, you know. Doing whatever."

The small pause before Dame Elsebet's reply sounded like a generous dollop of disappointment. "Oh. Well, please do tell her how very glad we are that she introduced us."

"We? Us?"

"I'm with Mesir Hawberry, Malfred. We were out having a picnic and the most unbelievable thing happened. It has to do with Phantactive substances so we thought you ought to know about it. I'll put Stevie on."

Istivan Hawberry could draw as vividly with words as he could with a slate and stylus. Fred felt he was watching it happen: the meager rogue balloon approaching, the hurried setup of the spyglass, the magnified view of frantic engineers rescuing a sixtyish Eastern-faced gentleman with a pet magpie...

That was as far as he let Hawberry get.

"Wait! Stop! This is important! Where's that fellow now? You didn't lose track of him, did you?"

"Why, Your Highness, surely to the heavens Elsie would never let a poor gentleman who'd nearly fallen into a mine pit wander away! He's safe and sound. The chief engineer took him home for a guest. He was most appreciative of the curiosity the gentleman showed regarding—"

"That's Marshal Fo!"

Istivan Hawberry *had* seen almost the entire natural world, but he'd never yet had reason to learn of Abode. So he could be excused for saying "Who?". And as for Dame Elsebet, though bitter experience had taught her much about Abode, she could be excused for not knowing its Dictator was in Midlandis.

For his part, Fred decided he'd save all his questions about how Fo came to be riding to the Whellen Country aboard a Phlogistical balloon for some other, better time.

Right now His Highness, architect of the League For Peace, was hiding under the hallway snack table for privacy, twisting the tablecloth with one hand and yammering to Dame Elsebet that she shouldn't try sending Fo back to Coastwall. Not even under guard, he was telling her. Just keep him! I'll handle this myself! I'm coming up to Whellengood this very minute!

No, no, please don't put him in actual *jail!* That would be a diplomatic faux pas of gigantic— yes, in fact Corvinalias *does* know the magpie— just hold on tight, I'm on my way!

CHAPTER 36

OK STEPPED FROM HER POWER carriage down to the pavement in front of the Nautilus and caught Fred in her arms as he ran to her. Well, toward her, anyway. His goal was obviously to reach the vehicle.

"Easy, Fred, easy. Will you kindly explain why you want to borrow my rig?"

One of Dok's hands was warm and steady across his back, but the other one found the tiny travel kit he was trying to hide behind him. "Aha. *This* tells me you're rushing off to deal with something. I may as well forget asking you to explain— you won't. You'll just give me a bunch of hocka bocka."

Fred scowled as he squirmed from her grasp. He took the travel kit away and tossed it into the power carriage, then climbed into the driver's seat himself.

"So let's skip the hocka bocka. I promise I'll only be gone a few days— I'm betting the League will be fine. At least as fine as they are now. In fact, I'm starting to think they'll spend the whole month arguing about what color ink is best to not sign a single agreement with."

He slammed the door of the vehicle. From the little storage compartment in its dashboard, he extracted Dok's sun goggles and pulled them on; he took hold of the steering tiller; but when he reached out to release the brake, he found Dok's hand blocking the lever. And by bending herself this way and that, she forced him to look at her face. It held the strangest, strongest mixture of emotions.

"We've switched places, haven't we, Agent Murd? Now you're the one with the Utmost Secret and I'm the one with no need to know."

Guilt churned in Fred's chest. "Come on, now, Dok— don't even joke about that. The only reason I'm not telling you where I'm going is because I don't want your life full of my problems. This is nothing. Just a little mess I have to clean up."

He'd meant that to sound breezy, careless, reassuringly inconsequential. But the word *mess*— and worse, *clean up*— had precisely the opposite effect.

As Dok slowly withdrew her hand from the brake release, Fred thought he could feel the air between them reverberate to the pounding of her heart.

"That's what I was afraid of," she whispered. She reached into her sleeve."I hope you won't need this, but take it with you. In case the mess gets bad." And just like the little girl outside the meeting chamber, she pressed something into his hand.

It was small but heavy, made of wood and steel: a compact hand-bombard. The very one an Abodean had once aimed directly at Fred.

With the lightning reflexes of a seasoned juggler, he froze in horror.

"Go ahead, hold onto it," said Dok. "No? Fine, I'll hold it, then. Now look here: these are the projectile capsules you load it with. I'm giving you fifteen. They go in down below, so. And when you pull back this little spring-loaded deck on top..."

"I can't use that thing!"

"Why not? Every Lady carries some weapon. I don't see why a Gentleman—"

Belatedly Fred's limbs kicked into action. He swatted the hand-bombard from Dok's grip, sending it and its capsules scattering across the pavement.

"I mean I won't! I've had that awful thing pointed right in my face, remember? There's no way I'm doing that to anyone else! How long have you even been carrying it around? Gods' guts, I'm *trying* to bring this world some *peace!*"

"Please, Fred, please don't be stubborn! I've seen plenty of peaceful moments turn deadly."

He knew that was true.

With a sigh he engaged the power carriage's standing brake—the one meant to hold it in place when it had to stay somewhere a while. He got out and looked for the ugly little weapon, found it, picked it up. Then he kneeled to search between the paving stones for the dangerous pills it devoured and disgorged.

Dok said nothing, but she kneeled too, helping him. They crawled about together, working silently, buffeted by great waves of love and dread.

After a while the job was done. Fred wiped his hands on his breeches as he handed Dok the fifteenth capsule.

"I'm going to the Whellen Country," he said. "If you need to know why, you can ask Corvinalias to explain. And if I need to do violence, I'll ask Dame Elsebet to loan me a knight or an archer." He stood up and pulled Dok to her feet. "Will that suit you?"

She held the door of the power carriage open for him. "It would suit me better if you weren't in any danger at all."

He got in and tried a smile.

"Come on, now. I highly doubt I'll be in danger. Besides, you didn't mind it, back when I was a spy and you were my Controller."

Dok shook her head. "Oh, I minded. I minded a lot. I just couldn't show it— The Bureau had regulations against that. But now it's different, Fred. Now I'm free."

CHAPTER 37

THE MOMENT ALVERT PUSHED THE red checked curtain aside from the windowpane, a big square of sun came blasting through the dark wooden guesthouse and hit his wife right in the face.

"Sorry 'bout that, Maroo!" he exclaimed, in a voice that had carried over plenty of snowy mountains and deep down into many a flowery valley. The exclamation hit Ata Maroo just as hard as the sun and got the same response from her— pretty much nothing.

Till the incident, Alvert would have said that weren't like her. It were more like him: an upbringing as poor and hard and flinty as Yondstone itself had left his big nose and big jaw and round gray eyes ever prepared to settle into a natural expression of distraught blankness, as though any momentary lack of misfortune were a fleeting treasure not to be chased away by such rashness as reacting to stimuli. In fact his face looked exactly like that of the god worshiped in the Peaceful Ocean, and as such had come in handy among his wife's people. But now it looked as if they'd swapped places, like. Nowadays Alvert was lively, an' Maroo was still.

"So that sun ain't too bright?" he asked, picking his way to her.

He was a freakishly tall man and was easily able to step over the many stacks of expensive luggage that hadn't yet been unpacked. Once, not that long ago, Alvert's entire stock of worldly possessions would have consisted of a foot messenger's canvas bag, one pair of cleated goatskin shoes, and some short knitted pantaloons. Perhaps also a rain poncho, if his patron happened to offer one. But a very small incident had unfolded into surprisingly large implications and, one thing leading to another, he had ended up marrying Maroo, and with her money galore. So there were all kinds o' stuff in the luggage— Alvert had busted out and bought her a lot o' new things. Pretty lengths of fabric that could make sarongs, lovely pearls to set in necklaces, and exotic skins to turn into footgear she might wear out a-walkin', should she ever again decide to do so.

"You hear me, Maroo?"

She didn't answer, so Alvert thought of an answer for her.

Course this little sun ain't nothin'. She was born in a land o' sun. She's all made o' tropical flowers, sugar cane an' coral...

But the way that thought came out, it let the awful thought in.

About a year before, Maroo had left this earth. Left this whole reality, like. She and he and Malfred and Corvinalias had been a-tryin' to catch up to an Abodean warship as it raced to attack Midlandis. The warship was trailing a leak o' Phantactive fuel, smearing death behind it, burning a slot in the sea— and in a last-ditch effort to talk sense into its skipper, Ata Maroo had rowed across for a parley: a fatal decision, for as she pleaded, a single drop of that fuel had sprayed into her open mouth.

At its touch she'd flashed like lightning, had begun jittering in a furious unstoppable cascade through a twisting, blazing Universe of forms, some of them forms that would have terrified Alvert still, had his stolid mountain mind not simply rejected them out of hand. On and on Ata Maroo had churned, real and unreal by turns, till after horrific seemingly eternal minutes the cascade began to slow; she settled into a pattern of insensibility punctuated by aftershocks.

And then began the hard part.

This was not the hard fate endured by a Yondy farmer when the barn burns down and the herd-plague comes and an avalanche wipes the village away. Nor yet the hard fight of a messenger against the merciless clock. It was subtler, this hard part. It was a hard lesson, a hard reality. It was months of sitting beside an infirmary bed, not knowing what the next moment would bring.

Corvinalias came and went from the rest of Isladorro University, bringing Doktors and Prophessors with various new ideas about what was happening to Maroo. Alvert sang to her, told her stories. Through the window he saw the Isle of Gold's vaguely differentiated seasons go through a whole cycle. And finally, at long last, Alvert had to reckon with the possibility that after all this was over— even if the aftershocks ended, even if she woke again— afterward Maroo might be… different.

Oh, not different like *changed*. O' course he knew she'd be *changed*. O' course her powerful Peaceful Ocean body would be much weakened, and obviously she'd have white streaks here and there in the long, smooth blackness o' her hair, and naturally there would be a lack o' much expression on her golden face. She might not be able to stand, or walk, or talk, any o' that. That's not what Alvert worried about.

No, the awful thought was that, while she was out in those other worlds the Phantactive poison had sent her to, the Ata Maroo he had known— *his* Maroo— might have dissolved, or splintered apart, and been lost forever. The one in the infirmary at Isladorro, the one he sat with, the one he waited for, might turn out to be a completely different Maroo, not made o' the same pieces anymore.

Nothing in Alvert's life had ever prepared him for Ontologikal Philosophy. The closest most people in Yondstone ever came to such concerns was the classic riddle of whether a shepherd who'd loaned her friend a pair of o' wool shears, an' the friend havin' replaced both blades o' them, would be gettin' her own shears back or not; this question was typically posed after two or three drinks of *linkapaa*, and typically answered with: shears? That friend don't remember borrowin' no shears.

Alvert suppressed a sigh, then tried again.

"Maroo. Guess what else I saw in that window? Cowmaids, a-drivin' a herd! You'll want a look. I'll roll you out on the vur-randa."

He gripped the handles of Ata Maroo's wicker chair-cart, cleared a path by kicking aside a crate marked *fragile*, and brought her out onto the front porch.

Out there the sun was even stronger. It was shining away as hard as it could, coaxing smells from the thawing earth, straining to bring springtime into the picture.

The northern part of the Whellen Country had a strong resemblance to Yondstone, and this was exactly the kind of weather that would have made Yondy brats kick off their winter boots, strip off their winter coats and push one another giggling under the nearest waterfall. But there was no way Alvert would risk letting his Maroo take the slightest chill. "Let me fix you up," he said, rearranging the quilt that covered her from head to foot.

At last Ata Maroo spoke. She said "I not cold, Alvie."

But Alvert didn't hear her, because he'd darted back into the house for more quilts.

He returned with a great heap of them, which he began piling onto his wife as though readying her for a winter expedition. "I'm just a-makin' sure you're comfortable, like. I promised them Doktors I'd create you a sportive virament. Now! Let me sit-u-ate you where you can see them cattle beasts." He rolled the chair-cart a foot to the left, then a foot to the right, then back exactly where he'd started. "See that great big pen right across the yard there? If you can't see it, just say, an' I'll move you."

From under the quilts came "I see perf—"

"Wait, wait." He rolled her three feet further forward, right to the edge of the porch. "There! Now. Look a-here, Maroo! What have them goodwives put in that great big pen but a nice lot o' brown an' gold cows from your old herd. An' a good dozen have their calves wi' them..."

Here, upon reflection, Alvert was afraid one wheel of the chair-cart might be too close to the edge. He pulled it back a bit. "Don't you think so, Maroo? A good dozen, I'd guess..."

The voice from under the quilts said "There eleven."

Alvert counted, reflexively bending his fingers as he did so. "Why, that's true! Eleven! An' look at the colors." He bent to press his bony, tanned cheek against the quilts. "You seein' them colors, there? Know why some o' them calves is spotted?"

Perhaps the quilts answered, or perhaps not. It was impossible to tell, as Alvert did not even pause before finishing, "It's because *those* cows was bred to Mesir Whellen's long-horned black an' white bull!" He addressed the quilts. "Remember that bull we saw?"

The quilts were back to not saying anything. That worried Alvert.

"You know," he prompted. "When we first got here, like."

Still no reply.

"To the Whellen Ranch. You know the Whellen Ranch, Maroo?"

More silence.

Finally Alvert peeled back part of a quilt, as though he were peeling the birchbark wrapper from a chunk of Yondstone goat cheese. The face thus revealed was reassuringly round, and golden, and perhaps scowling a little bit. To it he said:

"I could go *get* Dame Elsebet de Whellen's brother Lorenz an' ask him for a map...."

"That enough, Alvie," said Ata Maroo. "You can stop."

"Enough? Stop?" Alvert tucked the quilts tighter around her face. "What's that mean, Maroo? You want me to quit tryin' to help you? It's my fault, ain't it? Give me another chance... I can work harder at creatin' you a sportive virament..."

"*Ai!* I say it before but you did not listen! This environment *too* supportive! It supportive like stack of brass ring around neck of Stretch Islander! How my neck get strong, Alvie, if it always held up, ah? I—"

"Hush, Maroo, shh! Don't cite yourself! It might bring on another one o' them flashes!" Alvert bit his tongue before he added *and whoever comes back from it might not be you.* Instead he just dug in, like a mountain goat in some inaccessible cleft, and said "I promised them Doktors I wouldn't go lettin' you cite yourself, an' that's that." And then he feared that she might already have excited herself, because the brief moment during which she'd sounded like his old Maroo had melted away. From under the quilt the exhausted voice was back.

"Ah yah. Fine."

"You say you're a-feelin' fine?"

At her lack of a reply, Alvert fell to rearranging the quilts with a fiercely purposeful air.

He was nearly satisfied with his handiwork, a fine warm windproof cylinder, when he heard the crisp sound of hoofs scraping to a halt on gravel footing. Tack jingled. A horse puffed.

Because Alvert was a freakishly tall man, as well as standing on a porch, he didn't have to raise his round gray eyes too far to meet a pair of dark, smiling ones set in deep sunburned creases. A gentleman mounted on a sorrel stallion held its reins lightly in one hand. With the other, he reached up to the crown of his big felt hat.

"Good day, Medame Ata, Mesir Dragonsson," he said, lifting the hat off his head to reveal silver hair that still held a good deal of its original honey brown. "Nice to see you've settled in. I came to invite you over to the main house— my cook's serving up some chow."

CHAPTER 38

LORENZ WHELLEN'S ESTATE WAS AS traditional as Dame Elsebet's was innovative. The main house was a great rambling structure, all white stucco arches and broad roofs and tawny brick courtyards, in the style of the Pashma Country from which he had imported his first cattle. The dining room was enormous, centering upon a dark wooden table of massive dignity, flanked not by chairs but by benches; one wall consisted entirely of stained-glass doors thrown open to let in the magnificent hilly panorama— plus plenty of cowmaids, still in their fringed leather leggings and jingling boots.

"Day to ya, Boss," they would say as they pulled off their broad-brimmed hats and hung them carefully on a long row of pegs near the sideboard. Sun-scorched and dusty, but aware that decorum was to be observed in the main house, the cowmaids would silently serve themselves little loaves of golden bread and bowls of spicy beef stew; then, sitting at the far end of the table, they would talk among themselves in words that were few but expressive.

Ata Maroo found herself listening more intently to them than to the gentlemen. In their laconic way the cowmaids discussed which cattle had been moved where, which horses had been schooled in what, how the various projects underway here and there on the property were coming along. Their talk sent turbulent waves through Ata Maroo's spirit: it would rise with the joy of remembering her own herds and holdings, then plunge with the bitterness of knowing those were in the past. Back and forth fought the feelings, till Alvert interrupted them with a question, and a spoon.

"Maroo, I'm a-tellin' Mesir Lorenz 'bout what happened at deCoastwel Bank last year. How many coffers full o' your money did them safe-breakers think they run off with?"

Ata Maroo opened her mouth to reply, but before she could, Alvert said "Oh, what am I doin', a-makin' you zert yourself! I'll tell it," and into her open mouth he shoveled a big spoonful of mashed beans.

Ata Maroo swallowed the beans in silent fury. They weren't even spicy— as though her husband's over-protectiveness extended to her taste buds. She re-opened her mouth, only to have it filled again as Alvert told Lorenz Whellen: "It were four coffers o' notes, an' eight o' coins. Grand Constable said them thieves was a-workin' for a boss name o' Granny Almantree. Well she must ha' been as surprised as a hen what laid a firewyrm egg— because the whole time, it were actually a under-cover operation! Grand Constable says they didn't actually catch this Granny, more's the pity, but they did get a good many o' her crooks who..."

The flow of unseasoned mush kept coming, as inexorable as a glacier. Every attempt Ata Maroo made to speak up was gently thwarted, and soon she lapsed back into abstraction, staring out the wide-open doors. She didn't even need to chew.

In from the sun and wind jingled two more cowmaids. Each carried a coil of rope slung over her shoulder and wore a scarf tied around her neck, patterned with the emblem of a cogwheel encircling a heart. Unlike those who had come before, neither of these women kept a respectful distance from Lorenz Whellen, nor addressed him as "Boss".

"Can't stop for food, Pa," said one.

"Just came by to tell the guests how-do," said the other.

"See you at supper," said both. And then, as if blown on their way by the cool spring wind, the future rulers of the Whellen Country vanished back out to whatever task pressed them.

Lorenz Whellen shook his head. "Sometimes I don't know whether it's a good thing after all, that our family is keeping its noble title. The Great God Almighty knows I'm glad I renounced it for myself— five years of running this country were more than enough to last me the rest of forever. And I never raised those two to do any such thing either, but now here they are, with a big future ahead. Thank Ye Gods their husbands are smart fellows. There's all kinds of modern stuff afoot nowadays. Like *that* thing." He pointed past the end of the great table, where a white-and-tawny corridor led away into the midst of the house.

Alvert's forehead wrinkled in perplexity. "What are you indicatin', Mesir Lorenz?"

"Ah, from where you're sitting you can't see it. Lean over this way... it's against the wall, there... oh, and please drop the 'mesir'."

This whole time, despite the flavorless beans and Alvert's well-intentioned coddling, the Whellen Ranch had been working its enchantment upon Ata Maroo. The lowing cattle, the horses trotting, the clouds in a brilliant sky; all were telling her: misfortunes be damned. She was still the Ox-Train Queen, who had spent twenty years driving freight across the Kingdom; still an heiress of Re Shipping, whose vessels supplied the vast Peaceful Ocean; still a former Headmother of the Hundred Clans, born to mediate between all the peoples of the Ocean Empire. *At-last-yes,* she thought, as the taste of the mushed beans faded from her tongue. No more of this. I will assert myself.

"See it, there? It's a talk booth," Lorenz Whellen was explaining to Alvert. "My sister had one of her engineers put it in, but I haven't managed to make a single call with the pocking gadgima-what'sit. All it does is make awful noises, like a duck trapped inside an accordion."

With a mighty effort Ata Maroo squirmed one hand free of the quilt roll and pushed away Alvert's latest spoonful.

"I help you," she said. "I know how RCD booth connector signal work."

Alvert's jaw dropped. The sunburned creases around Lorenz Whellen's eyes opened.

"You surprise, ah? I explain."

To the amazement of both gentlemen, Ata Maroo extracted her other hand from its captivity, then both her entire arms. Before they knew it she was gesturing and chattering.

"Lorenz, in Peaceful Ocean draft power come from animal call Cloud Whale— black and white, ah, look like you spotted bull. Except Cloud Whale pull not with neck in yoke, but with tusk in harness. And driver issue command using not voice, but instrument known as whale-pipe. It blow to make sound like whale language." Here, fearing that the gentlemen would interrupt her before she could reach the important part, she took a deep breath and hurried on.

"Well, about whale-pipe. Cargo shipping business use very large craft. For example, *Re Ideal* require not twelve whale, but twelve *team* of whale. It easy to blow one beast general command like, let us say, turn south. But what if harness in big tangle? How to give many whale different command at same moment?

"Answer is: multiple tone, like chord in music. Back at Whellengood Hall, when engineer was helping Alvie place call to Prince Malfred, I listen to RCD connector signal and recognize it as exact same system!"

And here Ata Maroo rose to her feet and began a description that went far beyond the gentlemen's understanding. "Let us say we wish to place call from here to Isladorro University. No single connection far enough, ah? And also: which booth we want? Seem like trouble. But it actually easy. We identify chain of individual connection possibility, add determiner for specific receiver, and activate all simultaneously. Signal begin with tone opening multiple channel…"

The excitement in her voice was so captivating that Alvert nearly forgot to protest. But protest he did.

"Maroo! Are you sure you ought to be talkin' so much? A-movin' your arms so much? A-standin' up? Doktor would say to avoid citement an' zertion!"

"It fine, *ipo.*"

"Doktor would say you ought to calm down, like!"

"It *fine*, Alvie!"

"Doktor would say— oh, Maroo!"

The quilt encasing Ata Maroo's legs had caught up in one wheel of her chair-cart and sent her off on a very short and well-padded tumble. Nothing at all was hurt except her pride, a thing of which she was very much the master. She scrambled from the broad whitewood boards of the floor up onto a bench with her eyes agleam.

"I not hurt, Alvie, my *ipo.* Thank you for concern, Lorenz. I say something now, ah? I have all respect for Doktors at Isladorro and how they heal me, and all sympathy for you, watching as I suffer. But I wish to become strong again, so I must have challenge. It time for me to get back in saddle."

Alvert and Lorenz glanced at one another, unsure how to take this news.

Ata Maroo tossed her head and smiled till the four of her teeth that were filed into sharp points, like the fangs of a friendly panther, all showed. "Ah yah, that not just expression! I mean what I say. I wish to ride again."

CHAPTER 39

D EEP IN THE HEART OF the earth run veins. They branch and they join, they freeze and they flow; they carry the dust that slowly grinds from the gem at the heart of creation. That dust is the Stuff of Magic, and when the gem has worn away, it will fill the Universe; and then, at last, everything can begin...

Or so a mystical being once told Corvinalias. The mystical being also told Corvinalias he was free to take its words metaphorically, as some people found it all a bit much.

No one gave a choice like that to Ata Maroo. She learned by doing.

After swallowing the Phantactive droplet, she ended and the Universe put her to other uses— not once, as it will do to us all, but over and over, sometimes thousands of permutations in the space of a heartbeat. And as if that were not enough, she was stuck in a loop, returning between bursts to her earthly shape and place: mute and immobile, but Ata Maroo.

Along the way her transcendental eye opened, gazed upon existence, got sleepy and closed again; she counted the petals of the cosmic lily, but forgot their number; she succeeded in dissolving her self, yet for reasons unknown, it came back.

The mystical being was right. It *was* a bit much.

After some months of this, however, it was over. And then came the task of living.

Ata Maroo no longer worried about the question of what happens once our time alive draws to an end; she was aware of having learned the thing. But it was not a thing that could be explained, and everyone else was afraid of it. Especially Alvert, on

her behalf. Though it was tedious when he coddled her, she pitied
and understood.

But *Ye Gods afar,* to use a Midlandic idiom— Ye Gods afar,
it got old.

Even while she was still in the infirmary at Isladorro, Ata Maroo
had become so bored with the coddling that she did something
about it. In the wee morning hours, while Alvert sprawled snoring in
his chair beside her bed, she began sitting upright. It was difficult at
first, but once she had mastered sitting, she began swinging her legs
to the side of the bed; in short order she had mastered that too, and
worked her way up to standing, then stepping, then walking laps
around the room. Once she'd even risked waking Alvert by opening
the window, and had been rewarded with a satisfying sight: out on
the darkened campus, in the middle of a shadowy lawn, Corvinalias
was practicing flight the way she practiced walking.

During the day, though, Alvert's protection remained in full
force. It took every bit of Ata Maroo's patience to bring him to the
point where he rubbed his chin, pursed his lips, thought it over for
several glacial minutes and finally agreed that a little sittin' up might
not be *too* dangerous. But after that was done, the ice was broken:
a few days later, he allowed that usin' a chair-cart might help her,
and then came Ata Maroo's triumph— she managed to convince her
husband that a change o' scenery would help her most of all.

Yes, taking care not to upset Alvie had been a long and weary
road. But now she stood in the victory circle: the sand-and-sawdust
footing of a horse trainer's round pen, between her chair-cart and a
geriatric pony.

"Promise you'll be careful, Maroo," said Alvert, propping her
up by the armpit. "Oh, how I hope that beast won't start kickin'. Or
buckin'. Or— maybe we should wait an' do this tomorrow."

Ata Maroo sighed. For twenty years she'd spent most of every day on the back of a bull aurochs.

Lorenz Whellen had slightly more confidence in her. After he tightened the cinch of the pony's saddle— a cowmaid's heavy, tall-horned leather bucket— he looked up at Alvert and said "Deep breath, friend. She can do this." But then he turned to her and added, "...and if you'd rather not, why, you just say so. Easy does it."

"Hear that, Maroo? If you'd rather not, then just say so! Easy does it!"

Ata Maroo was *sure* the pony exchanged a look with her.

Cow noises reached them from over the wooden wall of the round pen. Overhead, a few birds glided by. Ata Maroo tucked up the center of her sarong, broke free of Alvert's hold, and made one, two, three strides to the pony. She took the reins. She stepped into the stirrup.

She changed her mind.

Forget the stirrup— she swung a leg over.

"Maroo! You're a-ridin'!"

Ata Maroo sighed again. "Ah yah," she said. She was not so much riding the pony as standing over it. "This amazing. Whee, oho, hurrah."

The pony took a few steps; so did she; Lorenz Whellen hooked his thumbs over the big marbled steel buckle of his belt and nodded in approval. But Alvert found the great achievement more difficult to appreciate. He stood as rigid as a fencepost, fists clenched, shoulders tense. When a fly landed on the pony and made it twitch its skin, he shouted "It's nothin'! Stay calm!"

Staying calm was not difficult.

While the pony inched along the perimeter of the round pen, Ata Maroo lifted her chin and looked over the boards. The Whellen Ranch, she found, was a place of solitude: only a single, narrow road connected it to the rest of the Kingdom. That was all right. It was good, sometimes, to be in places where it was easy to see all that came and went...

From one end of the road squawked the din of geese. Out rang the howl of a hound. A cowmaid leading a string of horses yelled as something on wheels shot from behind an outbuilding. In moments the thing was flying past the round pen— crunching gravel, flinging dust— and as it went, it honked out a trumpeting noise that actually startled the pony. Before Ata Maroo knew what was happening, she was on the ground.

Alvert was beside her, kneeling, wailing.

"Oh, Maroo! No! It's all my fault!"

"Stop crying, Alvie. I not hurt."

"—weren't payin' tension—"

"Everything fine."

"—set off another one o' them flashin's—"

"Hush, Alvie! Come here. Let me hug you, ah!"

While Lorenz Whellen caught the pony and led it a polite distance away, Ata Maroo wrapped her arms around Alvert's neck. She pulled him close, and held him there as the wind mingled his golden curls with her inky and snowy tresses, held him till his breathing slowed to match hers.

"Let's have no more o' this devils'-dare stuff, Maroo. I can't risk you goin' out again an' never comin' back. Just how you are, right now— I want that to stay."

His words were soft, his embrace was soft. But there was tension behind them; he was ready to fight for his wishes. So it surprised him, greatly surprised him, when she gave in.

"I understand, *ipo.*"

"Why not? I mean, what? I mean..."

"I understand. I change my mind."

"Really? I, ah, I hope that don't make you..."

"Nothing I want is important enough that it worth hurting you."

ATA MAROO WAS SETTLED IN the chair-cart, eyes half closed, completely still. She let herself be rolled out the gate of the round pen, onto the road. Taken toward the guest house with its calm, cool shadows...

But then the geese and the hound and the rolling noise all happened again. Except this time, the thing with wheels skidded to a halt in a great cloud of dust, and the dust drifted away to reveal one of Dame Elsebet de Whellen's power carriages.

Driving it was the engineer who'd placed the talk booth call which had reminded Ata Maroo of the whale-pipe. But it was most unexpected to see Mesir Jo, that friendly, pudgy, bookish and proper gentleman, whipped up into a lathering rage. He stood on his seat and roared at the party of three stunned observers and an apologetic-looking pony.

"Tell me you saw him! He came through here, I know it! There's no other road!"

Lorenz Whellen stepped forward. "What's this about, Jo? Saw who?"

"*Him!* The foreign oik who stole my new four-door model with the Alkemikal drive!"

"Slow down, Jo..."

Jo sped up, if anything. "Those thieving, spying devils might have stolen our wyrmlight and feather-steel and loom cards but by Ye Gods' twisted livers they won't get my compact Alkemikal..."

And here a second man popped up from where he'd been rummaging under the dashboard of the power carriage.

Despite the months they'd spent on their spy mission with Malfred Murd, neither Ata Maroo nor Alvert were completely sure the face behind the dark, blank sun goggles was his. Not until he leaned out over the passenger door and pulled the goggles off to reveal a weary, bloodshot stare. Then they knew him.

"Malfred!"

"We meet again, my fellow former Agents. Want to help me out? Tell me if another machine like this one came through here."

"Ah yah, it come through just now."

Alvert had rolled Ata Maroo's chair-cart right up to the door of the power carriage. "That thing dis-a-rupted Maroo's horse ridin'," he said. "What was it? What's goin' on?"

Fred came right out with it. "Marshal Fo is in Midlandis."

"*Marshal Fo?*"

Lorenz Whellen stopped patting the pony. "Martial foe?"

Out came the explanations, and in a moment everyone was clamoring: Alvert and Ata Maroo, growling angry remarks about the Abodean Dictator they remembered only too well. Fred, bemoaning the fact that he needed to tell someone where he was, but couldn't make his Twin Can place outgoing calls. Mesir Jo, ranting about his guest-turned-enemy's perfidy. Lorenz Whellen, loudly explaining that cattle hated noise.

Alvert found himself holding Ata Maroo's hand, but not in the gentle way one cradles the hand of an invalid. Instead he and she were sharing a fierce and determined grip. And when he felt her put her weight against it, rise to her feet, step across to stand right beside Fred in that carriage what's-it — well, he didn't try a-stoppin' her.

"Malfred, ah. You say you need help? Come in house. There is RCD booth. I can call Bureau— *ai!*"

Mesir Jo was through with this. He had sat back down, squeezed the throttle. The power carriage had begun to roll and Ata Maroo, leaning on the door frame beside Fred, had to think fast as it pulled her along in one two three strides wait wait wait and then she'd made a choice and hopped up onto the little platform that ran along the lower edge of the bodywork.

She held on tight. As the vehicle accelerated, the great black and white flag of her hair whipped across her face and her flowery sarong vibrated in the wind. Behind her chased Alvert, still a powerful runner— even after sitting for a year, even wearing expensive dress shoes.

"Listen to Maroo, Malfred!" he yelled. "She can help you, like!"

"She can? Uh, you can? Can you call the Bureau and tell them I'm after Fo?"

"Yes! I will call! You need other help?"

"Ha, well, you wouldn't by chance know someone who could cover for me at the League For Peace..."

"That no problem. Alvie and I know everybody!"

Alvert was alongside the power carriage now, arms and legs whirling as smoothly as its wheels. His face was level with Fred's and plainly showed what a toll the past year had taken on him: bony, stony, hollow... but something else, too. Fred could see it dawning, returning like the sun after a long night.

"Maroo ain't a-jokin'— she used to be Headmother o' them Hundred Clans. One o' your envoys is her cousin, two more are connected by way o' marryin' family, an' we're friends wi' both them Feud Islanders— though it might rile 'em up to say so." He smiled. "We'll head back to Coastwall tonight, like! I mean, if that's fine wi' you, Maroo."

Ata Maroo was swinging her head this way and that, trying to clear away her blowing hair without releasing either of her hands from their places on the carriage door. "It fine— *pffft*— there just one problem, ah?"

"What?"

"How I get off this thing?"

Mesir Jo squeezed the brake handle. Ata Maroo flew forward off the step. Alvert's hands flashed out and his stride turned into a powerful leap as he caught her.

As the carriage resumed its flight up the road and away from the Whellen Country, Fred turned back to see his friends the Ox-Train Queen and the island god— also known as Agents Ata and Dragonsson, interim delegates to the League For Peace— come tumbling to a stop in the dust, tangled together, aglow with anticipation.

CHAPTER 40

ROOKI WAS TIRED OF IT all, just so thoroughly tired. Lucky wasn't worth all this trouble.

Here's what Lucky did.

First of all, he went home from the mining pit with a local Uman, a male whose business was tinkering. Nothing wrong with that, except once at the fellow's cottage Lucky set out on a whole lot of the same meddlesome antics he'd pulled with the students at Mitsa-Konig.

Exhausting. Drove his host's mate crazy. Food devoured, pig let escape, neighbors' brats taught nasty tricks. And the next day at his host's place of work— a Laboratorium in the pretty glass palace that was the centerpiece of the estate— Lucky drove the assistants crazy too: gear broken, materials tampered with, here and there small fires.

Rooki had by then withered in importance to nothing more than a fluttering bystander who apologized for her pet almost continuously, though it was obvious that none of the Umans knew or cared what she was saying: her voice had given out, making her speech no more than a series of caws and gargles.

But honestly, Lucky's host was more than a little to blame for what happened next. Given Lucky's proclivities, the tinkering Uman probably should have known that showing off a series of power carriages, in all their continuously improving iterations, would be like letting a meldragore smell honey. Of course the moment the fellow's back was turned, Lucky leaped into a power carriage— the fastest one, as it happened— and sure enough, because ape see, ape do, he imitated the motions of driving it.

It didn't take sharp magpie vision to see what would happen after that. The power carriage was easily able to cross a lawn; it proved much stronger than a gate; it showed itself quite capable of accelerating and jumping a ditch. A knight, who happened to be schooling her chestnut mare when the power carriage whizzed past her, was the only Uman who came close to capturing Lucky. But as the knight galloped alongside him with sword drawn, she was unsure what to do and the moment slipped away. Lucky left her in the dust and sped off into the wilderness, emitting yelps of delight.

All this time Rooki had her nails hooked into the shoulder of Lucky's garment, afraid to let go— the wind rushing over the power carriage was dealing her a terrible buffeting, and she was by no means sure she could catch up to the machine again if she lost it; besides how fast the thing was, she'd been too busy to map out where in the world they might be.

Lucky himself seemed not to care at all where he was. He just loved his freedom. League after league he rolled, staring around himself in wonder. With the box containing its mechanical heart humming and ticking and ringing out a tone like that of a delicate bell, the power carriage— the *Alkemikal* power carriage, Rooki recalled its inventor having called it— bounced and bumped along with swift ceaseless energy.

It rolled up a long zigzag road cut into a birch forest, there to overlook a weird and twisted limestone valley full of waterfalls and monoliths. One of these stones was enormous, rosy pink, and to Rooki's wind-scraped eyes had something strange about it, as though it were alive; Umans had built a circle of buildings around that one, where they seemed to be busy with more of their tinkering, and Rooki was glad Lucky's eyesight was too dull to let him see it. She breathed a sigh of relief when they left the valley behind.

The carriage glided over deep green hills and entered a country filled with lush folds of grazing land. The road became smooth. Lucky became more confident, and drove faster.

By now Rooki had clawed her way down from her pet's shoulder to traverse his chest, his belly, and one of his thighs. With a clumsy flare of wings, she leaped from his knee to the leather bench seat and from there into the lee of the vehicle's front wall. From there it was hard to see anything, apart from backward glances at the places they passed through, but at least it was out of the wind. A huge farm disappeared behind them— barns and pens and cattle, and some commotion with Umans riding a pony. Then they were through the farm, the afternoon wore on, and as the leagues kept on rolling, the road dwindled to a path, then a track, then a trail.

The trail entered a maze of valleys, heavy with the scent of resin, and as darkness drew in Lucky was forced to slow down. Rooki dared to poke her head up over the edge of the dashboard and was just able to spot the sun before it sank into a notch among ranks of pine-sided mountains.

Rooki had never experienced a sunset like this. For all the majesty of fiefs like Upper and Lower Cloudyblue, the Isle of Gold was a speck in the midst of the wide-open sea and night came to it gently, in slowly diminishing sheets of color that tapered off to starlight. Here it was as though the sun dropped dead. As it fell behind a mountain all light and warmth suddenly vanished and in the cold, blue gloom Lucky— who had over the course of the day become most complacent about his ability to steer the power carriage— finally lost control. He misjudged the space between two shadowy pines, clipped the carriage against one of them, and began a wildly swerving attempt at recovery. The carriage was aimed directly at a third pine, a massive and immovable prickly-topped pillar.

"Lucky!" shrieked Rooki, putting the last strength she possessed into flinging herself at the hand with which her Uman gripped the steering tiller.

She clawed and slashed. With a yelp of pain, Marshal Fo jerked the stick that steered the exciting wagon and— that big tree came out of *nowhere!*

The wagon hit one side of it. There was a crash of metal twisting and wood cracking. Fo flew off the seat and through the air. He landed skidding and tumbling through a mass of dry needles and pine cones, which were very scratchy but had a delicious smell, and behind him a flare of light flooded the shadows.

After he came to rest, Fo turned his head, opened one eye and noticed something.

The light which had just come on gleamed upward like a great big bright yellow lamp, making a swirling oval spot on the sky. Everywhere rang a noise that reminded Fo of the gong his generals had used to carry before him, whenever he went walking in the courtyard of the Supreme Palace of the Citizens of Abode. The noise and light both came from the wreck of the wagon.

No more wagon? Fo was enraged. The wagon was the most fun he'd ever had in his life, even more fun than commanding the inmates of Do What Fo Says or Else Camp. And he'd still be enjoying it if it hadn't been for the bird! Damn that bird!

Marshal Fo felt a little sparkle of happiness when he noticed two more things: most of the stick with which he had steered the exciting wagon was still in his hand. And the bird was lying beside him, close enough to bash with the stick.

CHAPTER 41

MESIR JO'S POWER CARRIAGE MIGHT not have been quite as fast as Fo's, but it too was one of the new Alkemikal models, with plenty of power and no need to stop for winding. A great wave of energy had pushed Fred back into his seat when Mesir Jo twisted its throttle. The Whellen Ranch had disappeared behind them and on they'd flown, threading their way among the valleys that straddled the border between the Whellen Country and the Vonn Country.

Fred began to worry. It was getting late, and in these valleys darkness fell fast; and while it was true that their vehicle, unlike Fo's, was fitted with wyrmlight lamps, Mesir Jo was of two minds about whether to uncover them.

"Certainly lights would help us find our way. But they might also scare this Fo blister into hiding from us, see what I mean? And it might not be manly to use violence, but by Ye Gods I'd really hate to miss him. I want to express my opinion of thieving foreign oiks."

Here Mesir Jo let go of the steering mechanism for long enough to brandish both fists as though he were a male prizefighter; those few seconds of uncontrolled flight in the darkness gave Fred an awful fright.

He had something to be frightened about, in general. He knew the borderlands to be a hazardous place, inhabited by sparsely scattered but fiercely territorial freeholders— self-styled sovereigns of the hollows, who disliked strangers. When it came to borderlander hospitality, he could tell some extremely grim tales.

"Your Highness." Mesir Jo broke in upon his thoughts. "I hear your RCD signaling for a connection."

"My what? Oh! The Can." Fred scrabbled in his pocket. "Hello?"

From the depths of the spellbound tankard, a sharply pointed voice said "Listen! He's on!" and a quiet, strangely penetrating one said, "Oh, dear. This is— ah, greetings, Agent Your Highness. It's Agents Moktabelli and Dimachi, from the C. A. I."

Fred could picture the two Bureau operatives: Nicolo with his short, sharp nose and geometrically perfect black wig, Rhonso with his elaborate courtesy. They were probably packed into some dreary little closet of an office, three or four basements below the very chambers where, for all Fred knew, the envoys of the world were still arguing about nothing.

"Hoy, gents," he said. "Good to hear from you. I assume Agent Ata called to fill you in? Yes, the situation is far from ideal but I think I've got about as good a handle on it as possible— Dame Elsebet's chief engineer is driving me on the route Fo probably took. I really hope we find him soon— the sun's just setting and this is pretty rough country. No telling what might happen if one of the locals got hold of him." *Or us,* he added, but only to himself.

The silence at the other end of the call was ominous. Most ominous indeed. Fred shook the Can and asked it, "Still there?"

And then Rhonso's voice poured into his ear like lava.

"I'll speak plainly. We've completed a preliminary analysis. With the inclusion of recent information from Grand Constable Gino V. Doak, Agents Petir and Kestrella de Brewel, and witnesses from various parts of the Brewel and Whellen Countries, our reading of the situation is that "Granny" Almantree and "Hamflesh" Fliss, rival bosses of the Kingdom's two most powerful crime syndicates, are on the move and vying to capture Marshal Bu-Ta Fo, the nominal Dictator of Abode."

Fred felt ill.

"Your Highness!" exclaimed Mesir Jo. "Are you all right?"

Granny Almantree and Hamel Fliss? Hells afar, great gods' gizzards, holy smoking seven-sided pock! Forget what some deranged trapper or angry hermit might do *to* Fo, thought Fred— imagine what a master criminal might do *with* him! The vision of Granny's withered finger, hooked into the detonator pin of the Weapon, flashed into Fred's thoughts and he could hardly breathe. The lava flowed on.

"We must emphasize that the accuracy of this interpretation is not guaranteed. If you wish for greater certainty before making any decision, we could perform a second round of analysis, with the caveat that it might require up to twenty-four hours."

"And if you... if..."

Fred's mouth said this all by itself. His brain was racing ahead: a second analysis would only waste time— wouldn't it? And what if it contradicted the first one— would that be good or bad? How much confidence should he put in these analyses? Did it make any difference?

"Your skin looks clammy," said Mesir Jo. "I believe clamminess signifies fever. May I feel your forehead?"

The Can was droning on. Mesir Jo's hand was coming at him. The sun had gone behind a mountain. Fred's ears were ringing... his head felt light...

From the darkness ahead, a brilliant golden beacon pierced the sky.

Light.

And ringing.

From the spot of the beacon reverberated a crash, followed by the roar of a great, flat, shivering bell.

Mesir Jo didn't have to tell Fred what could cause such phenomena.

Somehow, he already knew.

CHAPTER 42

THE BEACON WAS EASY TO follow, the wreckage easy to find. A brilliant plume of golden light flaring up into the deep blue heavens is a pretty obvious thing.

"Ha! It works!" exclaimed Mesir Jo as he stood silhouetted against the beacon, swatting away some of the thousands of soulcomets that had come to dance around it. He pointed at something in the heart of the blaze. "Look down there, Your Highness— you *are* wearing your sun goggles, aren't you? See it? A little, sort of, well, it's hard to describe without resorting to technical terms. Of course I tested a smaller version in the Laboratorium, you know, but it's always nice to see emergency features operating properly under the, ah, actual conditions."

Whatever Mesir Jo was pointing at, Fred was sure it was fascinating. But something else was drawing his attention. Deep inside him, beyond his worry about whether Fo was alive and apart from the stomach-churning anxiety of imagining Granny and Fliss with their claws already in him, some finely tuned detector was ringing an alarm, calling him. He strode away from the light of the wreck, behind some bushes into a thicket of pitch blackness— and pitch was exactly what it smelled like— to follow a small, persistent beacon of feeling.

Fred couldn't see a thing. He moved forward step by step, groping about with his hands, in case he should run into something. He tripped over a log. Down on his knees, covered with crunching pine needles and various other woodsy shreds, he heard a weak little groan. A magpie groan.

"Rooki," he whispered. "That's your name, isn't it?"

Another groan, that sounded like "Yes."

"I don't want to step on you, Rooki— so I'm not going to stand up. I'm just going to reach out..."

The groan sounded like "Hiding. Under. Log."

It took some determined crawling about in piles of dark forest duff, but under a log just as advertised, Fred touched feathers. He called for Mesir Jo; in a few minutes they had carried the magpie back to the power carriage on a stretcher made from the door of the dashboard's storage compartment.

Mesir Jo uncovered the vehicle's wyrmlight lamps, detached one and brought it close to Rooki. "That wing looks pretty bad," he said. "So does the leg."

"Hoy, have you got a healing Doktorate?" snapped Fred. "Quit scaring her. Attitude is half the battle! Rooki, I'm going to ask this gentleman to take you back to Whellengood Hall— Dame Elsebet's people run a top-notch modern infirmary there. She'll make sure they take good care of you."

Mesir Jo aimed the wyrmlight globe away from Rooki and Fred, scanning the forest with it. "Uh, Your Highness, it's pretty well known that you're a big fan of magpies but are you sure that's our best course of action here? We still have to catch that thieving oik."

The magpie groaned again. "If you mean my pet, he went off with some wild Umans."

Fred shuddered. "Oh gods. That's what I was afraid of."

"I know," moaned Rooki. "Those poor animals have no idea what's about to happen to them."

Fred and Mesir Jo scavenged some seat cushions from the wreck and used them to fashion a bed for Rooki. Once it was strapped well into place on the seat of Mesir Jo's power carriage, Fred removed his overcloak and tucked it in around her. The

Castramars magpie embroidered on one lapel happened to land right where she could see it.

"Huh," she said. "That looks like Vinnie." The whiskers near her beak bristled with excitement. "Wait. I know. *You're* Vinnie's pet! Aren't you?"

"Shh..."

"That's how you knew my name. Did Vinnie mention me?"

"*Shh!* He, ah, only mentioned you in passing. No, um, stories about you or anything."

"He did? He mentioned me? Really?"

"Shh, Rooki! Save your energy! Mesir Jo is going to get in the power carriage now, and..."

"I *am?*"

"Yes, Jo, you are. And then, Rooki, he's going to drive you to..."

"Vinnie is my hero! My dream is to be just like him! My family doesn't understand— they want me to *marry* Vinnie, can you imagine? As if I'm just some social-climbing nitwit after a bigger title! Please! Last time my Auntie Chakda brought it up I gave her a real piece of my mind. I said—"

"Your Highness, are you seriously asking me to take this bird back to Whellengood and just leave *you* here in these dreadful valleys?"

Fred covered his ears, closed his eyes, took a long breath of the fragrant chilly air.

It is said that scent is the deepest of the senses, that it unlocks memories deep within us. It certainly did so for Fred. From start to finish, the breath he took couldn't have lasted more than a second. But that second held a lifetime.

"That's right, Jo," he said. "Please take her back, if you would. Don't worry about me. I'll know how to get along— one of these dreadful valleys is where I was born."

CHAPTER 43

D EEP IN THE WOODS, IN the shadows of the pine and
the blueneedle, a small band of travelers picked their
way westward. Their leader, a fellow of peasant type dressed in
surprisingly well-tailored clothes, was searching for someone and
a few locals had rallied to his aid— mostly for lack of anything
better to do, and perhaps out of grudging respect for him: in the
borderlands it was rare to meet a stranger at all, much less one who
didn't immediately make an enemy of himself.

This one had known how to approach borderlander
homesteads (very, very slowly and carefully) how to ask for help (best
done in a vague, roundabout way) and how to offer diverting songs
and dances as compensation for the trouble of not attacking him.
And once they were on the march, he entertained the little crew
with storytales, as was the custom in those parts.

"Where once there was, and now there's not," began Fred, "there
used to be a..."

"...a clever youth!"

"...a hardy maid!"

"...a scary monster!"

Fred's companions all blurted out their suggestions at once.
All except for the freckly boy, who waited till the old wight, the old
wench and the big round mother had finished. Then the boy looked
up at Fred and offered:

"...a cross-eyed magician who lived in a barrel, all alone except
for a gray cat wearing three wooden shoes?"

Fred had been about to say *a foundling who could juggle* but
instead he said, "That's the one! You tell it. I'll add sound effects."

For a few nights they camped: the old wight had a flint and striker, and the old wench had a knife; the big round mother could shy stones with great accuracy, and once the old wench had loaned him the knife for a minute, the boy could pull the overalls right off a squirrel with just one tug. Fred, meanwhile, surprised himself by remembering how to find wild onions, and how to tell the difference between the Beef Mushroom and the Liver-Kicker; and though the big round mother said there hadn't been longwolves in these parts for at least the past ten years, still they took turns watching for them as their cookfire died down and its smoke faded off into the sweet, brittle breath of the trees.

Where Fo might have gone, Fred could only guess. But his guesses were guided by the land— he went wherever the going was easiest. It made sense. His companions didn't disagree. On they went, till one morning they emerged from under a stand of whitewood saplings to find themselves looking down into a hollow with a village in it.

"New South Clodd," said Fred, more to himself than anyone.

He'd known it would look small, if ever he saw it again. That was common knowledge: every poem and pamphlet and theatrical always made a point of mentioning how, when characters finally found themselves once again looking upon their brathood homes, what once had seemed so big would now be very much otherwise. So yes. It did look small. But Fred hadn't been expecting it to *feel* so overwhelmingly massive, as though the shadow of Flat Mountain were crushing the village and its farmsteads and the little abbey beside them under the weight of the whole troubled world.

"Know that place?" asked the old wight.

"Yep." The local word for *yes* came naturally to Fred's lips.

"Want to ask there?"

"Nope."

So they gave New South Clodd a pass. Fred didn't think Fo had been there, anyway— he was sure any encounter with the Dictator would have left a mark, and the village looked pretty much undisturbed. The slate tiles were still in place on the steep roofs of every daub-and-timber cottage; manure piles stood unflung; geese and sheep had not been frightened off the mud streets, and carters still drove their stolid buckalopes. Fred shook his head at a suddenly revived memory: as a brat he'd tried to make his world a bit more exciting by imagining the common buckalope resembled that mythical beast, the nullicorn. But of course that was silly. The nullicorn was an antelope the color of a moonlit pearl, with a vast cape of mane and a long, spiraling beard— the touch of which, legend said, would grant wishes to a virgin pure of heart. A buckalope, by contrast, had no such beard. It had only a single dull and ugly horn sprouting from its forehead. And as for wishes— if a buckalope could have granted them, young Malfred would have been somewhere far better than New South Clodd.

Adult Malfred had a plan, but it meant leaving his crew.

Shortly before noon they reached a bridge where sentinels glared from slots in a black stone guardhouse. On the other side of a deep, rocky gorge loomed a great black fortress and from the spear of its tallest and sharpest tower flew the pink de Vonn flag, with its seven-pointed star.

Fred crouched and addressed the freckly boy.

"Hoy. That ring with the bird on it— I need it back now."

The boy scowled. "You said I could have it."

"I said you could hold onto it, but when it was time for me to go, I'd need it back. Remember?"

The boy scowled harder. "It isn't time yet."

In reply Fred held out one hand and waited. At last the freckly boy, with what Fred considered a really world-class scowl— one that, in a theatrical context, would have carried all the way to the back of the house— rummaged in the front pocket of his woolen shirt. He found the ring and ground it into Fred's hand.

"Thanks, son." The word had dropped from Fred's brain onto his tongue as mere slang, but it left an aftertaste. To cover it, he rummaged in his own pocket.

"Uh, watch this. I'm going to do a magic trick for you and your Ama and Omi and Opi."

He handed the boy a sharkskin purse, lumpy with golden coins, and hadn't quite decided whether saying *hocka, bocka, dominaka* would be a nice touch or over the top, when he was interrupted by a loud clank.

The spike-studded door of the guardhouse swung open. A big, fierce, truncheon-wielding armored wench emerged. As she strode toward Fred, a crossbow poked out of the guardhouse to cover her back. Two bows: the de Vonns were thorough.

"Who comes here?" demanded the sentinel. "You know the rules. We don't bother with commoners, cottagers, villagers, vagabonds… huh."

Her steel-backed glove closed around the wrist of the hand Fred extended toward her. Careless of the rest of him dangling from it, she pulled the hand closer to the eye slits of her helmet and examined the ring it bore. "*Huh.* All right, but that better not be a fake. Dungeon renovations still ain't finished."

CHAPTER 44

IT WAS TRUE THAT NO stranger had passed through the village of New South Clodd. But New North Clodd, Old South Clodd, and Clodd's Crossing all shared a very different fate.

These villages were stricken by crime. Food, drink, a pair of buckalopes hitched to a cart— one of which was later found all the way over in Beiken Dell, devouring a kitchen garden; such things went missing, and those who lost them had no idea that the culprits were not wicked poltergeists or envious neighbors but Marshal Fo, Granny Almantree and Hamel Fliss.

If the Vonn Country's farmers and blacksmiths, fishers and bakers, makers and merchants and all their husbands and brats had known what was happening in their very midst, they might have been frightened. But they didn't know. They only grumbled about how things these days were going straight to the hottest hindmost hell, unaware that a rogue despot and the two greatest fiends in Midlandis were right there among them— and moment by moment, drawing ever closer to one another.

CHAPTER 45

THE SENTINEL LED FRED INTO the forbidding black stone fortress that was Vonn Hall.

First they passed through a moderately sized barbican, well stocked with death traps. Fred noted iron tracks in the black stone walls, down which an iron grate suspended overhead might roll; the fact that the tracks were quite clean and showed evidence of having been recently lubricated was far more ominous than it would have been to see them creaky, crusty and rusted over. The same went for the holes through which archers might ply their craft, the overhanging balconies from which defenders might pour something hot or nasty or both; and the flagstones below his feet which showed signs of being trap doors. All looked to be in brisk working order and Fred wondered whether he would become the unlucky winner of a demonstration before he and his escort reached the other end. But eventually they did reach it. The final touch was a little paper ticket, pasted to the wall beside a second set of iron tracks, that bore a picture of what the descending grate would do to stray fingers; the stains on it were evidence that someone had failed to take note.

Then came a chamber within which a single pair of old-fashioned rush torches sputtered their gruesome light upon walls lined with plaster faces. Here the sentinel stopped. Clearly familiar with some procedure, she reached up to a niche in the wall and found a sandglass.

"What's *that* for?" asked Fred.

The sentinel only shrugged and spat a chaw of maidenroot into the shadows. She turned the glass over, and turned her back on Fred.

So he regarded the plaster faces. Their expressions were acutely serene, which made him wonder whether he were looking at mementos of honored guests or the death masks of executed ones; this thought naturally led to the unspoken but still unpleasant question of whether he would be joining the display; and by the time the timer ran out, Fred couldn't deny that the room had served its purpose admirably. He worked up the courage to comment on it, but before he did the sentinel pushed him through an iron-studded door. Alone, this time. She pulled it shut with a clang.

Now Fred was in a passageway, long and narrow and low enough to make him feel the urge to stoop. Upon its pink walls, block-printed with a star pattern, hung a series of portraits with cutout eyes. If he had wanted to spare the time, Fred probably could have figured out which cutouts were filled with paint and which really were observing him, but he decided against it. As he hurried along the passageway, a wisp of recollection tickled his mind: an image of the humorous fellow he had till recently been— the type who might have covered one of the portraits' eyes with his hands and cried "peek-a-lookie!" or even, Ye weeping Gods forbid, pretended to jab them with two fingers. A chill ran up his spine at the thought of making such a joke and he was grateful to have reached another door, through which he emerged into a great castle hall.

With a clash of broadspears, ceremonial guards strode into formation around Fred. There was no question as to where they would escort him next: the towering skylit stone-buttressed rush-matted tapestry-encrusted incense-scented cavern that gaped before him terminated in a pink carpeted dais, upon which stood two pink thrones before a pink brocade screen.

It struck Fred that life had led him to some very misguided notions concerning the color pink. He saw now that it was not the pretty hue of flowers, or the mellow warmth of sunset, or the gentle tone of a faded red anything. Pink was the color of raw flesh, stabbed and cut by seven pointed blades.

Some noises from behind the screen heralded the arrival of Their High Honors Dame Hizabel and Donn Kharl, the Domina and Seigneur of the Vonn Country.

The Seigneur's face had the shape of his daughter's, but none of its sweetness. As he flopped onto his throne, he cast a momentary glance down the steps at Fred.

"Who's that?"

Dame Hizabel gave her cushion a few vigorous whacks before gracing it with her bony bottom. "How would *I* know? Really, Kharl. Stop asking me everything— I'm not an oracle. You, down there on the steps! State your business."

Fred felt keenly aware of his dirty boots, faceful of stubble and pervasive reek of sweat and woodsmoke. But under them he was royalty, and besides that he had confidence in his oratorical skills. A little eloquence would go far. He even let his pronunciation edge toward a soft Vonnish drawl.

"My love and compliments, dear Kinfolk. You must wonder what I'm doing here, given that I'm supposed to be in Coastwall, presiding over the League For Peace convention. Well, to cut a long storytale short, we've had an emergency and dealing with it has brought me to your country. Time is pressing, and I decided my best course of action was to seek your help. It'll make all the difference, believe me— with the resources you command, I'll bet we get everything under control in a few hours. Let me explain what I need..."

Donn Kharl turned to his wife. "Do we know this wight?"

Dame Hizabel frowned. "*Now* do you see why I'm always telling you to think twice before you grant just anyone an audience? It's so tiresome. You get things like this. Have them take him away."

"But, Dame Hizabel! It's *me*, Prince Malfred."

Her face was blank.

Oh, Gods, thought Fred. This can't be happening.

He held up his hand, made sure the red and yellow enameled face of his royal ring was plain to see, and announced: "Malfred of Castramars."

Still blank.

"Remember? I was adopted last year? I'm the brother of Enrick?"

When even this got no reaction, Fred took a moment to breathe deliberately inward through his nose, a move recommended by every authority as deeply calming, before saying "You know, *King* Enrick. Who married your daughter. Your second daughter. Margadet."

"Ah!" exclaimed Donn Kharl, turning to his wife. "Didn't Moley send us some portraits of her husband's people recently?"

"Maybe she did. But don't tell me you put any stock in them— how would *she* know if a picture has the faintest resemblance to anything at all?"

"Good point. What about the ones by the documentary artist we sent to the wedding?"

"Oh, now those were very realistic."

"So do you think this wight looks like anyone in those pictures? Because *I* don't."

"Hm. You're right. He doesn't."

Donn Kharl de Vonn gestured to the guards. "Ladies...?"

"Wait!" yelled Fred. "Didn't you see my ring? Look again! It's ten generations old. It was originally made for Yigor of Castramars, and blessed by—"

Dame Hizabel scoffed. "Says you."

Breathing hard, Fred yanked the Twin Can from his pocket and took a few steps up the stairs, holding it out in both hands and trying to act as though he didn't notice the guards' broadspears hovering over him.

"Here, Your High Honors! This is another priceless Royal artifact! It's the original RCD device. It doesn't really place calls anymore but if you take it to Vonn University— not *now*, I mean, there isn't time, but—"

"What? This must be a joke." Dame Hizabel knocked the Can clattering aside. She was on the point of giving the guards an order when Donn Kharl literally hopped out of his pink velvet seat.

"Oh! I have it! *Joke!* The new Prince used to be Erick's—"

"Enrick. Really, Kharl. Enunciate."

"Fine. But here's the thing— Enrick's new brother used to be his personal Fool, don't you remember? A funnyman. A jester. With the jokes and the japes and the jingle jangle hat."

"And your point is...?"

"Here's my point, Hizabel. Get set for a brainwave. Ready?"

Donn Kharl de Vonn's cape of sheared longwolf, dyed the color of freshly butchered mutton, trailed down the steps as he walked around Fred, examining him from every angle. "We will ask *this* fellow here to give us a show," he said. "A royally entertaining show. I'd be satisfied as to his identity then. Wouldn't you?"

CHAPTER 46

Dame Hizabel de Vonn leaned back in her throne and regarded Fred. "Hmm," she said at last. "Very well. Let this stranger perform some amusing foolishness."

Donn Kharl spoke up. "Just a second." He caught the attention of an underling. "Grimmick, there! Fetch me that vessel."

Fred's innards flooded with sweet relief. The Seigneur wanted the Twin Can, which had rolled under a table containing some regalia. Perfect. Any Prophessor would recognize it; there might be an engineer on hand who could contact the RCD network, perhaps even reach the Queen. That would be ideal. If the de Vonns spoke directly to their daughter...

But no. The underling who picked up the Twin Can had a flagon in his hand. Donn Kharl wanted the can, all right. To hold a drink of wine.

"Ahh, delicious. Let me take my seat. And now, fellow: what my wife said. Amuse us."

Fred's long stint as a Fool hadn't been easy. He had, in fact, been far more than a Fool: his job had really been to bring joy to a wet rag of a kid who was about as easy to bring joy to as a mattress is easy to stuff in a thimble. But Fred had managed it, hadn't he? He'd worked the toughest room in showdom all day, every day for twenty years straight. He knew a thing or two about amusing people, starting with rule one: it has to look easy. No matter what kind of nausea storm is actually churning fearfully close to the surface.

"Amuse you?" asked Fred, with his teeth clenched in a brilliant smile. "How, I wonder?"

Rat-a-tat-tat went one of his feet, heel and toe, on the stones between the mats on the floor.

He froze, as if listening. "Did you hear something?"

Click-a-tick-tick replied the other foot.

Fred turned his gaze decisively down at the floor and then, after a heartbeat's pause, made his face light up with the joy of discovery when both feet shared in saying *clack, tack, a racka-ticka tack.*

And then, left and right, they were off to the races, glittering like the sticks of a dulcimer-drummer, making their own music.

Rat-tat tattering, tap stomp pattering... sweep and a step and a hop bang slide...

As the rhythm of Fred's boots grew more and more complex he began to sway his torso, pinwheel his arms. Louder, faster. And just when it seemed that no more could possibly be added to the outrageous, exuberant, frenetic barrage... Fred began to sing.

The song he belted was an old favorite, a party tune everyone knew. His voice was strong and bright. To sing along was as irresistible as a cold drink on a hot day.

The guards were already shifting their weight to the beat, humming behind their visors. One of them snapped her fingers. Another tapped her foot. There was no *way* the de Vonns wouldn't sing along— a dead buckalope would sing along. Here came the chorus.

"Lemme hear ya!"

But hear them, he did not.

And he continued not hearing them through one verse after another, till the song and dance ended.

"Well, that wasn't foolish at all," groused Dame Hizabel. "If you ask me, it was skillful. What was there to laugh at?"

Fortunately the Fools' Guild had an answer to this, and Fred quoted it.

"When the lamp of luck burns out,
we've got woes to laugh about:
trip and flop and stub our toes—
so our bad-luck laughing goes.
But when luck is shining bright,
then we laugh in sheer delight."

"The fellow makes a point," said Donn Kharl. "Let's see some blunders. Real bungles, you know? Ghastly floaters."

That was, of course, exactly the opposite of the point Fred was trying to make, but if blunders would secure the de Vonns' help then he was happy to generate as many of them as required. Well, he wasn't *really* happy to. He'd just *look* happy. Or not. Whatever got the deep-damned laughs.

Ye Gods knew he tried. He threw everything he had into it. In answer to the de Vonns' suggestions, Fred contrived an ever-deepening series of ludicrously incompetent mistakes: loudly declaimed but rotten poetry, clumsily floundering conjurers' tricks, tumbling runs composed purely of pratfalls. It was painful, much of it literally, and had devolved fruitlessly to the level of animal noises and silly faces when Donn Kharl de Vonn suddenly exclaimed "Oh! Hizabel! I know what."

He tipped the last drops of wine down his throat, clapped the empty Twin Can down on a side table with a rap that made the memo book and spectacles lying beside it bounce, then leaned toward Fred with one hand planted on one knee and the other outstretched.

"Here, sir. Come closer, that's the way. Could you..."

Donn Kharl twirled his extended arm about, pointing at something. It took Fred a second to understand that he was miming, trying to put across the idea that Fred should reach out his own index finger. *Hells afar,* he thought, this has been a long way around just to show him my ring again— not that I'm complaining—

A sharp tug jerked Fred's finger. What?

"Come on, fellow!" snarled Donn Kharl. "Don't you know this one?" and he pulled again. So hard, Fred felt his knuckle crack.

Behind one of the guards, a faint rumble sounded and she muttered "Excuse me."

Fred was left adrift. That was the word for it, that was the sensation he had, of being afloat in a foreign element. What more could he do? How could he possibly convince these people that he was their son-in-law, their sovereign, their guardhouse reports His Highness Malfred of Castramars?

The words *guardhouse reports* sizzled in Fred's brain.

What a very strange phrase. It hadn't come from nowhere. What on earth had made him think it?

The answer lay right before his eyes: the memo book on Donn Kharl de Vonn's little side table. There, yet to be crossed off a list headed VISITORS, were the fateful words.

The rage that rose in Fred's gorge was so hard to push down that he actually gagged. So they'd known! They'd known the whole time!

He longed to see the imprint his royal ring would leave right in the middle of Donn Kharl's chin. A good, deep, perfectly reversed image of the Castramars magpie. And for all that Fred was only a man, so bony though she might be, Dame Hizabel could wipe the floor with him six ways from Solderday, still how thrilled he'd be to go down kicking her...

...and then what? How would *that* help keep Marshal Fo out of the wrong hands?

Diplomacy. He had to practice diplomacy. He was withering inside, but he did it.

"Ha ha ha! Oh ha ha *ha*, you had me there! Pretending you didn't recognize me! Now we're laughing, yes indeed!"

Donn Kharl wiped his eye. "You should have seen yourself."

"No doubt, no doubt!"

Dame Hizabel twiddled her fingers in glee. "We used to play pranks like that on Yoley and Moley."

"Bet they'll never forget 'em!"

"So. Malfred. Or do you go by Fred? I believe Erick calls you…"

"E*n*rick. Really, Kharl!"

Fred crouched between his parents-in-law, locking eyes intently with them, telling a storytale to a pair of vicious brats. "'Fred' is fine. Now. Want to have some real fun? Help me with something. I'm chasing a fugitive— we could have a good old-fashioned manhunt! Doesn't that sound like a kick?"

To Fred's astonishment, it apparently did not. The de Vonns' failure to react was inexplicable. A desperate edge crept into his delivery as he tried again.

"The man I'm after is a legitimate threat to world peace. He's a Dictator, who says what goes, in a country that might have the capability to rebuild its doomsday Weapon program— how about that! One of those babies turned the New Capital into a glass ashtray. Isn't that wild?"

The de Vonns did not appear to think it wild. They only sat.

Sweat was pouring down Fred's back. His heart was racing. But he put on a suave demeanor as he added, "And oh! Here's the best part. It's a *triple* manhunt— right this very minute, our Dictator friend is being pursued by two powerful criminal bosses who want to use him for their own ends. Dastardly ends! I mean— the only thing worse than a secretive dictatorship with a doomsday Weapon is a secretive *kleptocracy* with a doomsday Weapon— know what I mean?" Deep breath. Here comes the ask. "So I think you should send out some trackers, knights, archers, that sort of thing. Like you'd do if you were hunting a monster. Come on, let's start right away."

No. Reaction.

"Please, *please!* If this ends up saving the world, I'll give you all of the credit. All. Or— I'll grant you a boon. You know a boon? You-name-it, you-got-it kind of thing?"

At long last, the silence of his hosts, his relatives, his most powerful vassals grew so profound that Fred did the very thing he'd sworn he'd never do. He clenched his stubbly jaw, closed his weary eyes, drew a calming nose breath and said, "I'm through making friendly requests. I now issue a Royal command. You are hereby required and directed to obey me in all particulars, and should you fail, will answer the contrary at your peril—"

Impossible. *Impossible.* They were getting up and leaving.

"Hoy! Hear me? You will answer the contrary at your peril! Should you fail! To obey me!"

Fred's shout rang in the great pink bowels of Vonn Hall, its fading echoes heard by no one but the guards, who radiated the awkward air of having witnessed something private.

Their broadspears were mounted on pink-lacquered shafts, their armor engraved with seven-pointed stars. Fred had a ring with a bird on it and a— nope, that was all. Donn Kharl had taken the Twin Can away with him.

So.

Fred didn't know what the de Vonns were playing at, but he thought it over and concluded that no one would so flagrantly mistreat a superior unless they had some plan to later... clean up the mess.

Prince Malfred? Sorry, never saw him.

If they wanted to be especially thorough about it, it would cost them a few guards, but Fred had a feeling they wouldn't balk at the price. In fact, the notion of their being deterred by something so trivial *was* kind of funny.

CHAPTER 47

BUT SURPRISE, SURPRISE.

The de Vonns came back.

"So, Fred," said Donn Kharl, as though the terms on which they'd parted about an hour before had been perfectly cordial. "Hizabel and I have had a little talk with someone from our University…"

Fred interrupted. "Did you use the Can to call Margadet?"

"…who heads the department that's, well, I forget the name of it. But it's to do with political matters. About your House of Castramars, and so forth. The gentleman confirmed that…"

Fred tried again. "Donn Kharl, I command you to listen to me, all right?"

"…that, despite last year's adoption decree, and the revision of your vital records, and all of that paperwork which made it so you're now King Enrick's twin brother… hear that, Hizabel? I enunciated."

Dame Hizabel swooped in. "What Kharl's saying is that Your Highness is not in the line of succession. At all. You are, we find, the Esquire of someplace in the Whellen Country, and possess some holdings on the Isle of Gold, and have a few political functions, but any issue of your loins would have no place in the lineage of Castramars."

Fred was taken aback. *Loins?* Who said she could talk about those? He sat on the steps and crossed his legs.

"Well, of course not! I'm not making any claim to the throne— why would I want to interfere with little Nedward's future? I was never in this for the, ah, issue. Ricky made me his brother for personal reasons. We have a bond, you know? Hasn't always been the greatest one but it's what our Da would have—"

Donn Kharl and Dame Hizabel spoke at the same time, using slightly different words. Their pronouncement was a jumble, but Fred untangled its meaning: he was to understand that, owing to his lack of prospects, the de Vonns had decided not to offer him the hand of their daughter Yolanda.

"We feel we can do better," admitted Dame Hizabel.

"Sorry if that sounds blunt, but we're good honest simple people," said Donn Kharl.

"And speaking of better…!"

"Calm down, Hizabel. I'm sure Fred will tell us everything. Won't you? We'd love to know more about this gentleman you're after. You say he's the head of what sounds like a completely new country?"

"You can't be serious!" shouted Fred. "Tell me this isn't what it sounds like!" As he leaped to his feet, he stumbled down a step or two— whatever. This was madness. He cried out in protest. "And it's a stupid idea, anyhow! Even if Abode wasn't actually, you know, an enemy power that *attacked* us, you'd get nowhere trying to ally with Marshal Fo! He's not a real leader! You can see it all over his dimwitted face— he's only a mouthpiece, a figurehead, a puppet! He's never been anything but a front man for the real power, see what I mean?"

Dame Hizabel's eyes were bright. "Yep. We absolutely see what you mean."

"What a plum," gloated Donn Kharl. "An experienced puppet! A pre-set stage! How good that you told us. I'd call that lucky."

THE UNDERLING WHO TOOK FRED away was a dim-sighted old crone who had, from the looks of her equipment, once been a knight. She was not mounted; instead she escorted him on a long, long walking trek across the grounds of Vonn Hall, pointing out the various features of the property along the way. From her rambling mutters, Fred gathered that one feature was the tower in which Yolanda de Vonn was— for lack of a better term— imprisoned. *But of course she is,* he thought. If you're keeping your best loin-issue around for purposes of installing her behind an unhinged enemy tyrant, naturally you stash her in a tower. It's part of the bit.

By the time the old knight finally led Fred to the furthest extent of the de Vonn estate, wrestled a comically large and rusty old key from among the folds of her sash instead of a sword, and unlocked one of seven great big groaning wooden doors in a great big black stone retaining wall, he was feeling very much in the spirit of things. Was this the renovated dungeon he'd heard about? Would there be some tortures? Maybe a monster? The hand-bombard Dok had offered him might have been helpful against a monster, but thinking about her hurt too much so he didn't.

The door swung closed. The lock clanged shut. It certainly was very dark.

CHAPTER 48

THE DARKNESS WAS LONG. PHYSICALLY long— a tubular, mildewy darkness, lined with what sounded like tiles. At least that's the kind of echo they threw back to Fred, when he shouted "Hello? Anyone?"

The Queen would have been good at figuring this out. For her, life consisted of spaces heard and smelled and felt instead of seen— *it's kind of a blessing that she never saw Vonn Hall,* thought Fred. Leaving at least one of her senses untouched by that creepy place was probably why she even had a chance to grow up sweet and kind. And having Donn Kharl and Dame Hizabel as parents— gods' guts! She was right when she said that showed her exactly what sort of person never to be. Imagine growing up a de Vonn. And *I* thought *I* had it bad!

Fred reflected on his own upbringing. He had plenty of time to do so, considering that he would probably wither away to bones in this tunnel of a dungeon. He groped his way to the wall— yep, tile it was. Clammy.

Something that felt like it had lots of legs raced past his fingertips.

"Yagh!"

He yanked his hand away and ran a few steps— a bad idea, he knew. He could trip over something, and land in a whole nest of whatever creepy crawlies infested this... again the idea was borne in upon him that he was in a tunnel. Tunnels led places, didn't they? Did he have anything else to do, but walk?

So walk Fred did. Slowly at first, as his attention was split between reflecting on his upbringing, and making sure he didn't have to touch the walls *too* often.

He walked till his reflections had reached the age of thirteen: a momentous age, for on that birthday— or at least, the monks had designated it as that birthday; no one really knew, did they, it wasn't as though foundlings came with labels— on that day Fred had flunked his novice's exam for the ninth and final time and been carted away from Flat Mountain Abbey like a wisecracking, back-flipping little sack of dried peas. He was just getting set to reflect on the next thing, his awful seasick voyage to the Isle of Gold, when the tunnel curved a bit and a distant light broke the gloom before him.

Fred's reflections took a back burner to this new reach-the-exit concept.

He walked faster. For a long time the light didn't get much bigger, but pretty soon he noticed that the smell around him had certainly grown. By the time the light had taken on a definite semicircular shape, the odor of the tunnel was no longer mildew so much as the reek of a kennel. And, though he knew not from whence it came, Fred had the strangest notion that someone was with him.

"Hoy!" he shouted. "Anyone out there?"

The answer came from overhead, and it was deafening.

A shrill, shimmering, chattering wave overwhelmed Fred's ears. For the first time he looked straight up. The dim light of the exit raked the darkness just enough to show him that the ceiling was moving, crawling, absolutely alive.

Beiken Ridge, the mountain protecting Vonn Hall's western perimeter, is deeply forested and the trail which runs along the valley at its foot is rarely traveled. The seven tunnels running through it are even more rarely disturbed. The colonies of bat-serpents living there have a routine.

Well, so much for *that*— millions of them now burst from the central tunnel, in nearly a solid cylinder of wings and tails and claws, shrieking in an enormous choir of a voice which would have been even louder if the ears of the panic-stricken man sprinting through the very middle of it could have registered even a fraction of the noise they were making.

"Aaagh! Aaagh! Aaagh!" howled Fred, though not a single bat-serpent had actually come into contact with him. If Corvinalias had been with him, he would have learned that the creatures' high-pitched calls translated mostly to *what is it? it's disgusting! get away, quick, don't touch it!* but be that as it may, as Fred skidded to a halt on a lonely trail in the heart of the legendary Gray Forest, the important thing was this: he was free.

Free to sink to his knees in the undergrowth, free to feel like maybe puking a little, free to get up and go off the trail for a shaky latrine stop and then come back and stand there watching the last few bat-serpents floating up out of the middle tunnel in what looked like a wisp of smoke.

What. In the seven-sided pock. Had just happened.

Fred's brain didn't want to do any thinking. It protested to itself that it would rather just feel for a while. This clean air, smell it? This afternoon light, so much of it. And being alive. *How about we just experience those for a while,* pleaded his brain, and not go trying to figure out what's next, or where that fellow what's-his-name has gone? Or those two, what are they, criminal masterminds...? Oh for all that's holy, fine. *Fine.* We have to think about it.

Fred wiped his face with both hands and looked around him. That wall of forest, those openings in it... he'd seen a picture of this somewhere... he remembered one of the books he'd read, back in another lifetime, back in the study of his townhome in Coastwall, next door to Dok who would sometimes pop in and find him hidden behind those desks he'd pushed together, and force him to take a few minutes out of his frantic studying for the League For Peace. Wonder what the League is doing right now... wonder what Dok is doing... stop that. This place, you've seen this place, this is Beiken Ridge at the back of Vonn Hall and that means this trail leads north into the Gray Forest, and south past the Beikenrock Falls.

Has Fo been here? Which way did he go?

Fred didn't have the faintest idea anymore. Obviously then, neither did the de Vonns. Had they let him out so they could follow him? If so, they were about to get a great big random guess. Fred turned south.

Before the trail curved out of view around a big tree, a purring noise from deep in the mountainside made him stop and look back.

Like the crescendo of a drum corps, the noise grew and grew until it was absolute thunder.

Abruptly it was joined by a trumpet blast of bat-serpents' shrieks: six tunnels' worth, six claws of black stabbing forth and curling upward like pillars of smoke; and then through this curtain exploded a mass of cavalry such as Fred had never in his life— never in pictures or on stage or even in his poet's imagination— seen.

Swordmaids from the northern tunnels, archers from the south, packed so tightly that the horn of each rider's buckalope threatened to stab the back of the rider before her, yet locked into perfect formation. As one, the columns of cavalry turned, six fingers of a huge, questing, malformed hand; the fingers broke apart and became massive beads, sliding along a cable, alternating as they fell in one behind another.

It was Fred's training as an acrobat that let him climb the tree in just three leaps— though something far more primal, yelping from the very root of him, had come up with the idea. He clung hidden in the branches as the beads rushing along the trail below him fused into a rail of pink enameled steel, pouring from the forge of Vonn Hall, on and on and on.

Finally it ended.

The trail was no longer a dim little track through the woods but a great river of earth churned up by thousands of cloven hoofs.

Pretty easy for a fellow to climb down out of a tree and follow.

Especially easy for the single rider who emerged from the middle tunnel long after all the others had gone, who kept her distance from Fred but who, he knew, was watching and following no one but him.

CHAPTER 49

As the river of hoofprints rolled on, smaller flows diverged from it. Fred could read them plainly: here one had turned down a valley, there another had gone up a ridge; given time, the whole Vonn Country would be thoroughly flooded with trackers and anyone hiding would be flushed out.

Was there any point anymore, in trying to direct the flow of history to peaceful channels? The de Vonns would surely become the next puppeteers of Abode, and should they choose to break with the Kingdom, their way would be clear. Fred supposed there was a chance the Queen could prevail on them to behave favorably toward the rest of her husband's Federation, but what would become of the League For Peace or its naive goal was anyone's guess. He was sure the de Vonns would delight in the Weapon— wasn't the engineer who Abode had kidnapped and forced to develop it in the first place a Vonn University man? Good old V. U., with its emblem the lorro leaf. Victory.

Fred trudged along till the sun was casting low golden beams through the branches. In their light, he came upon a waymarker shaped like a pointing finger.

The finger had clearly been carved by a true hullabaloo artist, a master of the craft. Its bright pink sleeve and cheekily braced posture all but guaranteed that passers-by would stop whatever they were doing and make the effort to go see whatever it indicated.

Most villagers couldn't read, so the finger was unlabeled— but it was famous enough just by itself, another of those sights Fred recognized from his books; its presence, plus the fresh, cold haze of spray blooming up like perfume from behind a screen of nearby boulders, assured him that if he followed the finger, he'd soon be looking upon the sublime Beikenrock Falls.

Why not. We pass this way but once.

He slipped behind the boulders.

His assassin dismounted and followed him.

Seconds later, the forest rang to a man's full-throated scream.

CHAPTER 50

THE BEIKENROCK FALLS IS A powerful spring, pouring from a cliffside to strike seven ledges of stone in its hissing white plunge to the bottom of a gorge, thus forming the headwaters of the river Clodd.

But surrounding the Falls, there are scenic overlooks aplenty—large and numerous enough to hold a force of mounted archers. And one, lower down, was large enough to hold Marshal Fo, who stood screaming as dozens of arrows rushed past him to stick bristling in the bodies of Granny Almantree and Hamel Fliss.

After years of shadow war, the two of them had finally come clashing together to grab the world's benniest prize. Granny had taken hold of Fo by the right arm, and Fliss by the left; back and forth they had pulled him; and though such a confrontation had long been the stuff of both their dread and their dreams, neither had ever imagined that, far away from their strongholds of Coastwall and Spireburgh, there might loom a power against whom they were nothing. Yet it was so. Now the two great crimelords of Midlandis were pincushions of dead flesh, their reign and rivalry over.

From his own place on the cliffside above, Fred watched as a dozen de Vonn knights sent their buckalopes straight down the rocks to finish the job. The tough mountain beasts fell and sprang from ledge to ledge like water. Even as they went, the knights' swords were flashing forth; in moments they had Fo surrounded; Fred was so absorbed in watching two of them swing from their saddles and kick the crimelords' bodies away to vanish in the Beikenrock Falls, that when a hand fell upon his shoulder, he nearly pitched into the gorge himself.

Fred turned around to look and it was Margadet de Vonn—except with piercing olive-green eyes.

Only after she'd thrown a sinewy arm around him and pulled him to a safe distance, did he figure it out. Of course, it helped that she introduced herself.

"I'm Yolanda, Your Highness. Margadet's sister. You've probably never even seen my portrait— my folks don't let me send anything to anyone. Are you going to be all right? Sit down there against the boulders, that's good. Ladies!"

Knights and archers all whirled to face her, their attention as sharp as their mounts' single horns.

"Sound the bugle— have all search parties rejoin. My orders are these: none of you will be returning to Vonn Hall. Instead you will serve as my guards on a journey to a place known as The Nautilus, located in the city of Coastwall, capital of the Brewel Country."

Fred watched as the knights clapped manacles onto Fo, loaded him upon a buckalope as though he were a sack of grain and packed him up the cliff. How completely vacant the wight looked— he might have lost his mind, not that there ever was so terribly much of it to begin with.

As Fo and his captors withdrew, Fred relaxed against the spray-dampened boulders and listened as the most senior knight argued with the Dominelle of the Vonn Country.

"With all due respect, Medame, I don't believe we have the option to obey you. Your parents' orders were clear: we were to capture the foreigner and dispose of the criminals. You aren't even supposed to be out here. You're supposed to be at home, locked in— ah, I mean, resting in your very, very lovely and comfortably furnished tower."

"Pocks to my tower," growled Yolanda de Vonn. "I *told* Ama and Da-Da I wanted to serve as our country's envoy to the League For

Peace. I told them repeatedly. Well, they can kiss my hand. From now on I'm through telling— I'm just doing."

"But Medame, it's impossible! We must take you home."

"Oh? Were you ordered to take me home? Don't bother answering, because I know you weren't. You said it yourself: they don't even know I'm gone. Just like they don't know I've had a copy of the key to that scab-flapping tower for *years.*" She turned her sharp eyes to Fred: they held a cutthroat, de Vonn kind of glow. "Of course the tunnels were a harder nut to crack. My folks never open those things, never! But they did it today, because of you. The news you brought gave me my chance— I am forever grateful, Your Highness. I feel as though you rescued me."

Fred would have commented on this but for the knight, who had to keep trying.

"It's no good, Medame! We are pledged to obey your parents! They are our Domina and Seigneur. We do fealty to them!"

Yolanda de Vonn crossed her arms, tossed her head and said "and *they* do fealty to the House of Castramars. So if Prince Malfred here says we're all going to the Nautilus, you have to obey him. Isn't that right, Your Highness." It wasn't so much of a question as a statement.

"Uh... yep."

"But Medame! I really must protest! The foreigner was being pursued by two notorious outlaws. How am I to know this— this—" the knight struggled to describe what looked like a filthy but admittedly well-dressed laborer— "this individual before me is not another outlaw, some sort of impostor, instead of the, ah, the, ah..."

"Don't be stupid," snapped Yolanda de Vonn. "If he weren't really Malfred of Castramars, would I do *this*?"

And there, in the evening's dying light, she crouched to her knees and bowed down her head.

"Your Highness, I am at your command."

"Seriously? Oh, come on now, Yolanda…"

She didn't move. The knight, too, was waiting. Fred shrugged.

"Uh, all right then. First let's get up… I mean, uh, *arise,* my good vassal, sister of— hoy, that was some fast arising! Listen, I feel a little shaky. Would you mind helping me…?"

As the Dominelle clasped Fred's hand and pulled him to his feet, she took the opportunity to kiss his ring, a most unexpected act that gave him a bit of a turn.

"*Yagh!* Stop that! You don't know where it's been!"

"My liege. State your command. Good and loud, so everyone can hear it."

"Well, I'm kind of new at this," Fred admitted. "But I'll start by formally appointing you as the Vonn Country's envoy to the League For Peace, and directing you to make haste to the conference, accompanied by all present. Anyone have a problem with that? If so, tough beans."

Yolanda de Vonn laughed. Her laughter had a harder edge than Margadet's, but somehow Fred could tell that it came from the same sort of heart.

When the two of them emerged onto the trail, they found that the riders had deployed travel lanterns: wyrmlight globes, fitted to little leather sockets at the tip of each buckalope's horn. The sheer vast number of these gave the impression of a summer night, as though the cavalry were a swarm of oversized flashbugs flowing through the depths of the forest. Fred found it surprisingly beautiful. Well, most of it.

When he found the buckalope toting Fo, his chest was seized with a cramping feeling which he identified as a longing for justice.

He addressed the nearest knight.

"Good Lady, would you please take a moment to twist this fellow's arm? And his leg, too. Hard. Really give it to him. I happen to know he deserves it— a little bird told me so."

CHAPTER 51

The morning air that Fred drew into his lungs when he opened the flap of his tent was bracingly cold. It made his nose tingle; he could see his outward breath. However, the fluffy woolen blanket wrapped around him from neck to knee was delightfully cozy. Likewise the felt slippers he wore, though they were borrowed and far too big.

Yolanda de Vonn had already been at her broadspear practice. Her cheeks glowed; as she strode over to stand beside Fred she radiated heat.

"I trust you slept well, Your Highness. Your clothing has been cleaned and will be brought to you directly, but your boots are taking longer— removing bat-serpent guano is notoriously difficult. In the meantime, please feel free to continue wearing my slippers." She gestured at a cookfire busily roasting various species of game. "Would you care for breakfast?"

For the first time in his life, Fred didn't think so— but he didn't want to go hungry, either. Likewise, he wanted to get dressed and hit the trail, but he also wanted to stay rolled up in the blanket. He didn't know *what* he wanted anymore. It was weird.

The shirt and breeches brought to him were still warm from the hot rocks they'd been dried with. The washbowl and basin were warm too, with some scent cubes floating in the water along with a chunk of army soap. Someone had even cut him a sassafras twig, to scrub his teeth with. Ah, comfort. A wight could get used to this. Maybe this was what he wanted.

Well, this plus Dok.

Great God Almighty that's around and within and between, he said to himself, however it is that you've set yourself up, I hope it includes me making it back to her. Great God, Ye Gods, and whoever's assigned to me— all of you, from the top to the bottom, I promise I'll never bug you again. Just take me back to Dok. Damn me deep, I love her.

Yolanda de Vonn, now sitting on a camp stool beside Fred's tent sipping a mug of sassafras tea, turned to him. "Tell me more about this Dok, with whom you pray to be reunited."

Fred blushed. He hadn't realized he was saying it out loud.

"I'm intrigued," continued Yolanda de Vonn. "Of course my folks don't know it, but I have secret advisers who tell me all the news— so I'm pretty well informed. Yet even so, I was unaware that Your Highness had married."

Fred bit the sassafras twig, hard. This again. Maybe Yolanda would let it go.

But no. Her sharp eyes were riveted on him; her ears, laden with rings full of starry pink sapphires, seemed perked to listen.

Finally Fred made a stab at it. "Um, no. We haven't made any plans in that direction. Dok is totally free."

Yolanda de Vonn seemed disappointed. "Oh. But isn't your country one of those where equals marry for love? You *did* just proclaim you loved her."

"Well, yes— I mean yep— that's true, I did proclaim it. In fact we both proclaim it pretty much constantly. Not always in words but, uh. Well. Thing is. My proclaiming doesn't have to, you know, *obligate* her to anything."

"Your Highness is unclear. Is Dok not worthy to be Princess Consort?"

"What? No! I mean yep! Of course she's worthy! More worthy than I am to be her— her— whatever it is I'm not."

From across the camp, a bugle began to sound. Yolanda de Vonn stood up and reached for the broadspear leaning against Fred's tent. "I can't say I understand, Your Highness. But I do admire the ways of our Kingdom's other lands. I have lots of ideas— my folks won't live forever, you know. Margadet and I are the Vonn Country's future."

THEY SADDLED THEIR BUCKALOPES AND moved out. The sun made an early try, but clouds soon covered it; the air stayed cold, and wind gusts rattled the pink star flag a bannermaid carried at the front of the unit. Yolanda de Vonn was apologetic.

"I regret that we don't have anything red and yellow. If we had, your colors would certainly fly above ours." She brightened up. "I know. I'll send a herald ahead of us. Though I blush to say it," —she definitely did *not*, noticed Fred— "my country's peasants are very backward and most have not even heard of your adoption and investiture as Prince. We'll be passing through some villages soon, and they ought to make obeisance to you."

Though Fred shook his head, a raindrop still managed to hit the tip of his nose. "No, no, don't worry about it. In fact, can we, ah, soft-pedal me altogether? I'd rather blend in." More raindrops invaded his collar, trickled through the hair of his chest.

"As Your Highness wishes."

"Thanks."

"I will bring Your Highness a rain poncho."

"Uh, could you? If it isn't too much trouble."

The parade of troops, complete with a sullen Marshal Fo stumbling along in their midst, formed the most exciting event of the past decade. In the tiny hamlet of Beiken Dell its whole score of inhabitants, wights and wenches and brats alike, came to stand by the muddy track that wound between their huts, staring in awe at all the armor, and swords, and daggers, and bows, and broadspears, and baggage, and flags. Fred, swathed in a flap of waxed muslin and sitting his buckalope with the tentative crouch of one who isn't used to riding, attracted no attention at all. Then they were through Beiken Dell and the cold, gray, drizzly spring morning wore on.

The Gray Forest receded. They passed through more settlements, slightly larger ones now, each blasted with rain from blustering skies. Fred pulled the drawstring of his poncho's hood good and tight, and viewed the passing world through a waxy, puckered hole. When the spire of Flat Mountain Abbey came into this frame, he lowered his head so as not to see it; along the main street of New South Clodd, there were a few familiar sights — young Fred had been allowed to go to the market once a month with the abbot, a cheerful old codger named Benedek Drum— but most of the town had changed and soon it, too, was left behind.

Foragers had ranged ahead of the unit. In the afternoon another meal, this time not only of game but also of villagers' stores, awaited them. Yolanda de Vonn found Fred where he was sitting apart, and carried a stack of smoky corncakes to him in the bowl of a knight's buckler.

"Here, Your Highness. Please eat. You grow thin."

"That's all right. I could stand to be a little less— you know. Built." But Fred did take a corncake. Two, in fact.

She crouched beside him. "I hope you don't think it rude of me to break in on your thoughts, but I was hoping that you and I would talk as we made this journey. I take my duties as envoy with the utmost seriousness, and I've tried my best to study— but I was somewhat restricted in my freedom to learn."

"Mm. I can see how being stuck in a castle full of towers and monsters and creepy plaster death faces might hold you back."

"It *was* extremely tiresome. I now look forward to having the same complete freedom as your Lady Dok. I assume she assists you in every particular of the League For Peace?"

"Well, ah, she would, I'm sure. I mean, if I let her."

This actually startled Yolanda de Vonn. The hand in which she held her own corncake dropped from her lips to her knee. "Let her? How so? What about the freedom?"

"Oh, but that's the thing! I can't go letting Dok get mixed up in my troubles. She had a really stressful life before— I mean like really, *really* stressful. Plus paperwork."

"So she is not free."

"But she *is!* Just— not free to throw the rest of her freedom away on me, see what I mean? She can do better."

Yolanda de Vonn stood up and dusted her fingers. "I fail to see what you mean, Your Highness. What better can there be, for your loved one to do?"

Fred had one bite of corncake left and he debated throwing it. Throw? Eat? He ended up doing neither, instead crushing it to crumbs as he blurted out the shame in his heart.

"Well, for one thing she deserves a wight with the guts to actually *look* at the place where he grew up. Someone who isn't too much of a deep-damned coward to just *go* to the pocking Abbey and finally after twenty-whatever years *ask* who the white-hot hells it was that threw him away, and why. A real prince, a brave one. That's what she deserves, but she isn't getting it!"

A rush of wind carried Yolanda de Vonn's reply to Fred. "And why not? It is entirely within your power to give her such a man."

CHAPTER 52

As the day grew late, the sun and rain did that trick they sometimes do: the one where the light manages to come from beneath the clouds, making it seem as though tears are falling from sunshine. Fred stood outside the cottage that served as the visitors' office of Flat Mountain Abbey, shuffling his feet in the gravel of its courtyard.

Now or never. He took a deep breath and pushed open the pickled whitewood door.

The row of garment hooks was still there, just where he remembered them; he pulled off his rain poncho and hung it to drip; he turned to face the front desk.

The monk who looked up from writing in his ledgers was not much older than Fred, and obviously annoyed.

"What is it, fellow? I'm about to lock up here and go to supper."

When Fred failed to reply instantaneously, the monk sighed and rose to his feet, throwing down his quill with one hand and rubbing his respectable gentlemanly paunch with the other.

"If you want to put some soup in that flat gut of yours, this isn't the place. Go back out the front, then come around to the almshouse on the eastern side. And bring your own bowl. We're through loaning out crockery, it just gets stolen."

Fred took a small step forward. The creak of the floor, the boiled-egg smell of rock oil burning in the lamp, the shelves full of inspirational figurines... after everything he'd been and seen and done, here he was again. It was as though a big chunk had been cut from his life, leaving a fresh stump that hadn't yet begun to bleed, or ooze, or itch. He extended his hand, but finding himself still a little too far from the desk he pulled it back in. The monk glared. Fred breathed deep and spoke up— his hands would have to get by on their own.

"Uh, hello. I don't know if anyone here remembers me, but I'm, ah..."

"Oho! Now it's coming to me! I think what I see here is one Malfred Murd. Isn't it? If I recall, you got packed off to be some sort of household entertainer for the Royals. Hence the fop togs and— *that*." The monk pointed at Fred's left hand. "Pretty fancy for a servingman's seal-ring, but I suppose it's to be expected. And listen to the accent you've picked up... ooh dee dah, it's so crusted with Isle of Gold I can hardly stand it! What are you doing back here, Murd?"

Fred opened his mouth but the monk went on: "Don't tell me: you got sacked. Well, that's no surprise— *I* never found your antics all that entertaining."

Fred's brow creased in dismay. "Really? Gods, I mean pocks, I mean hoy, I'm sorry, Cob." The name had come to him all by itself, occasioned by something in the monk's glowering square face.

"*Father* Cob. After I got out of your deep-damned shadow, I showed 'em what I could do! In fact our brewing operation is running so well I wish we had the means to expand. Baking, too— if you're looking for a loaf of bread, I'll have to disappoint you. They're all gone for the day. Hence the need to expand, see?" Cob slammed the desk drawer. "All right, Murd. Time for me to close up shop. Go around outside if you want soup."

"Actually, I came to ask for something else."

"Beer's all gone too. That runs out even faster than the bread."

"Uh, nope. I just ate, I'm fine. What I wanted was, well, I, ah..."

The monk looked smug. "Hmph. Did a magpie steal your tongue? You used to be a witty little brute."

Fred pushed it all out in one piece. "I want to know who dumped me here and why. I mean, I figured out that much... I know I was, well, handed over. Anonymous donation. Flung across the back fence, sort of thing. But being, well, unwanted... always kind of bothered me... and since I found myself in the neighborhood..."

As he rambled, Cob's face went through a series of evolutions Fred found it impossible to interpret. His training in reading audiences' reactions had been top-notch, but something here was wrong: Cob looked as though he were listening to nonsense. Worse, in fact: he looked indignant, as though he were being lied to. His fists were even clenched. Fred willed his heart to slow down and gulped, "You... ah... can't tell me anything?"

"Oh, I can *tell* you something, all right— I can tell you find it amusing to torment me! What's so fun about that, Murd? What do you *get* from it?"

"Huh?"

"Twenty years, that's what I call a long setup for a joke. But did you really think I believed all of that dumped-here, woe-is-me oxshit? Well, I might have had to struggle along in your shadow when we were boys but I've finally come into my own, Murd. Unwanted foundling, my bouncing double-dipped beans!"

"*Huh?*"

"Don't keep 'huh'-ing at me. The favoritism you got was unreal! All of us were sick to death of it.... well, *I* was, anyhow. Toil in the field. Clean stalls. Wash clothes. My hands were as big and raw as a girl's, but oh! precious little *Malfred* was free to do whatever he wanted! Clever little *Freddie* could bounce around and sing and play from morning till midnight! And *who* got first crack at the paper, the pens, the ink? *Who* got his very own key to the library?"

Fred suddenly remembered the shape of the key, the way it had felt clicking into the lock, the cool, dusty emptiness among sweet-smelling books in the only room where being alone wasn't unbearable.

"Huh. Cob, I really didn't..."

"*Father* Cob!"

"Sorry, sorry. Well, ah. Let's be honest, Father: fat lot of good the library did me, right? I never even passed the novice exam..."

Fred had meant this to be self-deprecating, disarming, a peace offering. But it had the opposite effect on Cob, who gripped the edge of his desk as though it were the only thing stopping him from flying away.

"Don't even start with that! *That* was the most flagrant abuse of power I'd ever seen! If Father Benedek had failed you just one more time, I'd have... are you serious? You really don't know what I'm talking about? Come on, Murd, *think!* If you'd passed that exam you'd never have gotten away from here!"

Realizing how that sounded, Cob covered his faux pas by lunging to a display shelf, seizing a frosted glass figurine shaped like a kitten with wings, and polishing it with one corner of his robe.

"Not that getting away from here should be the goal. No, indeed! Now that I'm in charge, I see what a fulfilling challenge it is. I'm proud of how well I've brought things into line. Where would we *be*, Murd, if every man who ever bent his chastity vow wanted to keep his little souvenir close at hand? I tell you, your Da-da couldn't have got away with it if he weren't the abbot."

Cob looked up from his polishing.

"Oh, don't play 'surprised face' with me, Murd. I suppose old Father Benedek thought nobody suspected— but everyone knows a man can be as old as rocks, and still manage to cause one last brat. Which is well enough, but bring you to live with us? Now *that* was risking a date with the pillory, wasn't it, and an end to his days in the poorhouse! The only thing that saved the fellow was that everyone liked him. Otherwise I'd have spoken up at the funeral, I'll tell you that for a cut-down penny."

"Uh, can I sit in this…"

"Help yourself, Murd. Want the footstool that goes with that chair? No? Why not make yourself at home? You always did. It must have been nice having dear old Da right there beside you. Handing you the best of everything. Finding you a place with the pocking King. And giving you his *name!* That was the crowning touch. Just to really rub the rest of our faces in it."

Fred felt as though he were spiraling out of the little chair with the needlepoint footstool, floating up to the smoke-blackened laths of the ceiling. He heard himself talking.

"What do you mean? My name doesn't sound anything like 'Benedek Drum'."

"Looks like you were right about all those library visits not helping you," snorted Cob. "Come on now, Malfred Murd. Try spelling your name backwards."

Fred blinked. "Derflam?"

"Your other name, Big Brain."

Fred pictured the four simple letters of the surname he'd hated all his life, the stubby lumpen word he'd always thought of as his truant mother's final mockery. But there it was, in a whole different light, like the light from the window where the rain had ended and something colorful was beginning to glow.

Fred dabbed his eyes dry as he stood up. "Hoy, Father— do you fellows need anything here? Anything at all? I suppose you could say I'm now in a position to help."

"*Are* you, now, Murd? Fine, I'll play along. How about something to help expand the brewery? You can donate a new vat."

"Done."

"Oh, that was easy. Let's do the bakery next— care to donate a nice new brick oven?"

"Absolutely. Just have it built, and send me the bill."

Cob practically trod on Fred's heels as he followed him to the hooks on the wall. "What's going on with you? Why are you looking so— so— *beatific?* These jokes must be giving you some sort of sick thrill. If I asked you to donate a hundred extra parcels of land, a new wine cellar, ten new hay sheds and a bell tower, would you fall on the floor in an ecstatic fit?"

Fred decided not to wear the rain poncho. Instead he just folded it over his arm.

"I wouldn't have a fit, Father, no. But I'm happy to give them to you— it's the least I could do. Like I say, just order whatever you need. And then write to 'HIS residence, Royal District, Coastwall'."

Cob glared at Fred, then heaved open the cottage door the way one does to let out an intrusive fly.

"Out, Murd. And wipe off that smile! Where'd you get the nerve, to come back here and tell me all these stories? Royal District, my arse— you haven't changed a bit. What a fool you are. A perfect, incredible fool."

PARTY BARGE MAKES UNEXPECTED VOYAGE

Multi-Extra!! — reported by M. I. Popper

Hot on the heels of this year's thrillingly successful Plum Blossom Festival, Coastwall got another treat last evening when the notorious "Party Barge", normally moored rock-steady at the foot of Holiday Street, actually cast off and made a cruise that brought joyous noise and excitement to Old Mama River.

The cacophonous craft was bedecked with colorful lights and banners: red and yellow, black and white— those are the Castramars colors, all right!— and from his zealously guarded secret lookout, your loyal reporter identified among its passengers the Royals (including our fair Queen's reclusive sister)... all the de Brewels... Dame Elsebet de Whellen (with her companion, the botanist who recently re-planted the blueneedle tree at Whellengood Hall)... shipping tycoon turned diplomat Ata Maroo, alongside her unmistakable husband... and Isladorro's famed magpie Prophessor, who made a short flight among the Phlogistical balloons and sparkling arrows that were released mid-channel to music provided by the wildly popular Slum Slim and the Fops.

(continues on other side of news sheet)

(continued from first side of news sheet)

Too noisy? Too bad! *The city's Grand Constable was off duty. He and his well-coiffed sweetheart were perhaps the most unbridled of all the guests aboard— and why not? He deserves a break, as crime in Coastwall is most unexpectedly down.*

Though exactly what was being celebrated remains unclear, this news hunter's eager peepers fell upon two sights that bear consideration.

First was the great, big grin on the face of His Highness, Prince Malfred of Castramars. And next were the hands of Leonne "Dok" Atler, the renowned Nameless Lady.

Was Medame Atler wearing embroidered gloves of translucent lace (the very hottest new fashion!) or are her hands now really decorated with the pattern of a jester's motley? **Keep reading my bulletins, because I plan to find out!** *Life, like spring weather, brings all sorts of surprises. You never know when there might be more to the story.*

The Heart of Stone Adventures began with

FOOL'S PROOF,
POWER'S PLAY

and

DOOM'S DAZE

Sign up for my newsletter, get updates,
and more at

evasandor.com